BREAKING
INTO
SUNLIGHT

JOHN COCHRAN

ALGONQUIN YOUNG READERS
WORKMAN PUBLISHING
NEW YORK

Algonquin Young Readers
Workman Publishing
Hachette Book Group, Inc.
1290 Avenue of the Americas
New York, NY 10104
workman.com

Algonquin Young Readers is an imprint of Workman Publishing, a division of Hachette Book Group, Inc. The Algonquin Young Readers name and logo are registered trademarks of Hachette Book Group, Inc.

Design by Andrew Wang

The publisher is not responsible for websites (or their content) that are not owned by the publisher.

Workman books may be purchased in bulk for business, educational, or promotional use. For information, please contact your local bookseller or the Hachette Book Group Special Markets Department at special.markets@hbgusa.com.

Library of Congress Cataloging-in-Publication Data is available.

ISBN 978-1-5235-2729-8

First Edition May 2024

Printed in the United States of America on responsibly sourced paper.

10 9 8 7 6 5 4 3 2 1

To Kelly, Maren, and Liam,
with love and gratitude

CHAPTER 1

They were together, the three of them, in the Barracuda—Reese with his mom and dad—following an empty country road into the setting sun. Reese's dad was driving, his mom beside him up front.

"Where are we going?" Reese asked from the back seat. "I don't recognize any of this."

"I told you it's a surprise," his dad said. "Seriously, I guarantee y'all are going to love this."

Reese's mom raised a hand to shield her eyes from the sun and squinted at his dad. "At least tell us how far we're going," she said. She had said she was tired from work and just wanted to lie on the couch and watch TV. But his dad had almost dragged them out of the apartment after supper, telling them to trust him and leave the dishes for later.

"We're two minutes away, I swear," he said. Then he gave her that smile of his: big and loose and charming, with a little devil in it. He looked up in the rearview mirror at Reese. "Okay, bud?"

Reese made himself smile back. "Okay," he said.

His dad was in a good place, and he had been for so long that Reese was beginning to believe he would stay there—clean and sober, working steady. And wherever he was taking them now, he clearly thought it was the best thing ever.

It was nearly summer, about a month before school let out. The evening was clear and warm. They had come south, through the ragged back end of Spendlowe, past the old brick shells of mills and warehouses, and then turned into the country. They were going by a cluster of little houses and mobile homes when Reese's phone buzzed. He had been texting his friends Tony and Ryan from the back seat, and Tony had just responded: **What do u mean u don't know where u are? Dude how can u not know where u are?**

Another buzz, Ryan this time: **HOME RUN!!!!!!! BRAVES!!!!!!!** He was home watching baseball with his cousins and kept texting about the game, as if Reese and Tony cared about the Braves as much as he did.

Then Reese's dad was slowing and turning, going hand over hand on the wheel, onto a dirt road. "We're here!" he announced, as if they had arrived someplace that Reese had been just dying to get to all along.

Reese looked up from his phone. "Where?"

"Skate Land!" his dad said. He turned left into a gravel parking lot, and Reese saw a cinder block building with a curved red metal roof. Over double metal doors in front was a neon sign glowing red: **SKATE LAND ROLLER RINK**.

The Barracuda slowed to a stop, and a cloud of dust raised by its fat tires drifted away. "Oh my Lord, Sam," said Reese's mom. "How did you find this place?"

"I just stumbled over it when I was out this way last month on a job. It's a palace, don't you think? Real old-school!"

It might have been old-school, but a palace it was not. Reese thought his dad had to be kidding. On the sign, the *K* and the *E* in *SKATE* were flickering like they were about to burn out, and the front of the building was streaked with rust that had run down from the roof. Off to one side was a metal bin overflowing with garbage.

And there was another problem that really made Reese's stomach drop: "I don't know how to skate," he said.

"We'll teach you!" his dad said. "Your mom and I, we used to do this all the time. It'll be like old times, early days!"

Clearly, he wasn't kidding, and incredibly, Reese's mom seemed to think the place was as awesome as his dad did. Suddenly she was smiling. "It's not that hard, Reese," she said. "You'll pick it up just like that." She snapped her fingers.

"So?" his dad said to her. "Is this okay?"

His mom shrugged, but Reese could tell it was okay by her. Her face had softened, relaxed. She was warming up.

His dad turned to look at him. "I probably shouldn't tell you this story because I don't want to scare you on your first time out, but this one time early on, I took your mom skating . . ."

Reese's mom laughed. "This was one of our first dates, your dad and me."

"It was our third date, actually," his dad said. "I took her to a rink in Goldsville. She'd never seen me skate, and I really wanted to impress her, so I was showing off, weaving in and out. And then I turned to skate backward, and I—"

"Wait a minute," Reese said. "You can skate backward?" He hadn't even known his dad could skate *forward*, and here he was talking about practically doing stunts.

"I can. Or I used to be able to, on a good day. So I turned, so smooth. I mean it was perfect, and I waved at your mom like, 'Check me out!' And then, *bam!* I hit the low wall around the rink and flipped. I actually flipped head over heels, right out of the rink."

Reese's mom laughed again. "He was waving at me like a fool, and then he hit that wall and went over. People screamed. Oh, the look on his face: total shock. I'll never forget it."

"Okay, *that* is funny," Reese said. "I would totally pay to see that."

"Right?" said his mom.

"I broke my wrist," his dad said.

"And we spent the rest of the date at the emergency room," his mom said. "The end."

"Not the end," his dad said. "Just the beginning!"

"My smooth operator." She leaned over to his dad, put one hand on his chin to turn his face to her, and kissed him.

It was honestly a little gross, but his dad, so healthy then, really at his best, had broken through. And just like that, they were a family again, like any other. Reese was not going to be the one who screwed that up, after everything they had gone through, after all the fights and the crying: He would go skating, if it could work this kind of magic. Or he would try.

He just hoped—*please*, God—that there was no one he knew inside.

His phone buzzed, a text from Tony: RU there yet?

Reese took a moment to respond before getting out: At a skating rink.

Tony texted back immediately: Dude can u even skate?

Reese put his phone in the pocket of his shorts, got out of the car, and followed his parents into the rink. Music was playing over the loudspeakers, a fast song, stuttering rock guitar. He smelled French fries and onion rings. The lights were up on the rink, and the skaters were gliding around. "Wow, it's got a beautiful old wood floor," his mom said.

When Reese looked out there, it wasn't the floor he focused on. It was a group of girls who skated by just then, laughing. They looked about his age, and they were skating as if they had been on wheels their whole lives. Instantly any small amount of confidence he might have had when he came into the rink drained away. He was almost thirteen and had grown nearly two inches since Christmas, which made him taller than his mom. He also had stretched thin as he shot up. He would look ridiculous out there on skates for the first time, as tall and skinny as he was, flailing around, falling probably, in front of those girls. He didn't know them, but still . . . He'd have nowhere to hide.

"Can I just watch for a while?" he asked.

"*What?*" His dad looked at him wide-eyed, making like he was shocked, outraged even, that Reese would think about sitting out the kind of fun he had lined up for them. "Nah, Reese. No way, man. You got to jump in there, and I'm going to help. Listen, two things to remember: First, there is always somebody else out there learning, usually more than one. Like that guy . . ." He nodded toward a balding, heavyset man, the tail of his shirt untucked, dark sweat stains under his arms, moving slowly and shakily toward them on the rink. "He's obviously learning, and he's older than me even. And number two, you have to remember that everyone is so focused on themselves that no one is focused on you."

He gave Reese that smile of his again. Reese's mom had said once that it was his dad's smile that had first made her love him. It made you want to let go of your fears and doubts and say yes. His mom was smiling still, too, nodding her head to the beat of the music as she watched the skaters going around, her exhaustion and worries apparently forgotten. Reese didn't want to bring her down. So he swallowed hard and nodded. "Okay."

His phone buzzed in his pocket again, but he ignored it. He followed his parents to the front counter to get their skates, and his mom showed him how to lace up. The skates felt heavy and clumsy. When he stood, his dad offered his hand, but Reese waved him away and clomped as best he could to the rink by himself, with his arms out from his side, stiff. On wheels, he felt about fifteen feet tall, and not in a good way. He probably looked like Frankenstein. Clutching the low wall around the rink and trying not to look at the girls skating by, he eased out onto the wood floor.

"Stick close to the edge until you get the hang of it," his dad told him. "Okay now, first: Bend your knees and turn your feet out a little, like a duck." He demonstrated for Reese. Then he showed him how to rock from side to side, pushing and gliding. "You're going to fall a few times. Everybody does, and if anybody even notices, all they're going to be thinking about is all the times *they* fell when they were learning. So just get up and keep going."

His mom glided up next to them. "If you two are okay, I'm going to practice on my own for a while."

"We're good," his dad said.

"Will you stay with me?" Reese asked him. As old as Reese was, this sounded pretty silly. It *was* silly. But exposed out there, he felt better, safer, with his dad at his side. If it weren't for those girls maybe seeing, he would have reached out and taken his dad's hand.

"I'm not going anywhere, bud," his dad said.

"Are you going to skate backward?" Reese asked. He would really like to see that. Now that he was on wheels himself, he could imagine how hard it must be—and how cool it would be to see his dad doing it. Without the crashing and falling, of course.

"Oh, I doubt it," his dad said. "It's been a long while since I was on skates. It was before you were born."

They made a circuit of the rink, and his dad stayed close, slightly behind Reese. By the time they had finished a second circuit, Reese was getting the hang of it. He was good at sports, especially basketball and swimming, and the side-to-side rhythm was coming to him fast. He hadn't fallen once. He moved away from the wall, and a nervous, happy feeling bubbled up inside him. He laughed.

"Having fun?" his dad asked. Reese nodded. "Well, you're doing great. Hey, Amanda, look at your kid. He's a natural."

"Good job, Reese!" she called. She applauded as she went by, and Reese was enjoying himself so much, this didn't embarrass him. Well, it was a little embarrassing, but he liked it anyway. She was wearing dangly earrings that flashed in the lights of the rink when she turned her head to watch him. She was smiling, *really* smiling.

After a while, they took a break and got lemonades from the grill. They sat on a wooden bench at the edge of the rink, and his dad put an arm around his shoulders and gave him a squeeze. "We need to do this more often," he said.

Just then, the lights dimmed, and a new song began to play. It was a slow one: soft keyboard, electric guitar. A man's voice came over the loudspeakers: "Slow skate! *Slooooow* skate! Grab your partners. Get out there, couples."

"Hey, Reese," his dad said. "Do you mind if your mom and I take this one together?"

Reese shook his head. "Have fun." He wanted to take a break. His thighs were starting to ache.

"You up to it, Amanda?" his dad asked.

"Sure," his mom said.

She stood, took his dad's hand, and the two of them clomped to the rink. Then they eased out onto the polished wood and glided away. They went around once, twice, three times, still holding hands. They waved at Reese each time they passed. They were smiling. A mirrored ball spinning above them scattered light like slivers of glass.

He took his phone out to text his friends, but just then, as his parents came out of a turn to pass him again, his dad reached across his mom, placing a hand on her hip, and with a turn that seemed effortless, he was facing her.

He was skating backward, both hands on her waist.

It was as cool as Reese had imagined. Cooler even. He laughed and stood up, went to the low wall beside the rink to take some pictures with his phone. When they came around to him again, he called to his dad: "Can you teach me to do that?" His dad smiled and gave him a thumbs-up.

Then they were past him, going around again, swaying in time with the song.

His phone buzzed, but he slipped it back into his pocket without looking at it. He would have felt stupid admitting this to Tony or Ryan or anybody else, because he wouldn't want people to think that watching his parents get all romantic and dance was his idea of a good time, but he wouldn't have been anywhere else right then. He thought his mom and dad were the handsomest couple and the best skaters out there, and standing in that dump of a rink, at that moment anyway, he was proud of his family. He thought he could watch his parents go around and around forever, like a dream that's so good you never want to wake up.

CHAPTER 2

Reese's dad was so good for so long. Then he wasn't, like someone had flipped a switch.

And this time it was Reese who found him.

He had just gotten home from school, and he had come into the apartment thinking about some leftover peach pie that was in the fridge. The first thing he did was look in the freezer in the kitchen, just inside their apartment door, to see if there was ice cream, too. He was happy to see there was.

The Barracuda had been parked outside their building, which was normal because his dad started his workdays early at the construction sites, leaving before dawn, and came home in the afternoons.

Reese called into the apartment: "Dad, I'm home!"

What his dad usually called back was, "Reese! Whatcha know? Good?" Or, "Howdy, bud! Talk to me!"

But this time there was only silence.

"Dad?"

Reese stepped into the dining room, and that was when he saw him: His dad was lying on his side in the bathroom, his legs sticking into the hallway. He still had his work boots on. For a moment—the amount of time it took Reese to drop his backpack and go to the bathroom door—he told himself that maybe his dad was down there working on the sink or the toilet, clearing a clogged pipe or something.

Then he got a good look at his dad's face: His eyes were closed. His skin was pale, his lips a little blue. Reese knew right away what had happened, because he had seen it before.

"Oh, no, no," he said. "Dad? Dad! Get up. You have to get up." He got down on his knees and touched his father's bare skin where his pants had ridden up. It was cool.

He shook his dad's leg. "Dad! Can you hear me? You have to get up!"

Nothing. There was no response. This time was the worst yet—and not just because Reese was by himself. The other times his mom had been able to get some sort of response from him: a raised hand, a flicker of the eyelids. This time he lay there like he was dead.

Reese made himself touch his dad's face, and he felt a flutter of breath from his nose. He was still breathing.

Reese stood, and for some reason he went to the kitchen to call for help even though he had his phone in his pocket, as if he needed privacy or something. He felt scared but also disconnected, as if he were standing outside himself, watching himself. He took his phone out of his pocket and dialed 911, and when a woman answered and asked for the address he was at, he gave it to her. Then he said, "My dad has overdosed."

The woman asked him if his dad was breathing. "Yes," he said. "Please send help."

She wanted to know what his dad had taken and how much, and Reese felt a flash of anger and frustration. Why wasn't she calling for help? "I don't know, I don't know," he said. "Pills, painkillers. Please, can you just send help?"

"Help is coming," she said. "I want you to stay on the line with me until the paramedics get there."

But he'd had enough of handling this alone. He couldn't do it anymore. "I have to call my mom," he said. His chest felt weird, as if someone were sitting on it.

"Son," the 911 woman said, "wait just a—"

Reese didn't let her finish. He hung up. Then he tried to dial his mom, but suddenly his hands were shaking. They had been steady up to then, but now they shook so hard that he touched Tony's number in his contacts instead of his mom's and had to hang up. He couldn't stop the shaking. He fumbled the phone. He cursed. Then he got it: The phone rang once, twice. His mom answered: "Reese? Are you home?"

"Dad's overdosed again," he said. "He's breathing, but I can't wake him up. I called 911."

For a moment there was no sound at all from the other end of the line, not even the sound of her breathing. "Mom?" he said. His voice rose and cracked. "Did you hear me? Dad overdosed, and I called 911."

When she spoke, her voice was weirdly calm. "You did just the right thing," she said. "I'm coming to you. When the ambulance gets there, let the medics in. Okay?"

Then suddenly Reese was yelling. He was shouting into the phone, as if he'd lost his mind: "*He was better! He was getting better! How could this happen?*"

"*REESE!*" She barked it. Reese flinched, as if she'd slapped him. "Listen to me," she said. "I'm going to hang up, and I'm going to come to you. I'll be there as quick as I can."

With a click she was gone.

He stood in the kitchen with the phone to his ear for a moment. His legs had gone weak, rubbery. Somehow, he managed to walk back to where his dad was lying. Looking at his face scared Reese, made him feel helpless, and he had an urge to walk away, go into the kitchen or out in the stairwell. But he couldn't leave him alone. He went into the bathroom and got down on his knees beside him. He held out his right hand, still shaking a little, and rested it on his dad's forehead. It was so cold.

He listened hard for an ambulance siren or the sound of his mom's footfalls on the stairs, terrified that his dad would stop breathing before help came, because he knew that was what happened sometimes. That was how the pills killed you: They stopped your breathing, and that was the end. He knew it because he had heard his mom yelling about it, shouting it at his dad to try to scare him into stopping.

His phone, which was still in his other hand, buzzed. Tony was texting: **Dude did u mean to call me?** Reese turned the phone over. He felt as if the room were spinning around him. He closed his eyes and whispered into the silence: "Please, Dad, wake up. Please, wake up."

CHAPTER 3

Reese was sitting in the ER waiting area on two chairs drawn together, his feet on one and his knees up to brace a clipboard that his mom had gotten from the nurse so he could draw. He had been doodling cars: muscle cars like the Barracuda, but crazy, souped up. Right then he was drawing a classic old Mustang with impossibly huge wheels, flames shooting from the exhaust pipes, flames painted on the sides and hood.

Sometimes he could lose himself in drawing, push the things he didn't want to think about to the back of his brain. But right then, out of the corner of his eye, he was watching his mom. She was in the hall with an older lady she had met at the church she had started going to. The woman's name was Mrs. Smith. Reese's mom had called her on the way to the hospital and asked her to come.

They were talking out there, although Reese couldn't hear what they were saying. Mrs. Smith was holding his mom's hands. Then they bowed their heads and closed their eyes, and Reese realized that they were praying. He looked away, felt his face get hot. It was embarrassing to see her doing it, in public like that, and it felt like a betrayal of his dad, who hated church people like Mrs. Smith. He called them busybodies and Holy Rollers.

When the prayer was over, his mom came and sat beside him. Her eyes were red and puffy from crying. She put a hand on his arm. Her fingers were cold, and he moved his arm away. She looked at his drawing. "Those are cool cars," she said. "I like the flames on the sides of that one. Is that a Mustang?"

He didn't answer. He knew what she was trying to do, talking about normal stuff to try to make him feel a little better—and make herself feel better, too. But he didn't want to play along. He was too angry at her for calling Mrs. Smith. Had *he* called or texted anyone? No, because this was their secret—his and his mom and dad's. He didn't want anyone to know about any of it. The anger was like a fist inside his chest.

He looked away, at the window beside him. Under the bright hospital lights he saw only his own reflection in the glass, floating against the darkness that had fallen outside. His skin, fair like his dad's, looked bluish white, and his blue eyes were hidden in dark hollows. His hair, dirty blond like his dad's, was a mess, sticking up on top and out on the sides. He thought he looked like a zombie.

"Reese?" his mom asked.

"Why is she here?" he asked.

"Who? Mrs. Smith? Because I need her here. I need her support."

"I don't want her here," he said. "Dad won't want her here."

"*I* need her here," his mom said again, and he knew the tone in her voice: She wasn't going to be moved, and if he pushed any more, she would yell and cause a big scene in front of the whole hospital. All he wanted to do was disappear.

He drew his legs tighter to his chest. "When can I see Dad?"

"Nothing has changed since the last time you asked me that. Soon, I hope. They have to watch him until they feel like he's in a safe place."

"Can he go home with us?"

"I told you, yes, I think so."

The only other person in the waiting room was a small man in a huge white cowboy hat, with a black eye and one hand wrapped in paper towels. He cleared his throat, got up, and walked into the hallway. Reese could hear the heels of his boots clicking on the floor tiles, fainter and fainter as he went down the hall. After a moment, his mom said, "Mrs. Smith went to look for something for us to eat."

"I don't want anything," Reese said.

His mom shook her head and drew back.

Two other times something like this had happened to his dad, back when they had been living in their old apartment on the other side of town, the place close to Tony and Ryan. His mom had been friendly then with an old lady, Miss Olive, who lived in the unit below them, and Reese had stayed with her those times while his mom went to the hospital with his dad. He had spent what felt like hours and hours with Miss Olive in her apartment, which smelled like mothballs and bacon, drawing and watching the old lady's game shows on TV, while he waited for his parents to come back. When his mom finally had come to get him, his dad had been in bed, with the bedroom door closed.

Now, though, they were living at the other end of town, in the smaller apartment they had moved into early the year before, when his dad had stopped working for a long time and his mom finally said they had to find someplace cheaper to live until they got back on their feet. She never spoke to anyone at the new complex, said the neighborhood was sketchy. And Reese wouldn't have agreed to stay with anybody else this time anyway. After what he had gone through, he couldn't pretend he was interested in TV or whatever. So they had driven together in her car behind the ambulance, all the way to Goldsville, which was the nearest city of any size to Spendlowe.

It was thirty minutes one way, with the ambulance in front of them, lights on but no siren. His mom had tried talking to him about what had just happened, had told him again all the things he already knew: that his dad was sick, that he couldn't stop taking the drugs on his own and he needed help. She blamed the doctors who had given him the painkillers when he had gotten hurt at work. She said Reese shouldn't blame his dad, because he was a good person. He just had to admit that he needed help if he wanted to get better.

She tried talking about it again at the hospital while they waited and waited for the doctors to finish with his dad. But Reese didn't want to talk about any of it—any more than he wanted to hold hands and pray.

When Mrs. Smith returned, she was carrying an orange plastic tray with drinks and plates of food. She was shorter than Reese's mom and had short, spiky gray hair. She moved in quick bursts, which made Reese think of a squirrel. She set the tray down. "I got a hot dog and a hamburger and a salad, so there's some choices," she said. "I got milk and lemonade. Reese, what would you like?"

He rolled his eyes and turned his face away, even though he knew it would upset his mom. Actually, he did it *because* it would upset his mom, so she'd really understand how much he wanted Mrs. Smith gone. "*Reese!*" his mom said, angry at his rudeness.

"It's okay, Amanda," Mrs. Smith said. "Reese, I'll set it here in case you change your mind." She put the tray on a table beside him, and then she just stood there for a moment, looking as if she were about to say something else. She knew their secret. She must know everything, Reese thought: the pills, the overdoses, the fights between his mom and dad. What was she thinking now, standing there looking at him? Maybe she was thinking about what it might be like to have a dad like Reese's and feeling—what? Pity? Disgust?

But she didn't say any of this. She just took a seat on the other side of his mom and took her hand. Reese looked away.

Outside the waiting room a cart clattered by, pushed by the nurse who had gotten him paper and a clipboard to draw with. She was younger even than Reese's mom. She smiled at him. She knew their secret, too. He closed his eyes and lowered his head, wishing he could sink through the floor.

Although he had been trying not to, he thought of his dad back at the apartment. The medics had gotten there quickly: a man and a woman hustling up the stairs with their gear. His mom had come running up behind them, out of breath, her face flushed. Reese was too upset and scared to watch them work, so he had gone outside to the stairwell and closed his eyes. He had heard one of the medics, the man, say, "Give it to him." Reese had known what "it" was: naloxone, the medicine they had given his dad the other times to wake him up.

Then he had heard his dad's voice, loud, angry, cursing: "Where am I? What the hell are you doing?"

"Saving your life," said the woman.

"Get that light out of my face. Let me up!"

"Stop fighting them, Sam, please," his mom had said. "Let them work."

Reese's heart had thumped hard against his chest, and he had felt as if he were sliding sideways, down the stairs, into deep darkness. The woman medic had said, "Restrain him! Hold him down!"

A hand on his cheek, warm and rough, brought him back to the ER waiting room. He heard his dad's voice: "Reese? Hey, Reese, buddy . . ."

His dad was beside him, touching his face. "I'm so sorry, Reese," he said.

He was in a wheelchair, and he looked sick, or as if he had gone a long, long time without sleep. His blue eyes were rimmed with red, his hair was a mess. From the wrist of the hand that touched Reese's face hung a white hospital bracelet. "Reese, buddy, I screwed up," he said. "I screwed up real big this time."

But Reese didn't want to talk. He didn't even want to look at his dad. It made him sick to see him, brought back the panicked feeling from the apartment. "Can we go now?" he said.

"Yeah, but I want to say—"

Reese cut him off: "*Can we go?*" He stood up so fast that the clipboard with his drawings on it fell to the floor with a clatter. His mom reached for him, but he shook her off. He didn't want another big scene, and he didn't want anyone touching him. He just wanted out of there. Mrs. Smith was gone; she must have slipped out before his dad came. But the young nurse was looking at him again from out in the hallway. He turned away, not wanting to meet her eyes.

"Reese, please," his dad said again.

"I don't want to talk about it," Reese said. "All I want is to go home."

CHAPTER 4

The next morning was rainy and so dark that when Reese woke up, he thought at first it was still nighttime. He lay there for a moment feeling blank, but then with a thud, everything from the day before came back to him. He sat up and looked at the clock on his bureau. It was a few minutes past seven in the morning on Friday, the last day of his last full week of seventh grade.

From the kitchen came the clink and clank of pots and pans, which he figured is what had woken him up. He heard his dad say, "Amanda, how many sausages do you want?"

"I don't want anything, Sam," she said. "I told you we don't have time."

"I want to do this," his dad said. "I *need* to do this for you. And we got time."

It was no surprise that his dad wasn't at work that morning after what had happened, but it was strange that he was up.

The other times he had spent most of the next day in bed, sleeping.

Reese's mom appeared at his bedroom door. She was dressed for work at the store, in her blue Kwik Stop shirt with the little yellow shell on the chest. She had dark rings under her eyes, like she hadn't gotten much sleep. Her hair was pulled back into a bun, but strands had come loose and were hanging around her heart-shaped face. "Your father is insisting on making breakfast before you go to school, so get up," she said. "I don't want to be late."

Reese wondered what his mom was thinking. But mostly what he wanted then was to get up, eat a bowl of Cheerios, which is what he usually had on school days, and pretend that everything that had happened the day before had been a bad dream.

"Reese!" his dad called from the kitchen. "How many sausages do you want?"

Reese looked at his mom, who shook her head and shrugged. "Tell him and let's get moving," she said.

"Two, I guess," he called back.

They had driven home from the hospital the night before in silence, and Reese had gone to his room and closed the door. Tony had been texting him, but he had ignored it. He had tried to draw for a while, but he had fallen asleep in his clothes, exhausted, with his face down on the paper. He got up now and changed into fresh clothes, moving like a robot, going through the motions of a normal weekday morning.

When he went into the kitchen, his dad, dressed in a white T-shirt and boxer shorts, was standing by the stove, mixing something in a bowl. Sausages whistled and popped in a pan on a back burner. His dad looked a little better than he had the night before; his face had some more color in it. But he had rings under his eyes like Reese's mom's, and his hair, which had gotten long in back, was sticking up all over the place. "Good morning, bud," he said. He gave Reese a smile, but not *the* smile. This one was there and then gone. He really looked like he should be in bed.

"What are you making?" Reese asked.

"I'm making you a pancake man," his dad said.

A pancake man was something his dad made on Sundays or holidays, a breakfast treat that Reese was too old for anyway. He still kind of liked it: It was something special his dad made only for him. But it wasn't a school-day thing.

"Do we have time?" he asked.

His dad waved away the question like he was shooing a fly. "You sound like your mother," he said. "Let me do this. I'm just about to pour the batter."

He didn't say a word about the day before, but Reese knew right then why he was out of bed, making them breakfast: He was trying to be the fun dad, trying to make Reese and his mom put all the bad stuff out of their minds, like hitting a reset button.

Reese watched him ladle the batter carefully into the big cast-iron skillet, first the body and then the head. He drizzled out another scoop to make the arms and legs, and there it was: a fat little man sizzling in oil. He shook the pan with the sausages in it, rolled them around. After a few moments, he leaned over the big skillet and poked the pancake man with one finger. "When it's ready to flip, do you want to do it?" he asked.

"No, you do it," Reese said. Flipping was the tricky part. No matter how many times Reese or his mom tried it, they never quite got the flip. They always lost something: an arm or a leg or even the head. But his dad was a wizard at it—a perfect pancake man nearly every time.

When it was ready, bubbling on the surface, he slid the spatula carefully under the man, flipped, and then: "Oh, crap."

"What happened?" Reese asked.

"I lost the leg," he said. Reese thought he saw something like a shadow move across his dad's face, but then he shook his head and tried to smile again. "We can fix it. Don't worry."

"I don't care," Reese said.

When the pancake man was done cooking, his dad put it on a plate, with the broken leg against the body. He got a can of whipped cream and a carton of blueberries from the fridge and went to work, with his back to Reese to block the view. Then he stepped back and smiled. "There!"

The pancake man had whipped-cream hair, blueberry eyes and shirt buttons. The broken leg had been rejoined to the body and covered with more whipped cream. "Well?" his dad said. "What do you think?"

"What's that supposed to be on his leg?" Reese asked.

"It's a cast," his dad said. "He broke his leg in a skiing accident."

Reese tried to make himself smile. He turned to his mom, who had come into the kitchen, and she looked so exhausted and sad that he suddenly wanted to try to help his dad make things better. "Check out what Dad made," he said.

She looked, but she didn't smile. It was like she was looking right though the pancake man and into the saddest thing she had ever seen. All she said was, "Hurry up and eat, will you? You're going to be late for school."

"Amanda . . ." his dad said.

"We're going to be late, Sam," she said.

Reese went to the dining table and ate fast. Then he got his backpack to go, but his mom said, "Go on out to the car. I'll be down in a minute. I need to talk to your dad."

"About what?" he asked.

"I just need to talk to your dad," she said. "Go on."

He went, and she closed the apartment door behind him. He walked down the stairs and out into the parking lot. His mom's car, the little red Ford Fiesta, was parked in front of their building next to the Barracuda. A light rain was falling from a low, gray sky, and Reese tried to open the Fiesta's door to get in out of the rain, but of course, the car was locked. A man in brown coveralls and a black baseball cap was in the doorway of the building next door, smoking a cigarette. The cap was pulled down low, and the man's eyes were in shadow, so Reese couldn't tell where he was looking, but he felt watched. He felt as if the smoking man was staring at him, the dumb kid standing by a locked car, getting rained on.

Where was his mom? She had been the one complaining about what a big hurry they were in, and now she wasn't coming out. He looked up at the windows of the apartments, empty squares of yellow light in the rainy morning. He kicked one of the Fiesta's tires. Then he went back into their building and up the dark stairwell to tell her to either get a move on or give him the keys so he could get into the car, out of the rain.

When he got to their apartment, on the second floor, he put a hand on the doorknob to go in, but just then he heard his mom through the closed door: "Enough," she was saying. "*Enough*, Sam."

She was standing just inside, and she sounded angry.

"You need to listen to me," Reese's dad said. "You're not listening."

Reese, alone in the stairwell, could have just walked down the stairs and out into the rain, not knowing. But he stood and listened, leaning in, his ear almost touching the door. He held his breath.

"*You* need to listen, Sam," his mom was saying. "You are sick. You need help. You need medical help. I've told you that and told you, but you haven't listened."

"You need to—" his dad began.

His mom cut him off: "Shut up and let me finish. I have lied for you. I have covered for you. I have lived with less while this drains away our money. And now I can't even let Reese walk home alone from school without worrying that he's going to find his father on the floor. What he saw yesterday no kid should ever see, and we are damn lucky that the hospital didn't call social services on us. So we're done with that. Either you get treatment now, *real help*, or we're out of here. I take Reese and we leave, period."

On the other side of the door, Reese had gone cold all over. She had never threatened to leave.

"You don't think this scared me, Amanda?" his dad said. "I know I have a problem. All I'm saying is I don't need the kind of help you're talking about. I can handle this in my own way."

"'Handle' this? I thought you were . . ." Her voice broke.

"I slipped up, Amanda," his dad said. "I let my guard down, and I had been clean for so long, it hit me harder than I expected. It was a mistake."

"Oh my God," his mom said. "A *mistake?* That's what you call what happened yesterday? That was you trying to handle this on your own, and you almost died this time. I wish I could reach in and just rip this thing out of you, so we can all be free of it. But I can't. I can't help you at all if you won't help yourself, and Reese and I cannot stand around and watch you do this to yourself. We *won't*. Yesterday might not have been the bottom for you, Sam, but it was for me."

"Amanda . . ." his dad said.

"We're done talking now," his mom said. "I've told you what you need to do. And I mean *today*, Sam. Now I've got to get Reese to school, and I've got to get to work."

Her voice got louder as she said this, as if she was stepping to the door to go out, and Reese's heart jumped. He didn't want her to catch him listening at the door, feared the scene spilling into the stairwell for the whole building to hear. So he went down the stairs as quickly and quietly as he could and out to the Fiesta.

The smoking man had gone inside. A few moments later, his mom came out. Her mouth was a thin, tight line. "I'm sorry to keep you waiting," she said.

She unlocked the car, and he got in. He didn't look at her. He didn't say anything about what he had heard, and he didn't want his mom to say anything. Not one word. What she had just threatened to do was too frightening to even talk about. Talking about it would make it more real, as if it were an actual possibility that could be discussed and considered.

She was just trying to scare his dad into getting better, Reese told himself. She must have been. She would never actually leave. She loved his dad, and his dad loved her. His dad also needed her. He needed both her and Reese. As horrible as it had been for Reese to find his dad on the floor, it was so much worse to think about what would have happened if he *hadn't* found him, if he and his mom had not been there to help. Hadn't his mom just said it herself, upstairs in the apartment? *"You almost died this time."*

Reese sat in the Fiesta beside her, staring straight ahead, hugging his backpack to his chest as if he were sitting next to a big box of explosives and unless he stayed absolutely quiet and still, it would blow them both sky high.

His mom didn't talk either. All the way to school, the only sounds were the hiss of the tires on the wet pavement and the squeaking of the windshield wipers going back and forth in the light rain.

He was relieved when they finally pulled up at Spendlowe Middle.

"Reese," his mom said when he had opened the car door to get out.

His heart turned over, afraid of what she was about to say. "What?"

"Just . . ." She stopped, and something about the break in her voice made him turn back to her. She shook her head. "Try to have a good day," she said. "That's all."

He got out and ran all the way to the doors of the school—and not because of the rain. He didn't even really mind when Mr. Rockers, the assistant principal, stopped him on the way in and told him to go to the office for a tardy slip because he was late for homeroom. It's not as if he exactly loved school, but one thing you could say about it: Nothing unexpected ever happened there. Every day was pretty much exactly like the day before. He knew what to do and where to go and didn't have to worry about anyone or take care of anyone but himself.

CHAPTER 5

It had stopped raining by the time recess came around, so Reese went out to the basketball court behind school. He hadn't had a chance to talk with Ryan and Tony, because he had gotten to school late and he didn't have any morning classes with them, but he knew they would meet him out there.

Ryan was under the basket when Reese came out, and then Tony appeared from the back door of the gym, dribbling a basketball. Tony always got the ball because he was the one Mrs. Brown, the gym teacher, trusted with gym equipment. Grownups loved Tony, because he was so polite and responsible. He was the oldest of four kids and sometimes acted and talked like he was a dad and about forty years old. He looked just like a younger version of his dad, too: same buzz cut, same serious brown eyes, same pointed chin.

He came up to Reese, still dribbling the ball, and the first thing he said was "Hey, how come you called me yesterday?"

"I didn't call you," Reese said.

"You did. I got a call from you right after school."

So much had happened that Reese had forgotten about accidentally dialing Tony the afternoon before. He remembered then, and a little prickle of worry ran up his neck. "Oh, right," he said. "I called by mistake." This was true, just not the whole truth.

"How come you didn't answer my texts?" Tony asked. He wouldn't drop it.

"I got busy," Reese said, irritated now. "I didn't see them."

He had never told Tony or Ryan or anyone else about his dad, and he wasn't going to start then. He knew he wasn't the only one who had a parent with a drug problem, but he didn't want to be that kid everyone felt sorry for—or worse, avoided, because other parents didn't want their kids hanging out with a kid from a messed-up family.

He thought sometimes about a boy who used to be in his class named Daryl Priddy. When they were in fifth grade, Daryl's father had showed up high at a school baseball game, passed out, and fallen off the bleachers. Reese saw how people treated Daryl after that, like he was the one with a problem or like he had a disease that they might catch. In sixth grade, Daryl's dad got arrested for selling drugs, and after that, kids wouldn't sit with Daryl at lunch or hang out with him at recess. Then, when seventh grade came around, no more Daryl Priddy: He had disappeared, moved away, Reese assumed. He didn't ask anyone about it because he didn't want to risk opening up the whole subject of drugs. He was just relieved not to have Daryl around.

"Think fast!" he said then, and he snatched the basketball from Tony. He dribbled once, twice, and broke quickly around for a tight pull-up jump shot before Tony or Ryan could take more than a couple steps. The swish of the ball going through the net gave Reese a satisfied feeling, and he had managed to distract Tony and change the subject, which felt good, too. Tony got the ball and came around to take a shot, but Reese poked the ball away and *swish*: another bucket.

Ryan laughed. "Nice one."

The feeling like a fist inside Reese started loosening, and for the first time since finding his dad, he could breathe a little easier. He passed the ball to Ryan, who was the smallest of the three of them, thin and wiry, with a big head of red hair that he never seemed to be able to get under control. He might have been short, but he was a good player, fast and aggressive. Ryan crossed over, dribbling left past Tony, and then sent up a hook shot that almost went in.

Reese got the rebound. "When are you supposed to go to Myrtle Beach?" he asked Ryan.

"Sunday, I think," Ryan said. His grandma had a beach house down there, and he and his family always went down at the start of the summer. This year, he was going to miss the last two days of school before summer break, but nothing ever happened then anyway.

"You'll be here for movie night tomorrow, right?" Reese asked.

"Yeah, I think so."

Movie night was kind of a regular thing, always at Tony's, because his house had an awesome rec room in the basement with a big-screen TV. "What are we watching anyway?" Reese asked.

"*John Wick*," Ryan said. He held his hands out together, arms straight, like he was holding a gun. He closed one eye to aim at the back of the field, past the court fence, and made like he was firing: "*Ka-pow!*"

"Be serious," Reese said. "It's R, and Tony's mom and dad would never let us watch that."

"How about *Fast & Furious?*" Ryan asked. "That's PG-13."

"That's R, too," Tony said.

"No, it's not."

"How could that not be R?" Reese said.

"Google it. It's PG-13, I swear."

"I don't think my mom would let us watch that anyway," Tony said.

"Your parents, man," Ryan said, shaking his head.

Reese saw Tony's face start to flush. He was getting mad. Ryan was always on Tony's case about how strict his family was, and Tony was touchy about it. Reese could feel a fight coming, and he'd had enough of fights. "Forget it," he said. "Let's play twenty-one."

That was okay by Ryan and Tony, so Reese walked to the top of the key and started things off with a shot that hit the rim and bounced off, just like it was supposed to: the tip-off. Ryan got the ball first, and he went in for a layup, but Tony blocked it and then he had the ball.

Sometimes guys played dirty at twenty-one, but Reese, Ryan, and Tony played it clean. No shoving, no elbows in the stomach or anything like that. You got one point a shot, and when you made a shot, you got to "make it, take it": You could take as many as three free throws, worth one point each, if you could make them without missing. The winner was the first player to get to twenty-one points, although most of the time they didn't bother to keep score; they were just messing around. As they played, Reese's worries about his mom and dad began to fade. When he made his first shot, he took the ball back to the free throw line and dribbled it once, twice, three times. He took a deep breath and let it out. Then he turned his back to the basket.

"You never quit trying, dude," Ryan said.

All school year, whenever they played twenty-one, Reese had been trying this trick: the backward free throw. The challenge he had set for himself, just for the fun of it, out there on the playground where no one was keeping score anyway, was to make all three shots in a row backward. His record was two.

"You'll never make all three," Ryan said. "But if you do, you get to choose the movie tomorrow."

"But no R," Tony said.

"Okay, okay," Ryan said, grinning. "No R. No G either, though."

Reese set his feet carefully, using the basket at the other end of the court to line himself up just right. Out on the field, past the court fence, he could see some boys playing soccer. A few were from his class, but most were eighth-graders. Behind them, above the trees, a little patch of blue sky had appeared.

He closed his eyes. He knew this court so well, had shot so many baskets there, that he could see every detail in his mind: the wood backboard, the rust-spotted rim. He took another breath and let it out. Then he shot, his right arm arching over his head. He heard the swish of the ball going through the net. He smiled.

"Nice!" said Tony. "All net. I wish I could do that."

Ryan passed the ball back, and Reese turned his back again to the basket and took another breath and let it out slowly. He closed his eyes and shot. He heard the ball hit the rim, and he thought he had missed. But Ryan shouted: "*Two!* You tied your record."

When he opened his eyes, he saw that some of the boys playing soccer in the field had stopped and turned to watch.

Ryan passed him the ball. "I think you got this," he said. "I think today is the day."

"You told me I'd never do it."

"I got a good feeling all of a sudden," Ryan said.

Mr. Nash, Reese's homeroom teacher, who was on recess duty that morning, had come over. Sometimes, when he wasn't on duty and didn't have papers to grade, Mr. Nash would shoot baskets with them. He knew Reese had been trying for three in a row. He called to him from the other side of the court fence: "Was that the second basket just now?"

"Yes, sir," Reese said.

"Good luck."

Some guys get wound tight when people watch them shoot free throws, and when they get tight, they miss. But Reese didn't mind being watched here on the court. He took another deep breath and let it out slowly.

"Take your time," Ryan said. "Don't rush. You got this. Just relax."

"Shut up and let him shoot," Tony said.

Reese smiled. He closed his eyes, and he visualized the basket. He let every detail of it fill his mind, and at that moment all the bad stuff was gone. He bent his knees a little. When he took the shot, he knew as soon as the ball left his hand that he was going to make it. His arm had hooked perfectly. And then: *swish*.

CHAPTER 6

Mr. Nash wondered what the record was for most backward free throws, and they looked it up on his phone before they went inside at the end of recess. The world record was thirteen in one minute by a guy from the United Kingdom named Tom "Conman" Connors. They watched a clip of it on Mr. Nash's phone. It was pretty incredible, although it wasn't all in a row. Someday, Reese thought, maybe he could break that record. Or he could set his own, like most backward free throws in a row by a kid. He could work on it over the summer, get Ryan and Tony to keep the balls coming to him as he shot.

That's what he was thinking about when he got home from school that afternoon. He was imagining what his name would look like in *Guinness World Records*: "Reese Thomas Buck, age twelve, from Spendlowe, North Carolina, USA." No, age thirteen, actually: His birthday was coming up. He wondered if there was a cash prize when you set a world record.

His mom's Fiesta was parked in front of their apartment building when he walked up. The Barracuda was gone, which Reese thought could mean that his dad had done what his mom wanted and gone to ask about getting help.

He went in and up the stairs to their apartment, No. 3. He let himself in with his key. He called out, "Hey, Mom! Guess what happened today?" He was going to tell her about the free throws.

But when he saw her, he forgot all about basketball and world records and anything else good.

She was in her bedroom, with a suitcase open on the bed, and she was folding clothes to pack them. Her eyes were red. She had been crying.

And just like that, everything flipped again, from good to bad. It happened so fast that Reese just stood there for a moment at the bedroom door staring at her. She didn't say anything either. She didn't even look up at first. She just looked down at the suitcase.

Finally Reese asked, "What are you doing?"

He wasn't stupid. He had heard what she had told his dad that morning about hitting bottom, about leaving, and here she was with a suitcase. But maybe she was just taking the threat to the next level, packing the suitcase to show his dad that she really, really was serious this time about him getting help.

She rubbed her eyes with the heel of her hand. "Sit down with me here, please, so we can talk about this."

"I don't want to sit down," he said. "I want to know where Dad is and why you're packing."

She sat on the edge of the bed anyway, alone. She put her hands on her knees, palms down, and she just sat like that for a few moments, looking at her hands. Then finally she said, "I told your father this morning that he needs to get into a drug treatment program. No questions or delays. He needs real help now."

"I heard you," Reese said.

She blinked and frowned. "When? This morning?"

"I came back upstairs because you didn't come out, and I heard you through the door."

She winced. "I'm sorry you had to hear that."

"But you're not serious about leaving," he said. "We can't actually leave."

"Let me finish, Reese. I had thought . . . I had hoped . . . that your father was scared enough by what happened yesterday that he would see that he needs to get treatment. But I guess that's still not the case. He made that very clear to me this afternoon when we talked about it again."

"He said what happened yesterday was a mistake," Reese said. "I heard him. He said he's going to get better. You have to give him a chance to do it. Where is he now? Where did he go?"

"He got upset and left."

"To go where?" Reese was starting to get really scared.

"Just out, Reese," she said.

"Text him. Call him."

"Reese, your father is sick," she said. "This thing . . . the pills, this addiction . . . it has its claws in him, and it's not letting go that easy. I think you know that. And I think your father knows it, too, deep down. But he's not willing to do what he needs to do to get better. Not yet. And until he is, we can't stay here. You can't go through again what you went through yesterday. I can't allow it. We're going to pack some things and go stay with Mrs. Smith and her family for a while. I called her, and she's expecting us."

Reese shook his head. They had slipped into some bizarre nightmare. Mrs. Smith? The church lady? "What are you talking about?" he said.

"We're going to go and stay with the Smiths, right now. I want you to pack your suitcase. I need time away to think, and Mrs. Smith has lots of room at her place. They live out in the country, and they have a trailer we can use. So that's where we're going."

She might as well have told him that they were taking her little Fiesta to the moon. It was impossible. The words, the threats, were one thing: *I will leave.* But to do it, to make plans—to call someone and arrange a place to stay . . . Reese had never, ever imagined she would actually do that. He felt light-headed, and something was wrong with his eyes suddenly: It was like he was squinting down the wrong end of a telescope, so that his mom looked small and far away. "You can't," he said. "We, we're . . ." Something was wrong with his voice, too: It cracked and caught.

"Reese—" She leaned forward and reached for his arm.

He pushed her hand away, and he found his voice: "We can't just *leave*," he said. "How can we just leave Dad? How could you do that?"

"What we've been doing is not working," she said. "Looking the other way is not working. Going around and around, up and down, from bad to good and then back to bad, is not working. I need to step away and figure out a better way. Okay? And I need your help."

"And what about Dad? Doesn't he need our help? What if he . . ." He couldn't finish the sentence. It was too scary to say out loud what might happen if they weren't there to find him, and he knew he didn't have to say it to his mom anyway. She knew what might happen, but here she was packing anyway. They couldn't just walk away and risk losing his dad forever. It was crazy. It was wrong.

"No," he said. "I'm not going."

"*Reese!*" She put a hand over her mouth and closed her eyes. She took a deep breath through her nose. When she brought her hand away, he saw a thumb-sized white spot on her cheek that darkened slowly to pink. She said, "I don't know what else to do right now. Please, we have to leave."

"I'm not going," he said again.

"Look, you sit," she said. "I'll pack your bag." She went to the closet in the hallway and took out another suitcase. She went into his bedroom—*his* room to pack *his* clothes. He followed her. She put the suitcase on his bed and opened it.

"Stop it," he said. "No."

Her hands were shaking. She opened his top dresser drawer, gathered up his underwear, and put them in the suitcase. Reese stood there for a moment, his face hot, both hands on his head, watching this. She had gone way over the line. She had lost her mind.

When she opened the next drawer and gathered up a bunch of his shirts, he went over to the suitcase, picked up the underwear, and put them back in the dresser. "We're staying with Dad," he said.

"Reese, we're going. Please. I need you to help me."

"No," he said. They were stuck in a horrible nightmare loop, and he was going around and around with it, powerless to stop.

"We're leaving," his mom said. She picked up the underwear and turned to put them back in the suitcase. But Reese grabbed the suitcase and moved it away from her. She dropped the underwear and tried to pull the suitcase from him. He pulled back, and then they were tugging it between them.

Reese heard himself yelling: "I'm not leaving!"

"Stop it!" His mom was yelling, too. *"Stop this!"*

Then she pulled with all her strength, and something about the look on her face, wild-eyed, her mouth screwed up, made Reese's whole body turn to ice. He had never seen her so upset and out of control. All the fight went out of him, and he let go.

His mom fell backward to the floor.

She sat wide-eyed for a moment, the overturned suitcase in front of her, and then she drew in her legs and lowered her head until it was almost touching her knees. Her shoulders began to shake. For half a moment, he thought she was laughing. Then he realized what was happening. "Oh, no," he said. "Oh, no, no. Mom, I'm sorry. Please, stop crying. Please stop."

He had done this, he thought. He had made his mother cry. He knelt beside her. He would have given anything to make things better, but he had no idea what to do. He just knelt there, his hands at his sides, and waited for her tears to stop.

CHAPTER 7

They were beyond the town limits on a country road running into the darkness. Reese was in the front passenger seat, slumped so low that the seatbelt cut across his throat. He was playing with his pocketknife, a Buck knife his dad had given him when he turned twelve. He was opening and closing the blade. He hadn't spoken for miles. But when his mom slowed and turned right onto a road that wasn't even two lanes—more like a lane and a half with ragged edges—he broke his silence: "Where the hell are we?"

"Watch your language, Reese," his mom said. "You should . . ."

She didn't finish.

"What?" Reese asked.

His mom shook her head. "Nothing. We're almost there." She wasn't going to take the bait and start fighting again.

Back at the apartment, when she had stopped crying, she

had gotten up and finished packing his suitcase. Then she had gone to the kitchen and put some food from the fridge in the cooler they used for camping trips. Reese had tried to argue again, tried to talk sense into her, and between that and her having to take everything down the stairs by herself—he certainly wasn't going to help—it was getting dark when she told him it was time to leave.

He had tried texting and calling his dad. He told him in his texts exactly what his mom was doing: Mom is freaking out. She is packing the car. WHERE RU? CALL HER. TEXT HER. But he got no response.

Reese had thought about just sitting on the floor of his bedroom and refusing to move. It's not as if his mom were strong enough to carry him out of the apartment. But then he had thought of that look on her face when he tried to wrestle the suitcase from her, and he couldn't go through that again, not then. And what was the alternative to going with her anyway? Staying alone with his dad? As much as he didn't want them leaving, he absolutely did not want to be on his own with his dad and try to handle things by himself. So he had gone with her finally, out of the apartment and down the dark stairs.

His last hope had been that his dad would reappear and talk his mom out of this, and he had held on to that hope until the moment she got into the Fiesta and turned the key in the ignition. Then, feeling like he had been twisted and wrung out, he had given up and climbed into the car with her, and they had headed out of the apartment parking lot and the neighborhood.

Turn by turn, everything familiar had dropped away, until the houses thinned out and it was all just empty fields and dark skies.

"I think this is our turn up ahead," his mom said.

Reese saw a street sign in their headlights, and his mom slowed and turned onto a narrow dirt road. The sign read, **SMITH FARM LANE**. The car bucked and swayed. Reese put one hand out the window to hold on to the roof of the car to steady himself. They had fallen off the map, and now they were breaking their butts rattling down some unpaved road. It took them across an open field to a line of trees, which were a deeper black against the night sky. They went through the trees, and then Reese saw a house, ahead and to the left. The windows, upstairs and down, were lit. Across the front was a long porch.

From tall weeds to the right, something small dashed into the road, and his mom slammed on the brakes to keep from hitting it. It was a cat. It stopped at the opposite edge of the road and looked at them, its eyes glowing green in their headlights. That cat was followed by another, stepping slowly, with its tail straight up. It stopped in front of the car and stared at them with glowing eyes. In the headlights it looked pure white. Reese's mom leaned out her window. "Shoo, get," she said to it. "I don't want to hit you."

The white cat blinked. Then it finished crossing, but in its own time, with one last look at them over its shoulder.

An outside light on a pole clicked on as they pulled in

beside the house, next to a hatchback, and his mom turned off the engine. The only sound then was a chorus of chirruping: frogs. His mom got out, but Reese stayed in the car and looked around angrily. Across the dirt road from the house was a mobile home, a trailer. Between it and the house stood a big tree with a homemade swing, an old tire on a rope, hanging from one of its lower branches. Next to the swing sat a picnic table, and beyond that was an old basketball hoop with no net.

A light came on next to the back door. The screen door opened, squeaking, and a boy stepped out onto the back steps. Another cat, a black one, came out behind him. Reese's mom had said nothing about other kids, and that was the last thing Reese needed right then: some kid getting into his business, trying to talk to him at a horrible time like this. The church lady, Mrs. Smith, was bad enough. Reese slid down in the seat to avoid being seen.

He couldn't tell how old the boy was, but he might have been about his age. He was Ryan's height probably. He was dressed in what looked like pajama pants and a T-shirt. His feet were bare. His hair was cut close. His eyes were in shadow.

Then Mrs. Smith came out behind him, dressed in a skirt and a white T-shirt. "Charlie," she said, "I told you to please stay inside. You can say hello tomorrow." She turned the boy around and steered him inside, her hands on his shoulders, like he was about five years old. She shut the door behind him and walked to meet them. The black cat followed her.

"Amanda, hello," she said. "And Reese . . ." She bent a little to see into the car, where he was still slumped in the passenger seat. "Reese, welcome."

He didn't answer.

His mom said, "Thank you, Mattie, for letting us stay."

"Have you eaten?"

"We're good," she said. "Thank you. We have some food in the cooler." She said this as if they had just dropped in for a friendly visit, as if their world had not just blown apart.

"That was my grandson, Charlie, who came out just now, wanting to say hello, but I figured you all would be exhausted. Tomorrow, though, if you're up to it, I know he and my granddaughter, Meg, would like to say hi." She ducked again to look into the car. "Charlie is fifteen, Reese. Meg is thirteen, which is about your age, I think. Is that right? Meg just finished seventh grade at Ogden Middle. Today was her last day."

Reese didn't answer that either. Why exactly would he care how old the kid on the porch and his sister were? Or want to meet them?

"Reese is about to turn thirteen," his mom said. "His birthday is in about two weeks. And he's just finishing seventh grade, too. Reese, why don't you get out?"

He didn't budge.

"Reese?" his mom said. "Please."

"Amanda, it's okay," said Mrs. Smith. Like his mom, she sounded as if she was trying to keep it breezy, cheerful, just chitchatting in the fake way grown-ups do with each other, no matter what's going on or what they're really feeling. But Mrs. Smith obviously knew what had just happened. She knew everything.

She was looking at him, her head cocked a little to one side, like she had at the ER, as if she was going to say something. Then she blinked and looked at his mom. "We could make space in the house, and you're welcome to stay in there if you want," she said. "But I thought maybe you'd want your own space, and the trailer is free. We rent our fields out to a neighbor, and he uses the trailer sometimes for seasonal workers he brings in later in the summer. But it's empty now. I carried in clean sheets and towels and tried to straighten up as much as I could after you called."

"Anything is fine," his mom said. "You shouldn't have gone to that trouble."

"Come on and I'll show you."

"Reese?" his mom said.

"He's fine, Amanda," said Mrs. Smith. "Reese, you're fine."

No, he wasn't. Did this lady think that he was stupid or that he was some little kid who didn't know exactly what was going on?

He didn't move as they began walking to the trailer without him. He looked at his phone for the millionth time to see if his dad had texted. Nothing. The only text was from Ryan, about the Braves again. Then the boy in the pajama pants came back, standing at the back door, looking out through the screen. Reese was afraid he might come out and try to talk to him, so he put his knife in his pocket, got out of the car, and followed his mom.

The trailer was white, with a metal skirt all around and four small windows along the side facing the house. Three wooden steps led up to the door at one end. The black cat walked alongside Mrs. Smith to the trailer.

"I hope you don't mind cats," she said. "They're Charlie's. He is absolutely crazy about cats. He picks them up as strays and rescues. He can't resist them. I've lost track of how many he has."

"I like cats," his mom said.

"I'm not a big fan, to be honest with you," Mrs. Smith said. "But they're important to Charlie. This black one here will get inside with you if you let her. Just give her a nudge with your toe if she gets too pushy. The only one you want to watch out for is a white one. He'll bite you if you try to touch him."

"I think we saw him coming in," Reese's mom said.

They went up the steps and in, Reese last. Mrs. Smith flipped a switch, and two fluorescent bulbs overhead buzzed and flickered on. Reese blinked in the sudden light. Mrs. Smith said, "I'm sorry I didn't have time to really clean up before you came. I can help you do that later on. It needs a good scrub and an airing-out."

Reese looked around, and although he didn't think he could possibly feel any sadder or more upset, his heart sank into the ground at what he saw. The floors in the front room and kitchen were covered with cracked brown-and-yellow linoleum.

The walls were bare except for a cheesy religious picture in the front room—a golden-haired Jesus holding a white lamb, rays of light streaming from his head like laser beams. For furniture, there was a blue sofa and a plaid recliner, both worn. On two stacked plastic milk crates was a small TV. In the kitchen were a wooden table and three chairs. These were worn, too, the wood chipped. On the table was a thick book with a black cover.

The stale air pressing in made him feel trapped. He thought his mom surely would come to her senses at last and say they couldn't possibly stay there. But what she said was, "It's great, Mattie. You don't have to clean it. We'll take care of that. We're just grateful to you for letting us stay for a while."

He wanted to yell and kick something, and he would have if Mrs. Smith hadn't been there.

The old lady was moving through the kitchen to the other end of the trailer. "The bathroom and bedrooms are back here," she said. Reese's mom followed. He went only as far as the kitchen. He turned to the table and picked up the book. Large silver letters on the cover read, *Sagrada Biblia*.

"It's a Spanish Bible," said Mrs. Smith, like he'd asked or cared. She had come back into the kitchen. His mom was behind her, the tour of this dump done. "The workers who stay here come from Mexico mostly. Or Guatemala."

Reese put the book down.

"What else can I tell you?" Mrs. Smith said. "The water's good. It's off the same well we're on at the house, and there should be plenty. There are dishes in the cabinets. You can use the washer and dryer at the house to do your laundry when you need to. Please just knock at the house if you need anything. Reese, that goes for you, too. Let us know if we can help."

He looked down at the linoleum floor, his face burning. He was so angry, it took everything he had not to yell at them both. His mom said to Mrs. Smith, "I'm sorry."

"There's nothing to apologize for," said Mrs. Smith.

His mom said good night and thank you again, and Mrs. Smith left them. As soon as she was gone, Reese turned on his mother. "What are you doing? We can't stay here. We have to go home."

Her face started to get red. She was angry, too. "Do you think I like this, Reese? I hate this. But don't be rude to the Smiths. They're putting themselves out for us when we need help."

"Dad needs help," Reese said. He was back to that. He was always going to come back to that.

"Reese, for God's sake."

"We have to go back to him," he said. "Why isn't he calling or texting? He could be hurt somewhere."

"Your father was upset and angry. When he calms down and wants to call, I have my phone. You have yours."

"I want to go home now," he said. "Call Dad. We can go."

"Reese, no," she said. "You and I—"

He walked out before she could finish. He let the trailer's

screen door fall shut with a bang behind him. His mom called after him: "Reese! Come back inside."

He took off running, past the swing and the house and then up the dirt road. He had no idea where he would go. He just ran. When he got to the trees, he slowed, afraid of stepping into a hole in the darkness and falling. He kept going until he reached the front road.

Then he squatted in the gravel at the edge of the road and just looked into the darkness. He could hear the frogs singing from the trees behind him. Above him was no moon, just stars—many, many more than he saw in town. He didn't know how far away town was. He had lost track on the drive. It was too far to walk anyway, he knew that much.

He took out his phone and tried to call his dad again. No answer. He texted him: Call mom. Now. When he looked up, his eyes were all messed up from the glare of the screen, and the night around him was darker than ever. He blinked hard, rubbed his eyes.

He pictured his mom alone now in the trailer that wasn't theirs, worrying about him, and he felt a mean sort of pleasure in making her worry. She was the one who had blown up their family. It was her fault he was stuck out there in a crummy trailer in the middle of nowhere. And if his dad wasn't hurt somewhere, she clearly had gotten him so upset that he wasn't texting or calling.

His dad had done something like that once before, early last year, when he had lost his job and Reese's mom had really let him have it about the drugs, about the money he was wasting on them and about how badly he was hurting himself. He got so angry then that he left and didn't call for two days. He said later he'd been upset and wasn't thinking straight. Reese also had figured it was probably the drugs: They had messed his dad up, made him lose track of time or something.

Reese told himself that this time was like that one, that his dad would call eventually. But he also was afraid that it was worse than that: Maybe his dad had overdosed again, and he was lying someplace where no one understood what was wrong or could reach him to try to help.

He felt a wave of anger at his mom again. But Reese also was angry at his dad. If his dad really loved them, wouldn't he just do what his mom wanted him to do and stop for good?

Reese hung his head. He was grateful for the darkness then because he started crying, like a little kid.

Exactly how long he was there he wasn't sure. No cars came. His phone stayed silent; there was no response from his dad to his text. The only sounds were the frogs singing, the breeze whispering through the field, and way off, a dog barking. When he stopped crying, he took out his Buck knife and fiddled with the blade, opening and closing it. At last he closed the knife and, putting it in his pocket, stood up and walked back to the trailer. Because where else could he go?

His mom heard him come through the door, and she called to him from the back bedroom. "Reese?"

He ducked into the bathroom, which was so small it felt

more like a closet, and he closed the door. He splashed water on his face and rubbed hard, trying to wash away any sign that he had been crying. He looked at himself in the tiny mirror over the sink, water dripping from the end of his nose. He had red rings under his eyes. He patted his face with a towel, wiped his nose, and tried to smooth his dirty-blond hair. He flushed the toilet on the way out and ran the water again to make it sound like he had gone in there to pee.

When he came out, his mom was at the kitchen table, with the Spanish Bible in front of her. "Have you been crying?" she asked.

"No," he lied.

"Where did you go?"

"Around," he said. Then: "You've been smoking." He could smell it. She had been promising to quit.

She frowned and opened her mouth to yell at him. She hated it when he got on her case about smoking. But then she shook her head and said, "Why don't you go lie down in your bedroom while I make us something to eat? I made your bed."

"It's not my bed," he said. "This isn't my home."

"No, it's not. But we'll get through this, Reese. We'll figure this out. Okay?" She stood and stretched out her arms to him. "Will you give me a hug, please?"

He let her draw him to her. He was exhausted suddenly, like all the blood had been sucked out of his body. He put his arms around her and rested his chin on her shoulder. He smelled cigarettes, but also all the good, familiar scents he knew: the soap she always used, the fabric softener she put in the laundry, a touch of the perfume that he thought smelled like a flower garden on a warm, sunny day.

He tried to forget where he was and imagine he was home.

CHAPTER 8

When Reese woke the next morning, on Saturday, the first thing he did was check his phone for messages from his dad. Still nothing. His heart sank.

He sat up and looked out the window, which he had opened overnight because the trailer was so stuffy. The hatchback was still out there, along with his mom's car. Next to them was a red pickup truck, which must have come in late the night before. The sides were splattered with mud. Beyond the cars was the house. It was white and tall, with a steep green roof and two brick chimneys, one at each end. It looked old. He looked at the tire swing and the basketball hoop. The hoop looked like it hadn't been used in ages: no net, paint peeling from the wooden backboard, with hard-packed dirt around the pole. Two cats were lying there in the sun.

Beyond the yard and the house, a field of bright green, close-mown grass sloped gently away, disappearing behind a clump of trees that grew along the other side of the road from the trailer. Across the field, against another line of trees, was an open barn with a metal roof and a tractor parked outside.

Nothing moved out there. He heard a bird calling out: *TEA-kettle TEA-kettle TEA-kettle.* A squirrel squawked, scolding the cats maybe.

Then he heard his mom moving around in the kitchen, clanking pots, and he got up and went to her. She was on her knees, rooting around in a cabinet. She was barefoot, in a T-shirt and shorts. "What are you doing?" he asked.

She sat back on her heels. "I'm looking for a frying pan. Do you want eggs if I make them?"

"I guess."

"You still want to go to Tony's for movie night?"

"Why wouldn't I?" The truth was he had forgotten about movie night after everything that had happened, but he would take any opportunity to get out of the trailer.

His mom ignored the rude edge in his voice. "I'm glad you're going. I told Larry I'd fill in for a few hours at the store this evening and I can just drop you at Tony's when I go in." Larry was her boss at the Kwik Stop, the son of the store's owner. She put the frying pan on the stove. "After breakfast, I'll clean this place up, make it more comfortable."

"Make it more comfortable for what?" Reese said. "I still don't know what we're doing, how long we're staying here. Have you tried calling Dad?"

"Don't start in on me again," she snapped. "I don't know

what the next move is, Reese. Okay? This is not forever. I told you that. But this is awful, and I'm making it up as I go."

"*Are* you going to call Dad today?"

"I know this isn't what you want to hear, but that won't help," she said. "He will call when he's ready to talk. I told him what he needs to do. The next move is up to him."

She looked so tired, and Reese knew he was making things harder on her. But that feeling like a fist was back inside him, so he just turned and went to the bedroom. If he had a door, he would have slammed it, but he didn't even have that.

He lay on the bed. A ceiling tile directly above him was stained a light brown, from an old leak in the trailer roof probably.

In the kitchen, his mom was pushing ahead with breakfast. He heard drawers opening and closing, forks or something clinking. After a moment, he rolled over and picked up the clipboard with the paper and pencil from the hospital, which his mom had put in his suitcase the day before. He started drawing again.

He almost always drew cars, airplanes, robots, tanks. It was what he was best at: gears, engines, metal. Sometimes he let his imagination carry him in strange directions, and he drew impossible machines, bigger and crazier than anything in real life.

This time, though, he wanted to draw something real: his dad's Barracuda, just as it was.

His dad loved that car. It was a 1971 Plymouth Barracuda,

metallic green, with double hood scoops. His dad had brought it back from the dead when Reese was younger. He had overhauled the engine, replaced the transmission, fixed the suspension, and reupholstered the interior. It had taken him forever, scrounging for parts and working on it weekends and evenings.

Reese loved the Barracuda, too, almost as much as his dad did. It was powerful, dramatic, and so much fun to ride in, especially on a sunny day, with the windows down and the stereo cranked. As soon as he was old enough, his dad had let him help with it. He had showed Reese how to change the oil, adjust the carburetor, rotate the tires. One of the beautiful things about the Barracuda, his dad had told him, was that it was a car you could work on yourself, with just your hands and simple tools. It had none of the fancy electronics and computers that were in modern cars.

Reese loved all its details, and he knew them well from studying them and drawing them: the slope of the hood scoops, the graceful curve of the fenders, the shine of the grip on the shifter inside between the front seats, the clean line of circular gauges along the dashboard. He drew it now traveling on an empty highway, a sun rising on the horizon behind it.

As he worked on the drawing, he thought about his dad and the conversation he had overheard through the closed door at their apartment. He thought of his mom, so tired and so angry at his dad: "*Either you get treatment, real help, or we're out of here.*"

He wished that his dad would call and say what his mom

needed to hear to realize that she had been wrong to leave. They could be back together in town, the three of them, before the day was out, if only his dad would say and do the right things and if only his mom would listen.

The pans clinked and clanked in the kitchen. The bird called again from outside: *TEA-kettle TEA-kettle*. Reese considered calling or texting his dad yet again to tell him to call his mom. But then he had another idea.

He pushed his drawing aside and reached for his phone. He called up the web browser and googled: *drug treatment help*. Then he added the name of their town, *Spendlowe*.

This brought up nothing in Spendlowe, but there were four results in Goldsville. He opened the link to one, a place called East Carolina Addiction Treatment Center. The home page read, "We provide counseling, psychotherapy, and testing and evaluation for adolescents and adults. Our caring licensed professionals will serve your needs with sensitivity and compassion."

That sounded promising. He went back to the search results and opened another link. It was a place called Lighthouse Health of Goldsville. On the home page was a picture of a smiling man who looked about the same age as Reese's dad, standing at a window with sunlight streaming in. Above the man were the words, "A Guiding Light to Recovery!" That was pretty cheesy, but the place looked good.

Reese pulled up his messaging app and considered for a moment what to say to his dad. He typed: Hi Dad. Here are some places to go for help like Mom wants. Will you call them? I will keep searching. Please read and CALL.

In the text, he pasted the links to Lighthouse Health and the other place. He hit send. He had no idea if his parents could afford places like those or whether they were what his dad needed, but he hoped that the links would at least get his dad looking, and then maybe he would see that getting help like his mom wanted wouldn't be so bad. The website for Lighthouse Health, with the sunshine and the smiling man, made it seem pretty nice, actually.

He tried to think of other search terms. He knew the name of a kind of pill his dad had taken, because he had heard his mom talking about it. He wasn't sure how to spell it, but autocorrect fixed it as he typed: *OxyContin treatment help*. This search brought up something called SAMHSA: Substance Abuse and Mental Health Services Administration. The home page had a phone number you could call for free help finding treatment and other information.

Reese typed a second text to his dad: Here's another. CALL. He pasted the new link and phone number into that message and hit send. He was starting to feel a little better. It looked like help was out there, and it felt good to *do* something, even if it was small, to try to fix this huge mess they were all in. And maybe these texts would cut through whatever haze or anger his dad was walking around in and get him to do something, too.

Reese decided it would be best to keep this between him and

his dad, at least for now. Partly this was because he thought his dad must still be mad at his mom and maybe would listen more if it was just Reese talking to him about this stuff. But he also thought his mom would need to see his dad getting treatment on his own, without knowing that Reese had been pushing him, before she would believe he was really serious.

Reese was scrolling through the search results again when suddenly someone spoke outside the trailer, a woman: "Just go up to the door with your brother, Meg, for goodness' sake. It won't kill you."

It was Mrs. Smith.

"Charlie," she said, "keep the plate level, please, or the cookies will slide off."

A girl spoke: "Why can't I just go back inside?"

"Just go, Meg," said Mrs. Smith. "You don't have to have a big conversation if you don't want to."

Reese remembered Mrs. Smith talking about her grandkids the night before: Meg and Charlie. He almost sat up, curious to get a look at them in daylight. But he didn't want to be seen and get dragged into coming out and talking with them.

A moment later there was a knock at the trailer's door. Reese's mom answered, and he heard her say, "Hey, y'all. Are those for us? That's really nice."

The boy, Charlie, spoke: "We can show you around if you want." Something was different about his voice, Reese thought. The words came out a little hard to understand, kind of like he had a marble or something in his mouth.

"I'm in the middle of cooking right now," Reese's mom said. "But Reese might. Can you wait a minute while I check? Do you want to come in?"

"Okay," Charlie said.

"No," said the girl, Meg. "No, Charlie. That's okay. We should wait here."

"It's no problem," Reese's mom said.

"No, thank you," said Meg.

His mom came to the bedroom. "It's Mrs. Smith's grandkids outside."

"I heard them," Reese said, not moving.

She motioned for him to keep his voice down. She came to the bed and leaned over to speak softly, so the kids outside wouldn't hear: "They have chocolate chip cookies for us, which is very nice. They want to know if you want to come out and look around. I think it would be polite. And you might enjoy it. I saw a basketball hoop out there, too. I bet there's a ball somewhere around, and maybe they would shoot baskets with you."

"Nope." He wanted no part of this place, and he wanted nothing to do with anyone living there.

His mom sighed, exasperated. She went back to the door. "I'm sorry," he heard her say. "Reese isn't feeling good right now."

"That's okay," Charlie said. Then: "Hey, have you seen my cats? Do you know how many I have?"

"Well, I don't know," Reese's mom said. "How many?"

"Take a guess," Charlie said.

"Hush, Charlie," Meg said. "She doesn't want to play games."

The edge in the girl's voice made Reese finally sit up to peek out. He couldn't see Charlie from that angle, but he could see Meg. She had brown hair pulled back in a ponytail, and she was tall, a little taller than him, Reese thought. She had long arms and legs, and she was wearing cutoff jean shorts, a green T-shirt, and red high-top sneakers.

But what Reese noticed most about her was the look on her face. Her eyes were down, and she was frowning. She looked mad or embarrassed, like she wanted to disappear, like she didn't want to be there any more than Reese did.

"Well, let me think," his mom was saying. "I've seen three cats. How about five? I'll guess that you have five cats."

"Ha!" Charlie laughed. "I have thirteen cats."

"Wow! Thirteen!" Reese's mom said in her fake cheerful voice. "And you take care of all of those?"

"I do," Charlie said.

"Well, I'll look forward to meeting all your cats when I have more time," Reese's mom said. "Thank you for the cookies. Tell your grandma we said thank you." The door closed, and Reese lay back quickly on the bed so his mom wouldn't catch him peeking out. When she came back to him, she stood in the doorway until he finally turned his head to look at her. "What?"

"You're really just going to lie there?"

"What else am I supposed to do? I'm stuck here. We're stuck here, until Dad calls."

"You could at least look around," she said. "Mrs. Smith says the river is close, just at the bottom of the field out there. She says there's a little dock, and you can go swimming. They have a canoe, too."

"No, thanks."

She sighed again. "Well, look, breakfast is just about ready. Come and eat."

He got up, but only because he was hungry. His mom had made toast and scrambled eggs and hash browns from a bag, browned in a pan. The cookies Meg and Charlie had brought were on the kitchen counter. He ate his breakfast quickly and in silence, his eyes down. Then, ignoring the cookies, he went to the bedroom and lay back down on the bed. He did nothing for a little while. But then he rolled over and continued searching on his phone for places his dad could go for help.

He heard his mom cleaning up in the kitchen. He didn't offer to help her, and she didn't ask.

CHAPTER 9

Normally, Reese would have just ridden his bike over to Tony's house for movie night. But because he and his mom were now way out in the middle of nowhere, his mom had to drive him into town. On the way there, slumped beside her in the front seat, Reese did some more searching on his phone for helpful links to send his dad. His dad hadn't responded to his earlier texts, and he hadn't picked up when he tried to call again, which upset and worried Reese. But he was going to keep trying.

His mom was watching him out of the corner of her eye while she drove, and finally, she said, "Whatcha looking at? You're really focused."

He didn't want to talk with her about his research, so he said, "Nothing." He put his phone face down in his lap.

"Okay, whatever," his mom said. She sounded a little annoyed—or hurt maybe, which made him almost reconsider and tell her what he was doing. But he kept his mouth shut the rest of the way to Spendlowe.

His mom dropped him off at Tony's on the way to the Kwik Stop. Tony's mom, Mrs. Alvarez, opened the door when Reese knocked. She was wearing a blue-and-white-striped apron, and she had a blue handkerchief tied over her hair. He could smell something good baking, pie maybe.

"Hi, Reese," she said. "The boys and Tony's dad are downstairs. They're trying to figure out something with the TV."

Reese took off his shoes at the door before going in, which was a strict rule at the Alvarez house. Mrs. Alvarez didn't want anyone tracking dirt on her white carpet. He walked down the front hall to the basement door. Maybe it was the carpet, but Tony's house was always very quiet. If Tony and Ryan were talking in the basement, he couldn't hear them. At his family's apartment, Reese heard the neighbors, upstairs and down, all the time, moving heavy things around, fighting sometimes. At the Alvarez place, it was so quiet that you could almost hear your own breathing.

"Oh, hey, Reese, do you like chili?" Mrs. Alvarez said when he got to the basement door. "I've got some going, and it's Tony's favorite. We were talking about having that for supper, but we could also order pizza if you want. Anything you guys want. It's a special occasion, after all."

"I like chili," Reese said. "But what's the special occasion?"

"The end of seventh grade," she said. "Just two more days next week and then you're done, right?"

"Yes, ma'am."

Reese went down the carpeted stairs to the basement rec room with the big-screen TV and a long, overstuffed sofa. There was a foosball table, too, and a dartboard on one wall. Ryan and Tony were playing foosball. "Hey, dude," Ryan said. Mr. Alvarez was on his knees fiddling with wires behind the TV. "What's going on with the TV?" Reese asked.

"We got a new whatchamacallit for streaming video," Mr. Alvarez said. "I've just about got it working, I think."

Reese hadn't seen him in a while. Mr. Alvarez worked a lot—he owned an auto-body shop and a laundry and some houses he rented out, in Spendlowe and Goldsville—so it was often just Mrs. Alvarez at the house when Reese came over. Mr. Alvarez's hair was black like Tony's, but sprinkled with gray. It seemed always to be the same length, like he got it cut every day.

"How are your mom and dad, Reese?" Mr. Alvarez asked.

Reese's lie was quick: "They're fine."

"Is your dad back to work? He was injured for a while, wasn't he?"

The Alvarezes were probably the best family Reese knew— certainly way better than his own, he thought. They were honest, always-there-when-you-need-them people. Lying to them felt like rubbing mud into Mrs. Alvarez's carpet upstairs. But he did it anyway. "He hurt his back at work," Reese said. "But he's working again."

He thought that was the story his mom had told most

recently. He had an uneasy feeling, though, that it wasn't. And then Ryan said, "Again?"

Reese felt a prickle of worry. "What?"

"Didn't he hurt his back a long time ago?" Ryan asked. He had his head down over the foosball game.

Reese's face got warm. This was just Ryan talking and not thinking, which he did a lot, but Reese couldn't help feeling that Ryan was calling him out. "He got hurt before," Reese said. "But it still hurts him sometimes."

"Well, I'm glad he's feeling better now," Mr. Alvarez said. There was something in his tone that made Reese think Tony's dad saw how uncomfortable he was and was trying to move things along. "Tony, take a break from your game for a minute and find me the remote for this thing, will you? The small one. I need to finish the setup."

"Hey, what are we watching anyway?" Ryan asked Reese. "It's your choice, remember?"

Reese had forgotten. He shrugged. "I don't know. I don't really care."

"You guys can browse and pick your movie after we eat," Mr. Alvarez said.

While he and Tony fiddled around with the TV, Reese played Ryan at foosball. Ryan won. Reese was way off his game. They played darts for a while, too. Reese won that, which made him feel a little better. Then they went upstairs to the kitchen to get something to drink. Tony's little brother, Joseph, wanted to help, and Tony let him get the ice. Ryan sat on the floor at the kitchen door and played with the Alvarezes' cat.

Mrs. Alvarez was stirring the chili at the stove. "Reese," she said, "I was just thinking that your birthday is coming up real soon. Isn't that right? I always remember because it's about the same time as Joey's."

"Yes, ma'am," Reese said.

"Do you have anything planned?"

"No," he said.

"Dude, you've got to do *something*," Ryan said.

Reese shrugged. "I don't know."

"How about paintball?" Ryan said. "I want to do paintball for my birthday. Or you could do laser tag. There's that laser-tag place in Goldsville."

"Those would both be cool," Tony said.

Reese shook his head. A birthday party felt impossible right then. His family had fallen apart. He felt like an alien, standing there in that clean kitchen with a bunch of normal, happy people.

"I'll think about it," he said. He grabbed for a distraction: "You want to play another game of foosball?" he asked Ryan. "I want a rematch."

"Whatever," Ryan said. "Sure."

They went back down to the basement, and Reese tried to lose himself in the game.

CHAPTER 10

The church that his mom had started going to, the one where she had met Mrs. Smith, was Spendlowe United Methodist Church, a big red-brick church with a white steeple, across the street from the county library in downtown Spendlowe. She said she had chosen it because she had been raised a Methodist and so it felt familiar.

This struck Reese as strange, because from what he had overheard her telling his dad, he would have thought she'd want to forget everything and everyone she had been raised with. Her father was an alcoholic—she called him a "mean drunk"—who used to hit her while her mother just stood by and let it happen. The first chance Reese's mom got, after high school, she had left home. She hadn't spoken to her parents or gone back to where she grew up, a place called Vera that was even smaller than Spendlowe, since before Reese was born. He had never met his grandparents.

She had not been to a church of any kind for years—for as long as Reese had been around, anyway. She had started going to Spendlowe United Methodist about the same time his dad got really bad and had overdosed the first time. One night, when Reese was supposed to be asleep, he had heard her and his dad arguing about it in their bedroom. "We don't need those Holy Rollers poking into our business," his dad had said. "I can't believe you'd have anything to do with people like that, Amanda. I thought you were smarter than that."

"Smarter than what, exactly?" his mom had asked.

"Smarter than those people in the churches going around shouting 'Amen' and 'Praise Jesus' and letting preachers lead them around by the nose."

"It wouldn't kill you to get some religion, Sam," his mom had said. "But whether you go or not, I need to. I'm smart enough to admit that I can't handle everything on my own right now. Maybe I could use some prayer and guidance."

Reese had gone with her once, at Easter the previous year. She went to the contemporary service, and she told him he would like it because it was more relaxed than a lot of church services, and the people were friendly and laid-back. But the place was so packed that they had to stand the whole time against a wall in back, and it was so hot and stuffy that he could barely breathe. He couldn't see much either, and standing still and quiet all that time made him want to jump and yell.

Several times after that, she had asked him to go back with her, but he had wanted to stay home with his dad, who usually slept in on Sundays, and draw or watch TV. Pretty soon she stopped asking.

Until that Sunday morning in the Smiths' trailer.

And when Reese said no to her then, she didn't ask again. She *told* him he was going with her.

"You lay here all day yesterday until it was time to go to Tony's," she said. "I won't let you do that again. Get up."

She couldn't be serious, Reese thought. She had dragged him away from town to this miserable trailer. They still didn't know where his dad was. And now she was making him go to church? "I'm not going," he said. "You go. Leave me alone."

"Get up, Reese."

He opened his mouth to tell her no again. But then he thought about how much they had been fighting, and it occurred to him that maybe his pushing and arguing all the time was only making her less likely to come around and reconsider leaving his dad on his own. Maybe he should try smoothing things over. So he said, "Okay, okay, I'm sorry. I'll get up."

His mom blinked. She seemed a little surprised at his sudden change of direction. Then she said, "Well, okay then. Thank you."

She went to the kitchen while he got up and got dressed.

When he came out of the bedroom, she said, "Look, I'm sorry to pick at you, but I'm upset and worried, too, Reese. I'm stressed, and I'm tired. And you lying in bed makes me worry even more. It would mean a lot to me to have you with me today."

"Can we at least not drive with the Smiths?" he asked.

"We can take our own car. That's fine. But we're going to sit with them at church, and please, just be civil. It's hard to explain, because I haven't known Mrs. Smith all that long, but we've got kind of a connection. Both our dads were alcoholics, so that's maybe part of it. But whatever it is, she's gotten to be kind of like a mom to me, and maybe I'm kind of like a daughter to her. She lost her daughter a while back . . . Meg and Charlie's mom."

"What do you mean she lost her?"

"Her daughter died. Both she and Meg and Charlie's dad were killed in a car accident."

Reese knew one kid at his school who had lost a mother to cancer. But he didn't know anyone who had lost both parents. "When was this? How long ago?"

"About a year and a half ago, maybe a little more. It was right before I met Mrs. Smith at church. Meg and Charlie were living somewhere outside Washington, D.C. Mr. and Mrs. Smith had to go up and bring the two of them back to live here."

"That's terrible," he said.

"It's very, very sad. I feel for Meg and Charlie, losing their parents and then having to uproot themselves and come here. And I feel for Mr. and Mrs. Smith, having to deal with all of this, particularly at their age."

Reese thought about this while he ate a bowl of Cheerios and his mom got dressed for church. He wondered what it must be like to lose both your mom and dad, and at the same time, and how exactly it had happened.

When they went outside to get in the car and head to church, Charlie was standing outside near the house's back steps. But he wasn't dressed for church. He was wearing pajama bottoms and a T-shirt, like the night Reese and his mom had arrived.

Reese realized then, when he got a good look at him in daylight, that Charlie had Down syndrome. Reese had seen a man with Down syndrome who worked at the Food Lion grocery store in town, and his mom had told him that Down syndrome is a way some people are born. Charlie had the same almond-shaped eyes as the man at the grocery store, the same round face and kind of small ears and nose.

He was petting a gray tabby cat. An older man came to the back door then and opened the screen door. It had to be Mr. Smith, Charlie and Meg's grandfather. He wasn't dressed for church either. He was wearing khaki shorts and a blue short-sleeve shirt, and his gray hair was mussed. He didn't look happy.

He said, "Charlie, the pants you want are wet, and they won't be dry in time for church. That's just the way it is. I'm sorry we didn't wash them last night. Couldn't you wear another pair just this once?"

"I'm not talking to you right now," Charlie said without looking back.

"Oh, for goodness' sake," said Mr. Smith, clearly irritated. He saw Reese and his mom then, and he tried to give them a smile. "Good morning," he said. "I'm sorry, but we're running a little behind here."

"Hello," Charlie said to Reese. "Do you want to see my cats?"

"Charlie, you can show them the cats later," Mr. Smith said. "You're making everyone late for church."

Mrs. Smith came to the door. She *was* dressed for church, in a tan skirt, white blouse, and dress shoes. She said, "Charlie, love, I think I have a solution. I found the old pants that you used to like downstairs, the blue ones with the tear in the pocket. I'll sew up the tear right quick and then you can wear those this morning. How does that sound?"

Charlie stopped petting the cat and stood up. He put his hands to the small of his back, and he looked up at the sky, as if he were thinking it over.

"Charlie?" Mrs. Smith said. "Everyone is waiting. We need to get going."

Charlie had made up his mind apparently, because he turned and went back to the house. "Just give us a few minutes," Mrs. Smith said to Reese and his mom. "We'll be out as quick as we can. Or you can just go on ahead if you want."

"We're fine," Reese's mom said. "Don't worry."

Mr. Smith came over to say hello. "Sorry I wasn't here when you got in," he said. "How is everything? Is the trailer okay?"

"It's great," Reese's mom said, and then she put an arm around Reese and squeezed, which he knew was a reminder to keep his mouth shut about the trailer and be civil.

"Have you been down to the river?" Mr. Smith asked. "It's just past the trees and down the field."

Reese shook his head. His mom said, "We'll have to check it out when we get back from church."

"There's a dock down there and a canoe," Mr. Smith said. "Meg and Charlie can show you where the paddles are and everything. Oh, and there's the basketball hoop right here, and I think we still have a basketball in the shed. The ball probably just needs pumping up. Do you play, Reese?"

Reese only shrugged.

His mom said, "Reese *loves* basketball. And he's very good."

"You'll have to show me your moves," said Mr. Smith. "I'm sorry we don't have a concrete court to play on, but the clay is pretty decent for just messing around."

Meg came out then. She was wearing a white dress that came down to just below her knees, and she had her head in a book. Her arrival pulled Mr. Smith's attention away from Reese. "There she is," Mr. Smith said. "Meg, can you say hello?"

The girl looked up. Her face was unsmiling, a mask that Reese couldn't read. "Hello," she said, like the word had been dragged out of her. Then she looked back at her book.

"Hmm," said Mr. Smith. "Well, she'll warm up, I'm sure."

Meg looked at him, her lips pursed, her eyebrows together, clearly irritated. Then she put her head down in her book again.

When Charlie and Mrs. Smith came back out, Charlie had on blue pants with black dress shoes and a blue short-sleeve shirt with a button-down collar. He seemed to have forgotten whatever he had been upset about, though Mrs. Smith looked rushed and annoyed. She was guiding him to the car with her hands on his shoulders.

"Can you say hello to everyone, Reese?" Reese's mom said.

"Hey," he said without enthusiasm.

"Reese is coming this morning purely to humor me," his mom said, "but I'm happy he is." She said this in that fake adult voice again, as if he were just some kid being lazy on a Sunday, as if their life weren't a huge mess.

"I know what that's like, believe me," Mrs. Smith said. She glanced at Meg when she said this, which made Reese take another look at the girl. Her eyes still were fixed down on her book. She seemed to be ignoring them all.

Mr. Smith, it appeared, didn't go to church. It was just Mrs. Smith and Meg and Charlie who got into the blue hatchback by the house. Reese's mom said she and Reese wanted to run some errands in town, so they would take her car.

When they pulled into the parking lot at Spendlowe United Methodist, the double side doors of the parish hall behind the church were open. That was where the contemporary service was held, with folding chairs and not pews. Reese and his mom went in behind the Smiths. A high school girl in a jean skirt and a red T-shirt was handing out programs, and she gave them a big goofy smile as if she couldn't be happier to be there and to see them. His mom took a program. Reese just kept his head down and slid past.

One good thing: The hall was less crowded than the other

time he had been there, probably because it was just a regular Sunday. His mom led him up the main aisle between the folding chairs.

"Hey there, Amanda," said a lady as they passed.

"Good morning, Amanda," said a man.

Another lady reached out and squeezed his mom's hand as they went by. "And who is this handsome young man?" she asked.

"This is my son, Reese," his mom said. "Reese, this is Miss Julia. Can you say hello?"

"Hey," Reese said, without really looking. His mom could make him go to church, but she couldn't make him be friendly, like he was going to make friends with a bunch of old church people anyway.

Up front, on a stage, a young man was tuning a guitar. An older man was at a keyboard. On the wall behind them was a gold cross. His mom followed the Smiths to seats just two rows back from the stage, way too close for Reese. "Amanda, after you," said Mrs. Smith. "Or do you want to sit on the end?"

"Whatever's fine," his mom said. She moved to step into the row, and Reese pushed in ahead of her, almost stepping on her toes, so he could get down the row of seats first and put her between him and the Smiths. He didn't want to sit next to Mrs. Smith's grandkids.

"Oh for goodness' sake, Reese," his mom whispered as he squeezed past her.

This made him remember what he had told himself about not fighting with her so much, so when the preacher came out and the guitarist and the keyboard player started in with the music, he kind of leaned over to look at his mom's program, which had the words to the song on it, like he was actually interested. He didn't know the song. It was slow, with pulsing piano and strummed guitar, and the words were all about Jesus and how he'll never let you down and how you're never really alone because he's with you no matter what.

His mom sang along loudly, and Reese saw a tear in the corner of her eye. She was getting weepy. He thought the song was pretty cheesy, but his mom and everyone else around them seemed to be eating it up, nodding their heads and swaying in time to the music.

Well, not everyone: When he looked down the row, he saw that Meg, who was sitting on the other side of his mom, wasn't singing. She had her head up, and her mouth was a hard, thin line. She looked like she was trying to keep herself from yelling at the whole church to shut up.

Reese let the rest of the songs and the words from the preacher slide over and around him. He looked up occasionally at his mom, who seemed to be enjoying herself. She didn't tear up again, thank goodness. She was smiling and nodding. She looked over at him from time to time and squeezed his hand, and he tried to smile back a little, because he knew that's what she wanted.

Charlie also seemed to enjoy the service, and he sang along

with Mrs. Smith and everybody. Meg, though, kept her mouth shut through most of it. When she was seated, she looked down at her hands in her lap. Once, out of the corner of his eye, Reese thought he caught her looking over at him, but when he turned his head, she looked away.

After the service they went to another room that smelled of coffee and cocoa. On folding tables lay open boxes of doughnuts. Reese took a glazed one, and he found a seat in a corner by himself to eat it. His mom was talking with some people by the coffeepot. He had to admit that she seemed happier than she had been for a while: Her eyes were brighter, and she was laughing.

Charlie came into the room. He was shaking his hands in front of him, like he had just washed them and was trying to dry them after going to the bathroom. Meg came in behind him. Charlie looked around, and when he saw Reese he headed straight for him. Reese turned away, but Charlie came to him and spoke: "Are you feeling better?"

"What?"

"We came over yesterday to the trailer and asked if you wanted to come out and look around. But your mom said you weren't feeling good."

"Oh," Reese said. "I'm okay now." He felt as if Charlie was standing too close to him, and it was making him uncomfortable.

Meg must have seen this because she said, "Back up and give him space, Charlie."

Charlie took a couple of steps back. But then he immediately took a step toward Reese again. "Do you like cats?" he asked.

Reese shrugged. "I guess."

Meg took Charlie's hand. "Come get a doughnut with me, Charlie. I want a chocolate one, and they're almost gone." She led him away without a look back.

Reese walked to his mom, hoping to take shelter in the little group of adults talking and wait it out. He looked at his phone to check the time: He would give her ten more minutes.

When he snuck a peek at Meg and Charlie, he saw they had gotten their doughnuts and were sitting together in the far corner of the room. They were playing rock, paper, scissors. As he watched, Meg held out "rock," and Charlie "paper." With a laugh, Charlie covered her hand with his, paper over rock, and Meg, who had been looking so serious and even angry, smiled.

She looked up then and saw Reese looking at her, and for a moment their eyes met. But then he looked away.

CHAPTER 11

Reese argued with his mom after church, although he had told himself he wouldn't. He wanted her to go by the apartment to check on his dad since they were in town, and when she said no again, that it was up to his dad to call *them* when he was serious about getting better, Reese lost it. He yelled. He threatened to get out of the car at the next light and walk to the apartment himself.

She just sat there with her mouth drawn tight, refusing to fight back but not giving in either, which made him angrier. But he didn't get out, and he finally gave up.

When they got to the Smiths' place, he changed into shorts and a T-shirt, took a stack of paper and some pencils to draw with, and went out to sit at the picnic table behind the Smiths' house to get away from her. He looked up at the cloudless sky. The day was hot. His mom had shut the windows in the trailer and turned on the air conditioner in the window at one end. Reese began drawing, sketches of robots this time, like Transformers, made of car parts: wheels for shoulders, exhaust pipes like cannons on their backs, shiny chrome headlights for eyes.

After a while the door to the house opened, and Meg and Charlie came out. They had changed into swimsuits, T-shirts, and flip-flops, and they were carrying towels. Meg's shirt had two words on it, red letters on blue: **WHITE OAK**. Charlie headed straight for Reese and asked him, "What are you doing?"

"Drawing," Reese said.

Charlie leaned in to see. "That's really good," he said. "Can you draw me something?"

"Like what?" Reese asked.

"How about my cats?" Charlie said.

"I can't do that. I can't really draw animals."

"You should try," Charlie said. "You're a really good artist. I think you could do it."

"Let's go, Charlie," Meg said. She came up and took his hand, just as she had after church.

"Hey, we're going swimming in the river," Charlie said to him. "You can come with us if you want."

"I don't know," Reese said, uncomfortable. "I don't have a swimsuit."

"You can go in your shorts," Charlie said.

Reese hesitated. Actually, swimming on such a hot day sounded good. But he was still feeling that he didn't . . . *shouldn't* . . . want any part of this place and these people.

He was supposed to be back in town, with his mom and dad together.

Meg was looking away, toward the barn across the yard. He wondered what she was thinking, and he wondered about the words on her shirt—what or where White Oak was.

"I guess I probably shouldn't," he said.

"Let's go, Charlie," Meg said.

"Come down if you change your mind," Charlie said.

Reese watched them go, their flip-flops snapping as they walked. They went through the grass, across the yard away from the house, and disappeared behind the trees. Reese was alone again. The air conditioner at the trailer hummed. A bird somewhere nearby murmured sleepily, and the sound made Reese feel lonely. He thought of going inside the trailer, but he didn't want to face his mom for a while. He thought about calling his dad yet again. But the last time he had tried, from outside the church after doughnuts, the call had clicked over immediately to voicemail, no ring, just a beep and then a message that his dad's voicemail was full. He considered texting his friends, but he didn't know what to say. In town, he could have texted them to meet at the town pool or the basketball courts and then jumped on his bike and ridden over. But here, he was stuck, unless he got a ride from his mom.

Faintly, he heard a splash, the sound of someone jumping into the water. He heard Charlie laugh.

After another minute or so, he stood up and found a stick to put on his stack of papers to keep it from blowing away. He couldn't take just sitting there any longer, so he walked the way Charlie and Meg had gone. When he came around the trees, he saw the river at the bottom of the field. A wooden dock extended over the water from the cleared grassy bank.

The river was sparkling in the afternoon sun. It was so bright that he had to put a hand up to his eyes and squint to make out Meg and Charlie clearly. Meg was in the river, with just her head out of the water. Her hair was wet, slicked back. Charlie had taken off his shirt, and he was standing on the dock. Beside him, on the bank, a red canoe lay upside down in the grass. Across the river was a line of trees, thick woods, that seemed to grow directly from the water.

Charlie walked to the back of the dock and then turned and took a running leap off the end. He pulled his legs in, wrapped his arms around them, and did a cannonball into the river, sending up a spout of water that caught Meg. She shrieked and then laughed.

Reese looked back toward the trailer and then made up his mind: He walked the rest of the way to the water.

Charlie saw him first when he stepped onto the dock. "Hey! Reese is here," he said. "Hey, Reese."

Meg squinted up at him from the water, one eye closed.

"Hey," Reese said.

"Can you swim?" Meg asked.

"Of course I can swim," Reese said.

"Prove it," she said.

"I don't have my swimsuit on."

"I bet you can't swim," she said.

"I can."

"Just jump in, then," she said. "Swim in your shorts."

That was enough: Reese was going to show this girl that not only could he swim, he actually was a good swimmer, strong. He took off his shoes and shirt and dropped them on the dock. He took his phone and his knife out of his pocket and put them carefully in one of his shoes. Then he went to the back of the dock, as Charlie had done, and he ran forward and jumped.

He went in feet first. He heard Charlie yell something just as he hit the water. Then the river closed over his head.

The cool water was a shock at first on his warm skin. But he let himself sink. He felt no bottom below him. His feet moved freely. He kept his eyes closed, his mouth shut tight. He moved his arms to push himself down, his toes pointed, searching for the bottom. Nothing. How deep was this river anyway?

He gave up finally and just floated in the silence between the sunlit surface and the bottom, wherever it was down there in the darkness. His skin adjusted quickly to the water, and he was now neither warm nor cold. That feeling like a fist that he had been carrying around again since the morning fight with his mom unclenched, and he relaxed. He imagined himself dissolving in the water.

Then he felt the water move around him. A hand touched his shoulder, and the spell was broken. Reese kicked himself to the surface and opened his mouth wide for a gulp of air.

Charlie popped up beside him, smiling.

Meg called, "Race to the other side!"

Then they were swimming, and Reese pulled hard through the water, moving ahead of both her and Charlie. They swam all the way to the other side of the river until they were under the shade of the trees. Reese came in first, and he finally felt bottom beneath him, mud that squished between his toes. It was still pretty deep: When he stood, the water came up almost to his neck.

Now that he was close to the trees, he also saw that the river seemed to have no edge on that side. It had left its banks and flooded the woods. It stretched away as far as he could see into the green shadows.

He turned and looked down the river, which bent to the left not far from them, disappearing around the shoulder of the woods. The water barely moved. The only ripples were from the light breeze. He looked across to the dock. "How deep is it out there, in the middle?" he asked. "I couldn't touch the bottom."

"It's really deep," Charlie said.

"My grandad says it's maybe thirty feet deep right here," Meg said. "And it's even deeper in some places. There's a spot downriver called Whitchard's Landing where it's supposed to be about eighty feet deep."

Reese tried to imagine that: He knew the deep end of the town pool in Spendlowe was eight feet, so the river was ten times that deep in parts. The black water reflecting the sky and the trees along the bank gave him no idea of the depth. He wondered what monsters might be living way down at the bottom. Giant catfish, maybe.

"I've tried to touch the bottom out there in the middle, but I never have," Meg said.

"I've tried, too," Charlie said.

Reese decided to see for himself. He swam to the middle, took a deep, deep breath, and dove. He kicked hard and pulled with his arms, hands reaching. He kicked and pulled, kicked and pulled, going deeper and deeper. He opened his eyes. The water was brown for a few feet below him, lit by the sun above, but then it darkened to black. He pulled and kicked a couple more times, going down, feeling nothing. The water got colder the deeper he went. When his lungs felt like they were going to burst, he pulled back to the surface.

"Did you do it?" Charlie asked.

"No," Reese said.

"That was a good try," Charlie said. "You were down a long time."

They swam awhile and then pulled themselves up onto the dock. Reese found that he felt good, better than he had since he and his mom left the apartment—almost normal. He sat on the edge of the dock, drying in the sun, while Meg and Charlie dried themselves with towels.

"Do you want to see my cats now?" Charlie said. "You can help me feed them."

Reese could have said he had to go in to help his mother with supper or help her clean or something. Part of him felt like that's what he *should* say, because it still felt wrong, him and his mom being there. But he also didn't want to go back and just sit in the trailer, especially if it meant arguing again with his mom. So he said, "Sure, I can help."

"I'll show you," Charlie said.

Reese pulled on his shirt and shoes, picked up his knife and phone, and followed Meg and Charlie to the house. Charlie went in the back door to get the cats' food. Meg stopped at the picnic table and pointed to his drawings. "Can I see?"

"I guess, sure," Reese said.

She moved the stick he had put on the stack of paper to keep it from blowing away. "I like these," she said. "I like the details. Did you just make these robots up?"

"Yes." He thought Meg seemed happier, more relaxed than she had since he met her.

Charlie came back with a plastic bin of food and a stack of bowls. He looked at Reese's drawings, too. "You really can't draw cats? Or any animals?"

Reese shrugged. "Not really. They just don't come out right."

One of Charlie's cats, a gray one, was lying on the ground nearby. It was bent double, licking its butt, one rear leg held straight up. Reese smiled at the strange pose, and while Meg and Charlie looked at his drawings, he studied the cat's lines and curves carefully. He had tried a few times to draw horses, for knights on horseback, but he never could get the lines right, particularly the back legs. It was hard, harder than anything else he had tried to draw, and he had given up.

Or maybe he had never looked closely enough, the way he looked at his dad's Barracuda, for example.

Another cat, one striped gray and brown, jumped onto the table and bumped its head against Charlie's arm. "The cats are hungry!" he said. "Are you ready? You can take the bowls if you want."

Reese picked them up and followed him to the tree. Charlie took the bowls and set them in a row near the tire swing. Meg was standing with her hands on her hips. "What do I do?" Reese asked her.

"Don't look at me," Meg said. "This is Charlie's thing."

"You have to give two scoops in each bowl," Charlie said. He opened the plastic bin, which was full of kibble, and he handed Reese a plastic scoop from inside. Reese scooped out some. The cats had begun drifting in from behind the trailer and under the cars. When he poured the kibble into the first bowl, they came running, tails up. He went back for more food and poured that into the next bowl.

Charlie smiled. "Do you know how many cats I have?"

"I heard you tell my mom you have thirteen," Reese said.

"That's a lot of cats," Charlie said.

"Where do they all come from?"

"I save them," Charlie said. "I do cat rescue."

"He's gotten some from the county shelter," Meg said. "A few of them have been dropped off by neighbors who found them wandering around. Some have just showed up and kind of rescued themselves."

Charlie laughed. "That's right."

Reese kept pouring the kibble, and the cats clustered in twos or threes at each bowl. Charlie was watching him closely as he did it. "Do you like cats?" he asked Reese again.

"Sure," he said, although he had never actually thought much about it. His dad didn't really like animals, so they'd never had any pets.

When Reese was done pouring, he squatted and watched as the cats crunched away at their food. Then he noticed one more cat, this one all black, moving in slowly, warily, its tail down. The other cats were sleek, but this cat was thick around the middle. Its belly dragged low. "What's wrong with that one?" Reese asked.

"She's scared," Charlie said. "I have to feed her special."

The cat stopped and sat on its haunches. "Why is she fat like that?" Reese asked.

Charlie laughed: "Ha! She's not fat!"

"Hush, Charlie," Meg said. "Don't be rude."

Charlie laughed again. Reese looked, puzzled, at Meg.

"She's going to have kittens," Meg said. "She's pregnant."

Reese studied the cat, who was casually licking one of her paws. "How do you feed her if she won't come to you?" he asked.

"I wait until everyone else is pretty much done and then I put a bowl out there," Charlie said. "She'll eat then. And every time, I can get a little bit closer to her." He held his thumb and forefinger up, almost touching, and squinted between them to show what he meant by a little bit.

"Why do you think she's scared?" Reese asked.

"Maybe somebody was mean to her," Charlie said. "Or maybe she's never been around people before."

The cat looked up, as if she knew Charlie was talking about her. She blinked. Actually, Reese could have sworn that she winked at Charlie. Then she went back to cleaning her paws.

"We don't know much about her," Meg said. "She showed up maybe two weeks ago. Right, Charlie?"

Charlie nodded. He filled a bowl for her then, and he brought it out to her and set it down. The cat moved off a few feet until he backed away. Then she came in and sniffed at the bowl. "What's her name?" Reese asked.

"I just call her Mama Cat," Charlie said. Another cat, the white one that Mrs. Smith had warned might bite, crept in to try to take food from the bowl, but the black cat hissed and batted at it, cuffing its head, chasing it off.

"Good for you, Mama Cat," Meg said.

Reese smiled at that, and he settled back to watch the cat eat. He could hear the crunch of her teeth on the kibble. He was already feeling pretty good after his swim, and hearing that sound made him feel even better, for a little while anyway. He sat down on the hard dirt and crossed his legs. He rested his elbows on his knees and put his chin in one hand. He stayed there like that, with Meg and Charlie, until the cats had eaten their fill and begun wandering away and his mom called him in to help with supper. "Bye," he said to Meg and Charlie.

"Okay, bye," Charlie said.

Reese's mom was putting a pot of water on for spaghetti when he came back inside.

"I was watching you out there with Meg and Charlie," she said. "I'm glad you spoke with them. Did you have fun?"

"Yes," he said. It was the truth, as strange and maybe wrong as it was, considering that nothing had changed about him and his mom and dad and that he had been trying to avoid Meg and Charlie since he got there.

"I'm really glad," she said. "You know, Mrs. Smith asked if we could come to supper at the house sometime soon. I told her I would ask you. What do you think?"

"Okay," Reese said.

"Really?" She looked a little shocked.

He shrugged and nodded.

Charlie had gone inside the house, but Meg was still outside, sitting on the tire swing. Reese could see her though the trailer's little kitchen window. She had put her T-shirt on over her swimsuit. Her hair had dried tangled, but she didn't seem to care. She was sitting with her hands on the swing's rope, one over the other, her forehead resting on them, and she was turning gently back and forth. She looked very alone out there, her head down.

"What did you guys talk about?" his mom asked him after a moment.

"Nothing really," Reese said. "The river, Charlie's cats."

One thing Reese had wanted to ask Meg and Charlie about was how exactly their parents had died and how it felt to be taken so far from home. But he had thought it wouldn't be right. Also, he didn't want to talk about his own family, and if he started asking about their parents, Meg and Charlie might have asked where his dad was.

"I need to walk down to the river," his mom said. "I bet it's beautiful."

"It is," he said. "And deep. Meg said it's eighty feet deep in one place."

"Wow," his mom said. "I had no idea."

Outside, Charlie came to the back door of the house, and he called out to Meg: "Grandma says *now*, Meg. It's not my turn to fold the laundry. It's yours."

"Yes, yes, okay," she said. She raised her head and got off the swing, and then, before going into the house, she looked over at the trailer. This time, Reese didn't hide or turn away. At the kitchen window, where she could see him, he raised a hand. She waved back. Then she turned and walked to the house and went inside.

CHAPTER 12

On Monday, with just one more day until school let out for summer break, Mr. Nash had all the kids help him clean and pack up his classroom. The school was getting new windows over the summer, so everything had to be put away before the workers got there. When the packing was done, they watched a movie from Mr. Nash's laptop, projected on the class whiteboard.

The movie was *The Princess Bride*, which was fine, but Reese had seen it a bunch of times. If Tony had been in his homeroom, maybe they would have sat in the back together and played paper football or something. But he wasn't, so Reese put his head down on his desk.

He thought about his dad, wondering what he was doing right then and why he still hadn't called or texted. Reese had texted him every day. When he closed his eyes there at school, he saw his dad lying on the bathroom floor at their apartment, and his heart thudded against his chest. What if he was on the floor right then, unconscious or worse, with no one to help him? Reese opened his eyes, sat up, and rubbed his face hard to make the image of his dad go away. He pulled out a sheet of paper and drew cars until the movie was over.

After school, he went out to the front, and Tony came out, too. Mrs. Alvarez was waiting to take Tony and his brother and sisters to Goldsville for an errand and supper with their dad. "Do you want a ride home?" she asked Reese. "We can drop you off on the way."

"No, thanks," Reese said. He was supposed to go to the Kwik Stop, where his mom wanted him to wait until the end of her shift, and then they would drive back to the Smiths' place.

"Later, dude," Tony said.

"Later," Reese said. He watched them pull away, and then he started toward his mom's store. At first he walked, but then he thought about his dad again and broke into a run. He wanted to know if his mom had heard from him.

When he got to the store, she was behind the counter, going through a stack of papers with Larry, her boss. Larry, who was tall and thin with stooped shoulders, could be disorganized and sometimes created problems for Reese's mom—forgetting to fill shifts or forgetting to order things or ordering too much. "You can see the way I've color-coded everything here," Reese's mom was saying to him, "and I'll tape the color guide to the desk in the office so we'll always know where to find orders and check on them before we put new ones in."

"That's good," Larry said. "That'll help."

"It'll also make it easier to track inventory flow over time," she said. "So right here, dairy products are in blue. Snacks are red."

Larry looked up then and saw Reese. "Hey, how's it going, buddy?"

"Fine," Reese said. "Mom, can I talk to you?"

Just then the door opened, and a big man in coveralls and a baseball cap came in to pay for gas. Half a moment later, the phone behind the counter rang. "Hang on a minute, Reese," his mom said. She took the call while Larry helped the customer. "It's a wonderful day at Kwik Stop," she said into the phone. "How can we help you?"

"Hey, Jackie," she said. She held one finger up to Reese: *Hang on a minute.* Then: "Oh no, not again." She put a hand over the mouthpiece and said to Larry, "Jackie can't get in for her shift tonight. Her boy has strep again so he can't go to the sitter's, and her husband is on the road. Is Andy maxed out on hours or can he come in?"

"Can you check his timesheet in the office?" Larry said.

The other line rang, and another customer came in. "Oh, Lord," Reese's mom said. "Jackie, hang on." She brushed her hair out of her eyes. "Reese, can we talk in a bit? Maybe after my shift?" Then before he could answer, she went ahead and picked up the other line: "It's a wonderful day at Kwik Stop . . ."

Reese grabbed a bag of pretzels from a display by the

counter, and since no one was paying any attention to him, he went outside with it.

He sat on the curb in front of the store. With every day that went by, he worried more about his dad, but his mom was too busy apparently to talk about him. Reese started to get mad at her all over again—for leaving, for not checking on his dad, and for putting Reese off now when he wanted to ask for news about him. He stuffed the last pretzels into his mouth, crumpled up the bag, and, because he was so angry, dropped it at the curb rather than putting it in the trash can. He wasn't going to pay for it either. He went inside to try to talk to his mom again, but it was just Larry at the counter, ringing up another customer. His mom was probably in the office in back dealing with Jackie and her sick kid, like that was more important than talking about his dad.

He took off his backpack and went around behind the counter.

"What can I do for you, buddy?" Larry asked.

"Nothing," Reese said. He put his backpack next to the stool Larry was sitting on. "Can I put this back here for a little while?"

"Sure, I'll keep my eye on it," Larry said.

Reese headed to his family's apartment. He would check on his dad himself.

He walked along the edges of the parking lots, past a liquor store, and down a dirt path that ran from the back of a vacant lot down a weedy slope to the rear of the Food Lion. Their apartment complex, which was called the Pines, was across the street. There were no pine trees at the Pines; there were just five buildings marked A through E, with four crummy apartments in each. Reese and his family were in building D.

The Barracuda was not outside, but Reese went in anyway and up the stairs. The people in the apartment below were fighting. He couldn't make out the words, but he could hear the anger in the muffled voices. He unlocked the door of his family's apartment and went in.

He called, "Dad? It's Reese."

He didn't expect to get an answer, since his dad's car wasn't outside. He spoke mostly because the silence made him feel uneasy. He went from room to room. The blinds were pulled over all the windows. The sheets on his parents' bed were pulled back to the foot. Dirty laundry was scattered on the floor.

He went to the living room, and he ran one finger through the dust on the table where the TV sat. He wrote his name in the dust. His dad would see it and know that he had been there.

He decided to leave an actual note. He went to his bedroom and found a sheet of paper and a pencil. He wrote:

Dad,

Where are you? We miss you and are worried about you. Did you get my texts? Please call us.

Love, Reese

He put the note on the dining table. He considered waiting around to see if his dad would show up, but the empty apartment gave him the creeps. Something heavy fell downstairs, with a *whump* that shook some glasses on the kitchen counter. That was it for Reese: He went out, locking the door behind him.

He stood outside the apartment building for another few moments, thinking about what to do. He decided to walk to a bar that his dad went to sometimes to see if maybe he had stopped in there after work. It was called the Elbow Room. It was a little box of a place farther up the road that he had taken from the Kwik Stop, almost to the highway bypass that you took to Goldsville. It wasn't far. Nothing was far from anything in Spendlowe.

When he got to the Elbow Room, there were three cars and a pickup truck in the gravel parking lot out front. No Barracuda. He walked around to the back to be sure his dad hadn't parked there. A muddy pickup was parked by the trash bin, and a man and a woman, who were probably about his parents' ages, were standing at the truck's back end, talking. They wore blue jeans and cowboy boots and black T-shirts. They were laughing when Reese came around the corner of the bar, but they stopped when they saw him.

Reese turned around to go, and the woman spoke to him: "Can I help you, kid?"

"I'm looking for my dad," he said, reluctantly. Maybe they knew him. "Sam Buck."

"Don't know him, haven't seen him," the man said. "Sorry."

"Thanks anyway," Reese said.

As he walked away, he heard the woman say, "Poor kid." Hearing that made him angry, mostly at his dad for dropping off the planet and forcing him to wander around like some lost, clueless kid looking for him. He also realized then that he didn't have his phone with him—he'd left it in his backpack— and he knew his mom would probably be trying to reach him and would be angry at him for walking away when he was supposed to wait for her at the store.

On top of everything else, it was about to rain. The sky was clouding up. But he decided to stop one other place to check on his dad, even though it was a long shot: a closed factory with a big parking lot where his dad sometimes took the Barracuda to work on it, since he wasn't allowed to do car maintenance in the apartment parking lot. By the time Reese got to the factory, the rising dark clouds had covered the sun. The property was surrounded by a high chain-link fence, but someone had cut the chain on the front gate at some point, and no one had come to lock it back up. A blue sign out front read, **BTI FABRICS**. Another sign next to it read, **INDUSTRIAL SITE FOR SALE**.

He walked in through the gate and went across the empty parking lot to the side where his dad would park the Barracuda, out of sight of the road. He found nothing. It was stupid to think he would be there on a workday, especially with the rain coming.

He stood there looking around, feeling as empty as the lot and the factory. Then he went back out the gate. The first drops of rain hit him when he was walking up to the Kwik Stop.

His mom's car wasn't outside. Inside, it was just Larry again behind the counter, reading a magazine, and when he heard Reese come in, he looked up. "Where have you been?" he said. "Your mom is awful worried."

"I was just walking," Reese said.

"Well, she's out looking for you. She said you were supposed to wait here for her."

Reese shrugged.

"Call her, will you?" Larry said. "She was really upset, especially when she found out you didn't have your phone. We could hear it buzzing in your backpack back here when she tried to reach you."

Reese called, and all she said to him over the phone was: "Meet me outside."

When she pulled up, it had really started to rain, and he was waiting for her under the store's eaves. She didn't get out of the car. She spoke through her open window: "Get in."

He got in quick. He could see how angry she was. She pulled away even before he'd had a chance to put his seatbelt on. "Don't you ever, *ever* walk away without telling me where you are going," she said. "Do you hear me?" She had her eyes fixed on the road. "I don't have enough to worry about without you disappearing, too?"

"I'm sorry," he said.

And he was. About everything.

CHAPTER 13

Reese's dad was missing for four days. He reappeared on the last day of seventh grade.

Reese's mom had arranged her work schedule that day so she could meet Reese at school in the car, because he had a lot to carry: all his work and folders and everything from the year. It was so much that he broke the zipper on his backpack when he tried to stuff it all inside. On top of everything, he had two little blue-and-red clay pots that he had made in art class; they had been sitting in the bottom of his locker for months, under an ever-deepening layer of returned tests and completed homework. The pots were pretty ugly, but he couldn't bring himself to throw them away, so he left school that last day stooped under his heavy backpack and with a stupid pot in each hand.

"I remember making those pots," Tony said. "That was, like, last fall. How come you're just bringing them home now?"

"I kept forgetting," Reese said.

Mrs. Brown, the gym teacher, came out of school behind them, holding her clipboard, with kids swirling around her on the sidewalk. "Bus riders, let's go," she called. Kids pushed past to the line of yellow school buses waiting with their doors open. Reese stood next to Tony, scanning the line of cars pulling in. It had rained hard overnight and into the morning, and the pavement was still wet. There was a big puddle at the bottom of the drive that the cars kept splashing through as they turned in to pick up kids.

"Where's your mom?" he asked Tony.

"She said she's going to be a little late. She had to pick up Joseph first."

Across the street from the school was a tree truck with a bucket crane on top and a wood chipper in tow. Its driver-side door was partway open, and the driver was at the back, doing something with the chipper. Cars had stacked up behind it, and one of them beeped.

"Hey, have you figured out what you're doing for your birthday?" Tony asked. "Ryan said you're thinking about paintball."

"No, I'm not thinking about paintball," Reese said, a little annoyed. "Ryan said *he* wants to do paintball for *his* birthday."

"Well, what are you going to do? It's, like, next week, right?"

Reese didn't want to talk about that, or even think about it any more than he had when Ryan asked about it at movie night. He looked down the block, hoping that his mom would appear. Across the street, the driver of the tree truck had finished whatever he was doing, and he climbed back into the truck's cab. The truck lurched forward, belching diesel smoke. Reese began to answer Tony: "I don't—"

He didn't finish, because right then, across the street, the tree truck rolled away to reveal a car parked behind it. And when he saw it, Reese froze. It was a Plymouth Barracuda, metallic green. Behind the wheel, smoking a cigarette, was his dad.

"You don't what?" Tony asked. "What were you going to say?"

Part of Reese was incredibly relieved that his dad was there, alive, and he wanted to run to him. Another part of him wanted to run away, because he didn't want a scene when his mom arrived, nothing that would attract the eyes of the people in front of the school and let everyone know just exactly how screwed up his family was. He just stood there, frozen, like a scared rabbit caught in the open.

His dad got out of the Barracuda, and Tony saw him then. "I thought you said your mom was picking you up," he said.

Reese's dad closed the car door. He took one last drag on the cigarette and flicked it away. Then he started to cross the street. For some reason, he was limping and—this was the worst part of all—he had a black eye, like he had gotten into a fight or something. Reese spotted it from all the way across the street, a dark bruise around his left eye, so he knew Tony and everyone else, if they hadn't seen it already, surely would in about half a second.

"I got to go," Reese said.

Tony looked across the street at Reese's dad and then back to him. He frowned. "What's wrong?"

"Nothing," Reese said. He tried to act like that was true, tried to say something normal: "I'll text you later." He hurried across the grass to the street, as fast as he could, bent over beneath his backpack, with those ugly pots in his hands, and he caught his dad just as he stepped onto the curb.

The first thing his dad said, like it was just some normal afternoon, was "Hey, Reese. You dropped something."

Reese had no idea what he was talking about. "What?"

His dad pointed behind him. "You dropped a notebook or something out of your backpack." He stepped forward, stooped to pick up the fallen notebook, and handed it to Reese. "Hey, look," he said, "I wanted to say first off that I'm really, really sorry I haven't called or texted. There's no excuse for that. I got your note at the apartment and your texts, with all those links, and I wanted to tell you that I . . ."

He didn't finish because right then he and Reese both saw a little red Ford Fiesta turn into the school's circular drive, the tires splashing through the puddle, and pull over to park. His mom had arrived, and when she got out and saw Reese's dad, she stopped dead. She put a hand to her mouth.

His dad touched Reese's shoulder. "Come on, let's go talk to your mom," he said.

Reese went with him, across the grass, which was a short distance but felt then like a thousand miles, with everybody at the school probably watching him. He could see Tony up there, definitely watching. He thought Mrs. Brown had noticed, too. She had a little frown on her face, like she could tell something strange was going on but wasn't exactly sure what it was.

His mom's hand was at her throat now. She looked as if she was about to cry, which was exactly the kind of scene Reese didn't want. When they got close, she said, "Just what the hell are you doing here, Sam? Just what do think you're doing?"

"Mom!" Reese hissed. "Keep your voice down." Everyone in the car pickup line and across the front of the school was going to hear her. He turned his back to the school, like he could block the view with his overstuffed backpack.

"I'm here to see you," his dad said. "You and Reese."

"And you couldn't have called? Or answered when I called?" Her face had gotten red, but she had lowered her voice at least. "You just appear in front of Reese's school, in front of all these people, with a . . . What the hell is this?" She pointed to his eye. "A black eye, Sam? What happened?"

His dad reached up and carefully put one finger to the bruise on his face, like he had forgotten it was there. "This was . . . It was nothing. It was just a dumb accident. I tripped over something in the dark. But that's—" He shook his head. "Look, what I came here to say is I'm sorry and I want another chance. I screwed up. I know that. And Amanda, I wanted to tell you that I called a place, like you wanted. I've called a place about getting help."

His words were coming fast, like he was trying to get everything out before Reese's mom tore into him again. He said, "I need us to be back together, and I will do anything to make that happen."

"When?" Reese said. "When can we be back together?" His dad was still a mess, but here he was, telling them he needed them. He *did* need them.

His mom said, "Reese, stop talking."

"Amanda . . ." said his dad.

"Sam, you, too. Both of you shut up."

His dad tried to speak again. "I want—"

His mom cut him off: "*Stop talking, Sam!*" She said it so loud that Reese had no doubt at all that the entire school had heard her. He turned and saw Tony watching. When Tony saw him looking at him, he put his head down and shuffled his feet.

Reese's mom said, "Look, we need to talk, but this is not the time or place." She brushed her hair from her eyes. "You could have called. You *should* have called."

"I know it," his dad said. "I'm sorry. I lost my phone, and I—"

"You couldn't call because you lost your phone," Reese's mom said. "That's a good one, Sam. That's real good."

"That's not an excuse," his dad said. "I should have called. I haven't been sleeping good because I missed you so much, so I haven't been thinking straight. Can we go to the apartment? Or look . . . look here . . . I can take you two somewhere to eat. Are you hungry, Reese? We can go to Hardee's or something. You can get a milkshake to celebrate the last day of school."

"Yes," Reese said. "We can go."

"No," his mom said. Her mouth had gone tight at the corners, and her eyes had narrowed. She would not be moved. "No, Sam," she said. "That's not how this is going to play out. Here's what *is* going to happen right now: I am going to take Reese back to where we're staying. I'm tired. When I get settled and I'm ready, then I will call you. Or do you still not have a phone?"

"I got one of those temporary prepay phones until I replace my phone for good," his dad said. "I can text you the number."

"*What are you doing?*" Reese said to his mom. He knew it was hopeless, but he couldn't stop himself from grabbing at the moment as it slipped away. "He's here. Dad is here, right now. We can—"

"Reese!" his mom snapped.

By then his dad had seen it was hopeless. He said, "Reese, it's okay. Your mom is right: It was wrong of me to just show up. I should have called. Look, Amanda, I will text you my number, and you can call me when you're ready."

His mom closed her eyes and took a long, deep breath. Then she nodded. "Reese, let's go. Say goodbye to your father for now and get in the car."

"See you soon, bud," his dad said. He went back to the Barracuda, turning once to raise a hand goodbye.

"Reese?" His mom was getting back into the car, and she stopped and looked at him over the top. "Get in." He took a last look at his dad and then did as he was told. "Please," his mom said before he could say another word, "just sit quietly.

Don't start in on me again. I will talk with your father, but I need space right now. Give me space."

She started the car and, looking both ways, backed out of the entrance of the drive into the street, rather than going around to the exit. And for that, at least, Reese was grateful: He couldn't bear to ride past all the watching eyes in front of the school.

He kept quiet through the ride back to the Smiths' place. When they got there and pulled in next to Mrs. Smith's hatchback, though, he couldn't hold it in any longer. "When are you going to call Dad? Would you look to see if he's texted his new number?"

She ignored him and went to the trailer like he hadn't spoken at all. He followed her. They went up the steps and in. "Will you call Dad?" he said again. He couldn't stop. He was back in that nightmare loop again. He had been so worried about his dad and now here he was, reachable again, and Reese couldn't let it go. "We can't leave Dad alone."

Then he pulled out the big one, the scariest thing of all, and he let her have it: "*You know what might happen.*"

"Stop it!" his mom snapped. She threw her keys on the kitchen counter and went to the bathroom. He stood there and waited for her to get out. She took forever. She was moving slowly on purpose, he thought.

When she finally came out, Reese started in on her again. "Dad is there, at the apartment, waiting. I'm sure he's texted you his number by now. Check and see."

"Stop pushing me!" Her voice rose. "You don't think this is hard for me? Don't you think I want everything to be okay with your father? I have been as worried about him as you. I have been worried sick, all the time. I didn't know where he was or what was happening to him. I was scared. I—" She put her hand to her mouth and closed her eyes.

She was about to cry again, but Reese was past the point of caring. "He needs us," he said. "You know that he does."

She moved her hand to her chest, palm down, like she was trying to hold down something inside her. "I miss your father," she said. "I want him to be better, and I'm scared about what will happen if he doesn't get better. Sometimes I think if I were a stronger person, I could fix what's wrong with him, just take it away. The fact that I can't makes me feel like I'm failing him and you both. But I don't know what to do to help him and help us. I don't know what the right thing is. I just don't."

"And leaving him on his own will help him?" Reese asked.

"I don't know, Reese. How many times do I need to say that to you? I told you that we will talk, and we will. But I can't say what's going to happen after that. Please, just go outside for a while and give me quiet."

He opened his mouth to say . . . what? He had run up against another dead end with her. He went out, letting the screen door fall shut behind him.

CHAPTER 14

Reese sat in the swing in the yard, the toes of his sneakers in the bare dirt. A breeze was up, and a flock of little gray birds flew past. He looked at his phone. Tony had been texting: **Dude what was that about?** And: **RU OK** And: **Hello? RU there?**

Reese texted back: **Just a dumb fight. I'm good.** Texting a lie like that was easy.

Tony texted back right away: **U want to come over?**

That made Reese feel really alone. Tony thought he was still at the apartment in town and could just bike over to his house. But he was miles away. **Can't,** he texted, which was true. He didn't want to say any more.

When can u? Tony texted.

IDK.

He thought about going back inside the trailer and getting paper to draw with, but he didn't want to see his mom. On top of being frustrated with her and angry at her for putting off his dad, he was also ashamed of the way he had yelled at her. Again. He understood she was stressed and scared.

He turned in the swing to face the line of trees at the back of the yard. He put his phone in his pocket and took out his knife. He opened the blade and ran his thumb gently down the cutting edge.

The screen door at the house squealed, and he turned to see Meg and her grandfather coming out. Mr. Smith was carrying a wooden bookshelf, and Meg had brushes, two paint cans, and a stack of newspapers. She was wearing her White Oak shirt again. Mr. Smith called to Reese, "Hey, son."

"Hey," Reese said.

They came out to the yard and put the things they were carrying on the ground. Reese, feeling self-conscious, got off the swing. He closed his knife and put it back in his pocket. The old man was wearing wire-rimmed half-moon glasses, and he lowered his head to look over them at Reese. "You okay, son?" he asked. "You got a face like thunder."

Reese shook his head. "What does that mean? A face like thunder?"

"It means you look upset."

"I'm fine," Reese lied. He changed the subject: "What are y'all doing?"

"Meg's about to get started painting a bookshelf I built for her room. You want to help?"

"I guess," he said.

"It's up to you," said Mr. Smith. "You don't have to."

"No, I'll help." Helping Meg was better than either sitting there watching her paint or wandering around this place by himself, which were his only other options as far as he could see.

"Good," the old man said, and he smiled. "Meg, why don't you spread the newspapers out? Reese, do you want to mix the paint? Just shake up the can."

The bookshelf was bare, light wood. It was wider than it was tall and had two shelves. Mr. Smith put it on the newspapers that Meg spread out. "You made this?" Reese asked him.

"I did. Meg has run out of space for books in her room."

Meg was putting sticks and rocks on the newspaper to hold down the edges. Mr. Smith opened the can when Reese was done shaking it. It was a primer to put on first so that the paint would go on smooth, Mr. Smith said. He showed them how to brush it on, back and forth. "Have at it," he said, handing Reese a brush.

The old man watched for a minute. "That looks good," he said. "Hey, Reese, when does your school let out for the summer?"

"Today was my last day," he said.

"Congratulations," Mr. Smith said. "Meg and Charlie finished up last week."

Reese didn't know what to say to that except "Thanks."

After a moment Mr. Smith said, "Well, I'll leave y'all to it and go in and get supper started. Meg, your grandma and Charlie should be home from his karate class shortly. I bet he will want to help with this."

When he had gone, Reese and Meg painted in silence for a few minutes, on opposite ends of the bookshelf, while Reese tried to think of something to say. Meg had her head down, the tip of her tongue out, concentrating.

Reese thought of the old basketball hoop in the yard. "Hey, do you play basketball?"

Meg looked up at him. It might have been a trick of the light, but Reese thought he saw flecks of gold in her brown eyes. "What?" she said. "Why?"

Reese pointed at the old hoop. "The basketball hoop right there. Do you ever use it?"

Meg looked at it as if she was seeing it for the very first time. "Oh," she said. "No, not really."

And that was that for basketball, it seemed. Reese tried to think of something else. After a moment, he asked, "What's White Oak? The words on your shirt. What is that?"

"It's my old school. Back home."

He dipped his brush in the can. "You go to Ogden Middle now, right?" He remembered Mrs. Smith saying that when he and his mom first arrived. "Do you like it?"

"No," Meg said.

"How come?"

She shrugged. "It's a dump."

Another flock of birds flew over them, headed for the end of the yard and the river. It was so quiet that Reese could hear the rustle of their feathers as they passed. Meg turned her head to watch them go. The birds disappeared behind the trees.

Meg looked at Reese without saying anything for a moment. "What?" Reese asked.

He thought she was going to tell him something else about her school. Instead she said, "Do you want to go canoeing?"

"Sure, okay," he said. "When?"

"Now."

"Now? Didn't your granddad just say Charlie was coming home? And shouldn't we finish painting?"

"We won't be gone long, and we can finish painting when we get back." She put her brush on the edge of the open can and stood up, brushing the dirt from her bare knees.

Reese thought maybe he should tell his mom where they were going, but he still didn't want to face her, so he put his brush beside Meg's on the can and followed her to the barn. Two wooden paddles and life jackets were leaning against a wall inside. She handed him one of each. "Do you know how to use them?" she asked.

"Maybe," he said. "I think so."

"You ever been canoeing?"

"No." He'd been fishing in a bass boat a couple of times with his dad and a friend of his, but that boat had a motor, no paddling. How hard could it be, though?

"I can show you," Meg said. "I love it. It's one of my favorite things to do. Come on."

They carried the paddles and the life jackets down the grassy slope to the riverbank, by the dock. More birds, fast ones, were zigzagging over the water and the bank, dipping low over the river, almost skimming it, and then rising and circling to come skimming in again. They made a burbling twitter as they flew.

After they put their life jackets on, Reese helped Meg flip the canoe and carry it out next to the dock. The canoe had two seats, front and back, wicker strung between bars of wood. Meg told him to sit up front, and she held the canoe steady against the dock while he climbed in. She got in the back, and they pushed away with their paddles.

The canoe rocked a little as she got settled, but then they slid smoothly and silently out across the river's black water. Meg pulled hard on her paddle, bringing them around so the bow of the canoe faced down the river. Then she showed him how to paddle: reach, dip, pull, then lift and reach again.

He dipped, pulled, lifted, and reached, then dipped and pulled again. "Keep going," Meg said.

And they were on their way, picking up speed, heading to the bend where the river went left, around the shoulder of the flooded woods. He felt his anger with his mom fading, as if he had left it at the dock and each stroke of the paddle was putting it farther behind. They sliced through the shining river, and it felt so good to reach and pull and move so effortlessly through the water that Reese laughed.

"You're doing really good," Meg said.

"Thanks," Reese said.

They rounded the bend, and she steered into it, keeping the canoe pointed down the river's deep middle.

"So you do this a lot?" Reese asked.

"As often as I can," she said.

"With Charlie?"

"Yep. He likes it, too. Here, paddle on your right. Aim for that big tree on your left." She was steering them toward the flooded woods. At the edge of the trees, they passed two white jugs, old bleach bottles attached to a rope stretched between two trees. It was a trot line, Meg said, set by a neighbor to catch catfish. The jugs were floats to keep the rope and the baited hooks hanging off it from sinking.

She dipped her paddle into the water near one of the jugs and lifted the rope. Hanging from it was a length of fishing line, and on the end was a fish head, the barbed end of a big fishhook sticking from one of its white eyes. Its mouth gaped open, as if it were surprised at how it had ended up, bait for some big catfish.

"Now that is disgusting," Reese said.

Meg laughed. "Right? I guess catfish love it, though. The stinkier, the better." She dropped it back into the river with a plop.

They went a little farther and then glided in among the trees. Reese felt something bump against the canoe's bottom and slide along its length, lifting them a little as it passed beneath them. He looked over the side to try to see what it was. "Just a branch," Meg said. "Hey, stop paddling for a minute."

He raised his paddle and lay it across the sides of the canoe. She did the same. They drifted forward, carried along by momentum, but then they bumped against a tree and stopped.

The back end of the canoe turned a little to the right, pointing them into the dim, flooded woods. Somewhere back in there something called out. It was a series of notes that rose in pitch and then fell: *Cuk-cuk-cukcukcuk-cuk-cuk.* Reese thought it was a bird maybe. It sounded like crazy laughter.

He looked back at Meg, wondering why she had wanted to stop paddling.

She said, "Can I ask you a question?"

"Okay," Reese said.

"How come you're here? Why are you staying with us?"

He looked away, into the trees, not sure what to say.

"You don't have to answer if you don't want to," Meg said. "My grandma just said you and your mom need a place to stay, and she said why was your business."

He was surprised that Mrs. Smith hadn't told her everything. He hadn't trusted the old woman to keep quiet about it. Now, in the silence among the trees, where it felt as if they were miles and miles from anything, just him and this girl he barely knew, he found himself thinking about telling the truth. He was sick and tired of carrying it around by himself, lying about it. But he still was afraid of letting the secret out, even though he couldn't say what he was afraid would actually happen if he told Meg. Who would she tell? She knew no one he knew.

He had to say something. He couldn't just tell her to mind her own business while he was sitting in her canoe. He didn't want her thinking he was a jerk. So he gave her some of the story, just a little: "My mom and dad have been fighting," he said. "We're just here while they work things out."

"I'm really sorry," she said. "What are they fighting about?"

Reese shrugged. This was a line he didn't want to cross. "I don't know," he lied. "Different things."

"Why did you look so mad just now when my grandad and I came out of the house?"

"We hadn't been able to reach my dad since Friday, and he showed up at school today, wanting to talk. But my mom yelled at him, in front of the whole school, for being gone and just showing up like that. The whole thing was embarrassing and stupid."

"Wow," Meg said. "What did you do?"

"I tried to get my mom to talk with him, but she wouldn't right then. I got pretty mad."

"I would have been mad, too," she said. She looked at him as if she were waiting for him to say more, but when he didn't, she blinked and looked away. Then she said, "My parents fought sometimes. One time my mom got so mad she walked out and took us to stay with my grandparents down here for, like, a whole month."

Reese turned sideways in his seat so he wouldn't have to keep twisting his neck to look at her. "What happened?" he asked. He really wanted to know.

"She went back to my dad, after a while. But I used to get scared sometimes that she wouldn't."

Reese was surprised that she would talk with him about

her dead parents. She was dry-eyed, her head turned toward the river, her chin up a little, as if she were listening for something.

She said, "They fought about different things, but one thing they fought about a lot was Charlie. They'd argue about what kind of help he needed. They'd argue about what he should be doing for school and how much he could do on his own. My dad thought my mom did too much for him, didn't let him do enough on his own, and that made my mom mad. She was the one who was at home with Charlie and me most, while my dad worked, and she'd get really upset when my dad told her maybe she should handle things different. Like he was telling her how to do her job."

"I'm sorry," Reese said. He didn't know what else to say.

Meg shrugged. "Do you think your parents will get back together?"

"Yes," he said, trying to sound surer about it than he was.

"That's good. I'm glad. It sucks when your family is split up."

He thought again that he wanted to ask her about her parents, how they had died exactly, how she felt about living without them now, far away from home. But it might be rude or make her sad. So he only nodded and said, "It does. It sucks."

That crazy laughter started again from back in the trees. Reese faced forward and peered into the trees, trying to see what was making that sound. "What is that?" he asked.

"It's a pileated woodpecker," she said. "Do you know Woody Woodpecker, with the goofy laugh? That's the kind of bird he's supposed to be."

"How do you know stuff like that?" he asked her.

"Just from reading," she said. "Hey, do you want to go back? Or keep going? I'm fine with either."

He thought of his mother, back in the trailer. He wanted to know what she would say to his dad when she called and what his dad would say to her. But he heard her words again: *Give me quiet.* She'd had enough of his pushing.

"Let's keep going," he told Meg.

They picked up their paddles and dipped them into the still water, and they eased their way out through the trees and into sunlight on the open river. Reese looked around, back the way they had come. The sun was getting lower, and all the colors were deeper, electric almost: the greens of the trees, the blue of the sky, the red letters on Meg's shirt.

Meg nodded then at something in front of them, and he turned to look. "Heron," she said. "To the left."

They were passing a stand of trees that stood out a little way into the river, and wading among the roots of the trees was a big bird with a long neck and long legs. When they got closer, it rose awkwardly, with a croak and a little splash, its wings beating hard, long legs dangling, spraying drops of water that caught the late-day sun and made Reese think of falling diamonds. "That's a great blue heron," Meg said.

The heron gathered itself as it caught air, tucking its head against its body, stretching its legs straight out behind. Free of the river, all its awkwardness vanished: It was flying, rising steadily above the treetops, its wide wings beating easily. Reese watched it, thinking about how he would draw the lines of it with his pencil and how hard it would be. Its shape had changed two or three times in just a few seconds as it took off. The bird went around a bend and was gone.

"That was cool," he said. His words felt flat and silly. He couldn't explain how he had felt when he saw the bird.

But Meg said, "It is cool. I don't think I could ever get tired of seeing that."

"What's the farthest you've ever gone down the river?" Reese asked.

"Pretty far, with my granddad and with my parents," she said. "My dad and mom one time went all the way to the ocean from here. Not with me, though. It was before I was born, before Charlie, too.

"In this canoe?"

"Yeah, I think so." The bow had begun to drift toward the trees, and she dipped and pulled left to straighten it out. "They took water and a cooler full of food, and they went all the way to the mouth of the river and out into the Albemarle Sound, and then across the sound to the ocean. It took them three days. They camped out at night."

Something in her voice made him look back at her. She was staring into the trees. Her hair was down around her shoulders. She had beads of sweat on her upper lip, and her face was flushed from paddling in the heat of the day. Reese's face felt hot and prickly, too. He bet it was red.

Meg looked at him. "My mom and dad used to talk about taking me and Charlie on the same trip, down the river," she said. "Just the four of us. They were talking about getting a second canoe, and we'd camp out just like they did."

She didn't sound sad exactly. She said it matter-of-factly. But Reese thought how that trip with her parents would never happen now, and he wanted to say something to try to make it a little better. "Maybe you and Charlie could do it someday," he said.

"Maybe," she said. Then she picked up her paddle to get moving again.

CHAPTER 15

The sun was starting to go down when they got back to the dock and pulled the canoe up the bank. Meg led the way to the barn, where they put the paddles and life jackets back. The screen door of the house screeched open as they came into the yard, and Mr. Smith came out. "Where did y'all go?" he asked. "We were starting to really worry."

"Nowhere," Meg said. "Just out in the canoe."

"You left Charlie hanging," Mr. Smith said. "You were gone when he got home, and we didn't know where to tell him you were. I think he was looking forward to seeing you and Reese. He said he had something he wanted to show you."

"I'm sorry," Meg said.

"I'm not the one you should apologize to. Reese, your mom was also out looking for you. You ought to go in."

"Yes, sir."

"I'll put the paint away," Meg said.

"I got it," Mr. Smith said. "And I finished the priming."

Reese wanted to slide away without another word from Mr. Smith. At the trailer steps, though, he felt a twinge of guilt for leaving Meg alone to take the consequences of their sneaking off. But it was too late: When he looked back, she and her grandfather were going inside. The screen door shut behind them.

Inside the trailer, his mom was in the kitchen, washing a pot. "Where were you?" she asked. "I texted."

"I went out canoeing with Meg." He hadn't thought to check his phone the whole time out.

"Please don't take off like that, particularly out on the river, without telling someone." She wiped her forehead with the back of her hand. "Look, come dry these dishes, and then we can eat." She handed him a dry dishrag. "Start with the pot."

He picked up the pot and wiped it, outside and in. He watched his mom, trying to read her face. He wanted to ask her if she had any news about his dad, but he was afraid of making her angrier than she already was. She was looking hard at a plate she was washing, her mouth set. She handed it to him to dry and grabbed another, without raising her head. Then she said, "I spoke with your father."

"Okay," said Reese, cautious. He felt as if they were standing on a narrow ledge or something. One false move and they might fall.

"We're going to keep talking," she said. "We discussed him meeting us for supper some place. Hub's maybe."

"When?"

"I don't know. Not tomorrow night, because I've already told the Smiths we'd go to their house for supper. But soon."

She handed him another plate to dry.

"And then what?" Reese asked. "Whenever we meet Dad for supper, what happens after that?"

"I don't know, Reese." She straightened up, wiped her forehead again. "We'll keep talking. That's all I can tell you. I know it's not what you want to hear."

It wasn't. But it was something, a small hopeful sign.

After supper, his mom told him to take a shower, and he did it without complaint. As he stood under the warm water, his thoughts turned from his dad to Meg and Charlie. He wondered again what it must be like to have no dad and no mom, and then, on top of that, to have to come to a little place like Spendlowe—actually, not even Spendlowe, but outside it, in the country—after living your whole life someplace big like Washington, D.C. He wondered what Meg thought of this place and small-town kids like him.

He wondered, too, how she felt about Charlie—about having a brother with Down syndrome. And he wondered how Charlie felt about having Down syndrome. Meg had said her parents argued about how to take care of him, and Reese had wanted to ask more about Charlie and Down syndrome, but again, he had thought it might be rude.

While he was drying off from his shower, someone knocked on the trailer door. A few moments later, his mom came to the bathroom door. "Reese? Are you almost done? Charlie's here, and he was wondering if you could come out for a minute. He says he wants to show you something."

"Is Meg with him?" he asked.

"I don't think so," his mom said. "I think it's just Charlie."

He grimaced at himself in the mirror. He felt a little shy around Charlie without Meg there.

"Reese?"

"Can you tell him I'm tired or sick or something?" he asked.

"I'm not going to lie to him again," she said. "Just pull on some shorts and a shirt and go see what he wants to show you. I'll tell him you'll be out in a few minutes."

Reluctantly, he got dressed and went outside. The air felt a little cooler, after his shower, and the frogs were singing. Charlie was sitting at the picnic table, under the light on the pole. He stood when Reese stepped out. He was holding a flashlight. "I can show you something, if you want," he said. "I came looking for you when I got home, but you and Meg were gone."

"What do you want to show me?" Reese asked.

"It's a surprise." Charlie was smiling. "I'll take you. Come on." Reese snuck a look back at the trailer. His mom was watching from the kitchen window. She pointed at Charlie: *Go.* So Reese went, following Charlie across the yard.

"Where's Meg?" Reese asked.

"Meg doesn't know about this," Charlie said. "It's a secret."

This wasn't an answer to his question, and Reese looked

over at the house. The lights were on in the kitchen and in a couple of windows upstairs, but he couldn't see anyone.

Charlie was headed to the barn, and he waited for Reese to catch up. They went around the barn, and Reese saw a wood-shed against the trees. It was open in front and had a sloped roof. It was about as tall as Reese was, and it was half full of split logs, firewood. Charlie turned and put a finger to his lips: *Quiet.* Then he motioned for Reese to come closer. Charlie squatted at the opening of the woodshed, and Reese squatted beside him, as quietly as he could.

Charlie lifted the flashlight and shone the beam down, at an angle, so it fell just over the edge of the woodshed. "There's the secret," he whispered.

Reese didn't see anything at first, except a jumble of shapes in among the logs. Then he saw something flash: two small lights, like bits of yellowish-green flame. All at once he realized what he was looking at: It was the black cat, Mama Cat, the pregnant one, lying on her side, on a pile of rags. Except she wasn't pregnant anymore.

She'd had her kittens.

They were huddled against her belly, four tiny balls of fur. Two were gray, one was white, and one was black like its mother.

Reese expected Mama Cat to run, but she didn't. She had turned her face away from the light, but she stayed where she was, with her kittens beside her, so tiny, no bigger than the palm of Reese's hand. He'd never seen anything like this in person, animals so newly born. They looked incredibly fragile.

"How come she's not running away?" Reese asked. He was whispering, too, like he was in church.

"I don't know," Charlie whispered. "But you have to be careful not to scare her, or she might take her kittens away."

"How did you find them?"

"She came out today by the house, and she wasn't fat anymore. And I followed her here. She wanted to show me her kittens. That's what I think."

Reese had forgotten all about being uncomfortable alone with Charlie. He leaned forward to try to get a better look at the kittens without scaring the mother. They were so small. One was lying sideways, and its eyes were tightly closed. Charlie held the flashlight higher, above his head, and moved closer to Reese. He brought his face in very close, so his nose was almost touching Reese's face.

"This is a secret," Charlie whispered again.

"What do you mean?" Reese asked.

"All this, the kittens. It's our secret. I didn't tell Meg."

"Why not? Why didn't you tell Meg?"

"She's already got a secret with you," Charlie said.

Reese shook his head. He didn't understand at first. "What secret do I have with Meg?"

Charlie only shrugged. But after Reese thought about it for a moment, he realized that Charlie was talking about him and Meg going off in the canoe without telling anyone. Suddenly, he felt ashamed for leaving Charlie behind. He said, "Thank you for showing me the kittens."

"That's okay," Charlie said. "Do you want to pick them up when it's time? You can help me feed Mama Cat and the other cats, too."

"Sure."

Mama Cat had turned her head at the sound of their voices, like she was listening and understood. Reese stayed with Charlie, watching her and her kittens for a while. Then he said good night and slipped back across the yard to the trailer.

CHAPTER 16

The next day Reese went into town with his mom and hung out with Tony for the first day of summer break, while she worked her shift at the Kwik Stop. They walked over to the town pool to mess around for a while, just like they had done almost every day the summer before. It was okay, but this time Reese kept thinking about swimming with Meg and Charlie in the river. The town pool, which didn't even have a diving board, seemed boring after that.

The pool had a snack bar run by high school kids every summer, in a wooden hut over in one corner. He and Tony got hot dogs and cheese fries there for lunch and then ice cream sandwiches. Tony's mom paid for it when she came over to the pool with his little brother, Joseph, and a couple of Joseph's friends.

Reese didn't really want to swim any more after lunch, and Tony didn't want to get dragged into playing in the pool with

Joseph and his little friends anyway, so the two of them got dressed and went down the block to the basketball courts. They met an older kid Reese knew from one of the apartment buildings his family used to live in, a guy named Mikey, and Mikey let them borrow one of his basketballs.

Reese messed around with his backward free throws a little. Mikey and some other guys playing a pickup game one court over stopped to watch, and they cheered and clapped whenever he made one. He made two in a row and six altogether before it was time to quit hogging the ball and pass it to Tony. They worked on their normal free throws for a while and played around the world, taking shot after shot around the basket from the three-point line.

It was fun, but Reese was still thinking about Meg and Charlie. He had this urge to tell Tony about them and about the river and the canoeing, but he couldn't without raising a whole bunch of questions he didn't want to answer about how he had met them in the first place. He also thought Tony would probably give him a hard time about hanging out with a girl. Still, Reese was actually looking forward to supper with them, and he was curious to see the inside of that big house.

After a while, they walked back to Tony's house, and when it was time for Reese to meet his mom, he texted her to say that he would walk to the Kwik Stop to meet her, even though she had said she would pick him up. It would probably raise questions about why she was driving him home when he could have walked if they had been at their apartment in town.

He and his mom didn't talk much as they rode back to the Smiths' place. Reese didn't push her to go back to the apartment to check on his dad, even though he wanted to. She was talking to his dad again anyway. That was *something*.

Charlie was out feeding his cats when they pulled in, and Reese helped. He also went up with Charlie to the woodshed to feed Mama Cat and look at the kittens. Then he went in and took a shower without his mom asking, because he was sweaty after playing basketball and didn't want to stink up the Smiths' house. He put on a clean shirt and shorts. When it was time to walk over, he offered to carry the pasta salad his mom had made.

Mrs. Smith met them at the door and let them in. Meg was at the counter with her grandfather, dishing green beans into a bowl. She looked up at Reese as he came in, and he thought maybe she smiled a little, but then she went back to her work.

"I brought some pasta salad," Reese's mom said. "I hope that's okay."

Charlie came out of the downstairs bathroom then. "I really don't like pasta salad," he said. "It can be kind of slimy."

Meg, Reese, and Reese's mom all laughed.

"Charlie, don't be rude," said Mrs. Smith. She put her arm around his shoulders and drew him close, patting his arm, just like Reese's mom did to him when she was trying to shut him up in front of company.

"It *can* be kinda slimy," Reese said. "Not yours, though, Mom. No offense."

"No offense taken," she said. "Charlie, you do not have to eat my pasta salad if you don't want."

Mrs. Smith said, "Well, thank you for coming, Amanda and Reese, and thank you for bringing the salad, which I know will be delicious *and not at all slimy.* Charlie, can you say thank you?"

"Thank you," Charlie said.

"Thank you for having us," said Reese's mom.

"I think we're just about ready to eat, if you are," said Mr. Smith. "Please, go on in."

Mrs. Smith led them out of the kitchen into a big dining room with a long table covered by a white tablecloth. "This is all so lovely," Reese's mom said. "You have a beautiful home."

"It's a money pit," said Mr. Smith, who had come into the dining room, carrying the bowl of green beans. "This place is way bigger than we need. It was built by my grandfather, and it passed to my father and then to me, furnishings and all. It's kind of a family white elephant."

Mrs. Smith snorted. "You will never get him out of here alive. He loves this place."

Reese had no idea what a "white elephant" had to do with the house. He looked at Meg, who had her eyes down. She was folding napkins to put on the table.

When supper was served, Mrs. Smith had Reese sit between Meg and his mom. His mom tapped a finger on his napkin, and he looked at her, puzzled. Yes, that was his napkin. He saw it. She frowned a little and pointed down, and Reese realized she wanted him to put the napkin on his lap, which is something she never had him do at home. Reese did it, but then he didn't know what to do with his hands. He always ate with his elbows on the table at home, but he figured his mom wouldn't want him doing that here either.

Spread out in front of them were a roast chicken and the green beans, fruit salad, and the pasta salad. Mrs. Smith stood up to carve the chicken, and Mr. Smith, who Reese figured didn't know his mom as well as Mrs. Smith because he didn't go to church, asked, "So, Amanda, Mattie tells me you work at the Kwik Stop in town."

"I do," his mom said. "I'm an assistant manager."

"She should run the place," said Mrs. Smith. "She ought to be manager, the way they depend on her."

"I don't know about that," his mom said.

"Well, I know it," Mrs. Smith. "I have been by multiple times, and I've seen the way what's-his-name, the owner's son, relies on you. That one day, the way you were handling the deliveries, all the paperwork, while he just stood around. He would be lost if you weren't there."

"Larry?" Reese asked.

"Yes, Larry," said Mrs. Smith. "That's his name. Clearly not the sharpest knife in the drawer."

Reese laughed at that, and his mom poked his thigh under the table. His dad was always telling her the same thing Mrs. Smith was: She needed to speak up for herself, tell the owner to at least give her a big raise for all the extra work she did to cover for Larry—or better yet, give her a raise and make *her* the boss. But she never had. Reese's dad said she lacked confidence, didn't believe in herself like she should.

There at the Smiths', she quickly changed the subject: "So tell me more about this house. When was it built?"

While the adults talked, Reese glanced at Meg, who was scooping out pasta salad for herself. She seemed to be watching him, too, out of the corner of her eye. But she didn't say much through supper, and neither did Reese. He felt awkward in front of the adults. Maybe she did also. Charlie spoke a lot, though: about his cats, about the karate class he took in Goldsville twice a week, about how much he liked his granddad's chicken.

When they were done eating, Mrs. Smith said, "Meg and Charlie, why don't you take Reese upstairs while we clear the dishes. I bet Reese would love to see the attic."

Meg pushed her chair back. "Do you want to go upstairs?"

"Okay," Reese said. He was relieved to get away from the adults and that fancy dining room. He had been worried the whole time that he was going to drop something on the white tablecloth and stain it.

Charlie got up, too. "We can see my room first!" he said. "Follow me."

They went out of the dining room and up the big staircase to a hallway above.

"Charlie, is your room halfway clean?" Meg asked. "You got any dirty underwear on the floor?"

"I cleaned up," Charlie said. He led them down the short hall past two other doors to a room with windows looking out onto the yard in front and the trees and field beyond. Charlie's bed, covered with a red bedspread, was against one wall, and on it, side by side, were a stuffed cat and a real one. The real cat was an orange tabby that Reese had never seen. It must be an indoor cat.

"This was our mom's room when she was a kid," Charlie said. "Now it's mine."

On a dresser were two trophies with figures on top doing karate kicks. On the bases were the words, **OUTSTANDING PROGRESS!** Beside them was a single photo in a frame. It was big, about the size of a page from a school notebook, and in it were a man and a woman in front of what looked like an altar in a church, with a large, plain gold cross on the wall behind them, like the one at United Methodist in town. They were smiling, standing shoulder to shoulder, holding hands. The man had red hair, and he was wearing a black tuxedo. The woman had dark brown hair and dark eyes, like Meg and Charlie and their grandma, and she wore a white dress that pooled around her feet. She was smiling, too. Meg had her nose: long, narrow, and straight.

Charlie saw where Reese was looking. "That's our mom and dad right there, from when they got married." He stepped forward and picked up the photo and brought it close to Reese.

No way did Reese want to stand there looking at a picture

of Meg and Charlie's dead parents. It made him uncomfortable and sad. But he didn't know what else to do other than pretend to look at it more closely. He could see his own face in the glass that covered the photo.

"They're dead," Charlie said. "They're in heaven now."

Reese felt as if maybe he should say something, offer his condolences or something, the way people do when someone dies, but he didn't know exactly what to say. All he did was nod like a dork. A clock on a table next to the bed was ticking. He heard Mrs. Smith laugh downstairs.

After a moment, Meg said, "Let's go see my room."

Reese followed her down the hall to a door that led to another, narrow flight of stairs. The ceiling of the staircase was low, so that the top of his head almost brushed it. They turned once at a landing and then came up through an opening in the floor, into one end of a long room with walls that angled in as they rose, meeting at the top, so the space formed an upside-down V.

"This is the coolest bedroom I've ever seen," he said.

It was like a hideout. At each short end of the room was a single window. At one end, opposite from where they were standing, was Meg's bed, with a little table and a dresser. The other end of the room was set up like a library. Reese could understand why Mr. Smith had to make another bookcase for her: She had shelves full of books along the wall, and more books stacked on a desk.

On the sloping walls Meg had thumbtacked maps. One, the

largest, was a map of the whole world. Others showed South America, Africa, and Australia in more detail. Pushed here and there into all the maps were push pins with brightly colored beads for heads—red, green, blue. "What are all the pins for?" Reese asked.

"They're places I want to see someday," she said. "I'm going to travel all over."

He leaned in close to the map of South America and squinted to make out the writing next to one of the pins. "That's Iguazú Falls," Meg said. She said it like she spoke Spanish or whatever it was people spoke down there: *ee-gwa-ZOO.* "It's one of the biggest waterfalls in the world. It's on the border between Brazil and Argentina."

"Our mom and dad went there," Charlie said. "They traveled all over South America before we were born."

"They were in the Peace Corps in Ecuador," Meg said. "That's how they met."

The farthest Reese had ever traveled, aside from a few visits to the beach, was to see an old aunt of his dad's in Richmond, Virginia, which was only about a four-hour drive away. It had never occurred to him that he could travel to a place like South America.

He looked around her room. On the desk was another photo of Meg and Charlie's parents, in shorts and T-shirts this time. Their dad was sitting in a lawn chair, and their mom was sitting in his lap. They both had big smiles on their faces again, bigger even than in the wedding photo. Reese thought about how Meg and Charlie had nothing left of their parents but these photos and stories.

"Meg? Charlie?" Mrs. Smith was calling them from downstairs. "Do you and Reese want ice cream?"

"Do you want ice cream?" Meg asked him.

"Sure," Reese said. They went downstairs, Charlie leading the way again. Reese's mom was in the kitchen helping Mrs. Smith wash the dishes. Mr. Smith was scooping ice cream.

"Hey, we were just talking about tomorrow," Reese's mom said. "Mr. Smith has to go to Goldsville to run an errand, and he was thinking about taking Meg and Charlie out to lunch at a restaurant they like. He was wondering if you want to go with them."

"Yes!" said Charlie. "You like Indian food, don't you?"

"Let him decide for himself, Charlie," Mrs. Smith said. "Reese, Meg and Charlie like Indian food, and there's a place in Goldsville where they're kind of regulars."

"Do you want to come with us?" Meg asked. "Sometimes we go to a comic book store there after lunch, a place called Mighty Comics."

"We can do that," Mr. Smith said.

"But you don't have to come if you don't want to," Meg said.

He wanted to go. He was a little surprised by that himself, especially because he had never had Indian food and didn't know if he would like it at all. The only kinds of food he'd had that weren't just plain old American were Chinese and

Mexican. He could have gotten out of it by saying he had other plans in town or something. But the whole time he had been in town that day, even when he was having fun, he still had felt wrong, like he was being fake, lying even, because Tony and everyone assumed he was still living in town and his parents were together.

Meg might not know everything, but she knew some, and she was so separate from town and his normal life that he felt kind of safe with her and Charlie.

"Okay, sure," he said.

Meg smiled. "Cool," she said.

CHAPTER 17

They were on their way to Goldsville in the Smiths' hatchback. Mr. Smith was driving. Charlie was beside him in the front seat, and Reese was sitting in the back with Meg. They had left about ten in the morning, not long after Reese's mom had gone to work, and now they were on the state highway headed to the city. Charlie was humming, his pitch matched to the whine of the tires on the road.

Mr. Smith looked at Reese in the rearview mirror. "This is your first time eating Indian food, right?"

"Yes," Reese said.

"Well, this place has a great buffet."

Charlie stopped humming and turned to look at him in the back seat. His seatbelt fell off his shoulder. "My favorite is butter chicken," he said. "Murgh makhani."

"What's that second one?" Reese asked.

"It's the same thing," Meg said. "It's just the Indian name for butter chicken."

Terrific: They weren't even in the restaurant yet, and he was making himself look like some dumb small-town kid. He was already feeling a little nervous about trying a strange food, especially in front of Meg, and saying or doing something stupid at the restaurant, like getting dessert first by accident.

"What's your favorite?" Charlie asked.

"Reese just said it's his first time eating Indian," Meg said, as if she were jumping in to save him. "How can he have a favorite if he's never had it before?"

"Oh, yeah," Charlie said. "Right."

"Okay, Meg, be nice," said Mr. Smith. He tapped Charlie's knee. "And you, face forward and fix your seatbelt. That's not safe." He looked in the rearview mirror again and changed the subject: "So, Reese, you have a birthday coming up, don't you? I think Meg and Charlie's grandma said you're about to turn thirteen. Is that right?"

He nodded. "Next week," he said. It was one week away exactly.

"What are you doing to celebrate? Are you getting together with your friends or something?"

"I don't know," he said. He looked down at his hands. He had been trying *not* to think about it, and he didn't want to talk about it with Mr. Smith any more than with Tony or Ryan. Mr. Smith wasn't picking up on this, though. It clearly didn't occur to him to think about how Reese might feel about a birthday party with his family split.

Out of the corner of his eye, he saw Meg looking at him. When he raised his head to look at her, she looked away, but then, whether she could tell what was going on with him or not, she saved him from any more questions. "You want me to read, Charlie?" she asked.

"Okay," Charlie said.

She reached into the pocket on the back of the seat in front of her and took out an old book, a green hardcover with a spine worn shiny. She showed Reese the cover: "It's *Anne of Green Gables*," she said. "Charlie and I both like it. We read it out loud sometimes. Have you read it?"

"No," Reese said. "I think I've heard of it, though."

"Do you want me to catch you up, tell you what the story is about?"

"Nah, that's okay," Reese said. "I'll just listen."

He leaned his head against the window as Meg opened the book and flipped through to find her place. Charlie began humming again softly, but Meg didn't seem to mind. "We're at Chapter 5," she said. "Charlie, this is the part where Marilla tries to take Anne back."

"I like this part," Charlie said.

Meg began reading: "'Do you know,' said Anne confidentially, 'I've made up my mind to enjoy this drive. It's been my experience that you can nearly always enjoy things if you make up your mind firmly that you will. Of course, you must make it up *firmly*. I am not going to think about going back to the asylum while we're having our drive. I'm just going to think about the drive. Oh, look, there's one little—'"

"What asylum are they talking about?" Reese asked.

Meg looked up from the book. "What?"

"Why are they taking her to an asylum? Like an insane asylum?"

"No, they're taking her back to the orphanage. Anne is an orphan. Her parents are dead. They called the orphanage an asylum back then."

"The word 'asylum' just means a safe place or a shelter," Mr. Smith said.

It seemed strange to Reese that Meg would just say all that about orphans and dead parents, like it was no big thing, like she and Charlie weren't orphans themselves. He looked at Charlie, wondering how he was reacting. He had his head back and his eyes closed, listening happily, as far as Reese could tell. "Don't worry," Charlie said then, as if he knew what Reese was thinking. "They don't take Anne back. Keep reading, Meg."

"Okay, so: 'Oh, look'—this is Anne talking—'there's one little early wild rose out! Isn't it lovely? Don't you think it must be glad to be a rose? Wouldn't it be nice if roses could talk? I'm sure they could tell us such lovely things. And isn't pink the most bewitching color in the world?'"

She read like that all the way to Goldsville. Reese was impressed. It was a cool thing for Meg to do. Some kids would be too embarrassed to read out loud to their brother in front of other people, particularly when they didn't know them all that well.

Meg kept reading while they waited in the car outside an AutoZone for Mr. Smith to get a part for his pickup. Then they went on to the restaurant. It was in a shopping center, between a liquor store and a Roses discount store. When they pulled into the parking lot, Meg carefully put a bookmark in her book and laid it on the seat. It really did look old. Reese touched it and turned it a little to look at the cover, which had old-fashioned gold lettering pressed into it: *Anne of Green Gables, L. M. Montgomery.*

"It was my mom's book," Meg said.

He pulled back, like the book might crumble into dust. He thought Meg might not want him touching something her mom had left behind. But she just rubbed her nose with the back of her hand and said, "Let's go. You're going to like lunch. I promise."

The restaurant's name was painted in red letters outlined with white on the plate-glass window: **KABAB AND CURRY**. Under the name, in smaller white letters, were the words **FINE INDIAN CUISINE, DINE-IN TAKE-OUT**. They went in, Meg first, and the aroma of the place hit Reese: a mix of roast chicken and freshly baked bread and cinnamon maybe and he didn't know what else. He breathed in deeply. It smelled good.

There were two other groups in the place: a man and a woman about his mom's and dad's age at one table near the buffet, and an older man and woman with a teenage girl at another table near the door. When Reese looked at the couple by the buffet, both the man and the woman were looking in his direction, but when they saw him looking back, they put their heads back down over their plates. It made him feel as if they had seen right through him and figured out that he really belonged at Hardee's eating a burger, not in an Indian restaurant eating whatever it was people ate in India.

Mr. Smith led the way to a table to the right. "Would y'all like mango lassis to start?" he said. "Reese, I think you'd enjoy a lassi."

"They're like milkshakes, kind of," Meg said. "I love them."

He swallowed his doubts and said okay.

"I have to go look at what they have today," Charlie said. He got up and went to the buffet table, moving from tray to tray, checking out the contents. He was rubbing his hands together. "Yes!" he said happily.

A man came out from a back room, and he spoke: "Good day, Charlie," he said. "It's very good to see you. How are you?"

"I'm hungry," Charlie said.

The man laughed.

"They know you?" Reese asked Meg.

"We come here a lot. Charlie especially. He completely loves Indian food."

"Hi, Dinesh," Mr. Smith said to the man. "Would you mind making us three mango lassis? I'll take a beer, a Tiger, I guess." The man nodded and went to the back. "You guys can go up and get started if you want. Meg, can you show Reese what's good?"

When Reese went to the buffet, the only thing he recognized were fried chicken strips. "You can have those if you want," Meg said. "But I bet you'd like the butter chicken. It's kind of sweet. The rice is good, too."

He looked at the rice a little suspiciously. "Why is it yellow?"

"Saffron," said Mr. Smith, who had come behind them. "It's just a spice. Very mild. It comes from flowers, crocuses, believe it or not—from the stigmas, little threads in the middle of the flower."

Reese picked up a plate from a stack at one end of the buffet, and he hovered for a moment over the chicken strips, which is what he probably would have taken if Meg weren't watching him. But he didn't want her to think he was boring or, worse, scared, so he dished out some of the yellow rice and the butter chicken, which did smell good.

"Here, try these, too," Meg said. With metal tongs, she put two little fritters on his plate. "They're pakoras."

Reese took his plate back to the table. At Mr. Smith's place was a bottle of beer. At the other places were slim, tall glasses filled with a bright orange drink, the lassis. Charlie had already piled his plate high with food, and he had dug in. He had shoved his napkin into the collar of his shirt, like a bib, which Reese thought looked a little silly. He was being a little loud, too. "Yes!" he said over his food. "Delicious!"

Reese glanced around to see if anyone was watching. The couple by the buffet were, he thought, and again, when he looked in their direction, they put their heads down. It occurred to Reese then that maybe they had been looking at Charlie all along.

Meg hadn't seemed to notice. She said, "Here, Charlie, let me cut that." She reached across, and with a fork and knife, she began to cut the meat off a chicken drumstick on his plate.

"Is India one of the places on your maps?" Reese asked her. "Is it one of the places you want to go someday?"

"Definitely," she said. "I want to see Jaipur."

"The Pink City," said Mr. Smith, who had come back with his plateful of food.

"The what?" Reese asked.

"Jaipur is called the Pink City because it has these amazing buildings that are pink, almost like huge fancy cakes with decoration and frosting all over them," Meg said.

Mr. Smith took out his phone and googled it. He slid the phone across the table so Reese could see for himself. The buildings really did look like cakes. They didn't look real.

He took a sip of his lassi while he scrolled through the photos. The drink was sweet, a little like orange juice. He took a bite of his chicken, and it was good, too. It was creamy and sweet and just a little tangy. The rice was fine. It didn't taste strange or like flowers. It was kind of nutty.

Mr. Smith took a sip of his beer. "How's the food?"

"I like it," Reese said.

"Better than chicken strips," Meg said, but not in a mean way like she was making fun of him. She looked happy that he liked it. She smiled, and Reese thought how nice her smile was: It was wide, with dimples on both cheeks.

They had a long, good lunch. Mr. Smith had just the one beer, but he ordered another round of mango lassis for the rest of them. Reese went back with Meg to the buffet for seconds, and this time he let her pick everything for him and put it on his plate, including a sort of green goop with white chunks in it that he would not have taken for himself in a million years. But it was good, too. It was called palak paneer, and he learned from Meg that *palak* was the word for "spinach" and paneer was a kind of cheese.

"It's cool that you eat at places like this," he said to her. "My family isn't too into trying different kinds of food. I didn't even know they had Indian food anywhere around here."

"Well, I'm glad you like it," she said. "You really do like it?"

"Definitely, sure."

After lunch, they said goodbye to the man who had greeted Charlie and brought them their drinks. Mr. Smith introduced him to Reese as Mr. Dinesh Chatterjee and said he was the owner of the restaurant. Mr. Chatterjee shook his hand, as if Reese was an important guest, and told him that he hoped he would come back soon. Reese said he would. His dad was all about burgers and fried chicken, but his mom liked Chinese, and he thought she'd like Indian, too.

Then they went to the comics store, which was a short drive away, in another shopping center by the Goldsville mall. A game was going on at a table in back, with a group of teenage boys talking over one another and laughing.

Reese looked around. There were superhero posters on the walls and action figures lined up on the front counter. In back were shelves of books and graphic novels and games. Up front were racks of comics and two tables with white boxes full of more comics, with handwritten signs on the tables that read, **BACK ISSUES, FROM $1**.

"What comics do you like?" Meg asked.

"I don't know," Reese said. He didn't really read comics. He liked that Meg did, though. He didn't know anyone else who read both comics and old-fashioned books like *Anne of Green Gables*. He also didn't know any girls who read comics.

"Do you not like them?" Meg asked.

"I just haven't really read comics much. I mean, I've seen the movies, though—the Avengers and stuff." Actually, Reese didn't do a ton of reading of any kind, but he never would have said *that* to Meg.

"Let me show you some," Meg said. She led him to the back, and after scanning the shelves, she picked a thin book and handed it to him. *"The Amazing Spider-Man."*

"I've seen those movies, too," he said.

"These are reprints of the original comics from the 1960s, his first appearance and then the first few issues. They're kind of over-the-top. But I think it's fun to see how it all started. We can get it for you, if you want. Or something else. It doesn't have to be this one."

"I'll get this one," Reese said. "I can buy it." He had decided right away to get it, partly because he was interested, but mostly because he figured it would make Meg happy. He thought he probably had enough money: His mom had given him fifteen dollars for lunch, but Mr. Smith had insisted on paying for that, so he still had the bills in his pocket. He didn't think his mom would mind if he spent the money on a book, even a comic book.

"My granddad probably won't let you pay for it," she said.

"I can pay," he said again.

"Whatever," she said, giving up. "Here, look, check this out. . . ." She flipped through the collection and read the title pages of one of the stories: "'The Uncanny Threat of the Terrible Tinkerer!'" She said it in a deep, over-the-top serious voice, which made Reese laugh. She flipped through and read another: "'Face-to-Face with the Lizard!' They're totally goofy, but they're fun. They make me laugh. Here's another one: 'Nothing Can Stop the Sandman!'"

He smiled and took the book from her. He flipped through the pages, scanning the panels of bold reds, greens, and yellows.

"I have this one at home," Meg said. "It was my dad's. But it's falling apart. The pages are coming out, so I don't read it much."

That wiped the smile off Reese's face for about half a moment, but then he made himself smile again so he wouldn't make her feel bad. No matter what, her parents seemed always right there with her, hovering over her, even when she was goofing around or smiling. Reese felt as if he kept bumping into them.

He looked out over the store. He saw Mr. Smith up front looking at a book. "Where's Charlie?" he asked.

"He's up front somewhere. He likes to look at the new comics. Do you want to look around some more?"

He wandered with her, checking out other comics. They watched the boys playing their game for a while. Then they circled to the front. They found Charlie sitting cross-legged on the floor near the boxes of back issues. He had one comic in his lap, and he was reading another, his head bent low over it.

Mr. Smith came over. "Y'all ready to go? Charlie, you found something you want to get?"

Charlie handed over the comic that was in his lap, and Meg said, "Reese wants this Spider-Man collection."

"I'll get it," Reese said.

"Give it here," said Mr. Smith. "Seriously, this is our treat."

Reese looked at Meg, who shrugged. "It can be an early birthday present," she said.

When she put it like that, it was okay. He didn't want to talk about his birthday plans or be reminded of it right then, but Meg wasn't trying to get into his business or push him to have a paintball party or whatever. She was just trying to give him something nice, without making a big deal out of it.

He smiled. "Okay," he said. "Thank you."

CHAPTER 18

"Please read, Meg," Charlie said. "Why won't you read?"

"You can read it to yourself, Charlie," Meg said. "Or read your comic book. I told you I need to give my voice a rest."

They were in the car, heading back from Goldsville. Charlie had asked three times for her to read. She had been nice at first, but now she was starting to sound a little annoyed. "I like to hear it the way you read it," Charlie said. "Please."

"You're being a pest," she said.

Mr. Smith cleared his throat and changed the subject: "Did you enjoy yourself, Reese?"

"Yes," he said. "Thanks for inviting me."

"Sure. And how about you, Charlie? Did you have fun?"

"Yes," Charlie said. He turned to look at Meg again, and he opened his mouth like he was going to ask her a fourth time to read to him. But then he turned to Reese. "Have you tried to draw my cats yet?" he asked.

"No," Reese said. "I haven't."

"You could try," Charlie said. "It would be a good picture."

"Maybe," Reese said. He really didn't want to. It wasn't what he liked to draw, and he wished Charlie would stop asking.

"Why *don't* you try?" Charlie said.

"Leave him be, Charlie," Meg said, clearly annoyed this time.

"Ease up, Meg," Mr. Smith said. "Charlie, let's just sit quietly and enjoy the ride for a while. Okay?"

They got to the state highway and went along silently for a time. Reese watched the fields passing, the view broken occasionally by billboards. They passed one advertising Virginia peanuts for sale and then a sign for a little town with a name Reese had always liked: Resolution. Just past it, Mr. Smith said, "You know what? I think I might get off at the next exit and take a scenic way back home. It's a beautiful day, and I'm sick of the highway. Reese, do you mind?"

He didn't. It *was* a beautiful day.

At the next exit, Mr. Smith slowed and went off. At the bottom of the ramp, he turned left onto a country road. The skies were high and blue, and here and there in the fields were pools of water left by the recent rains, reflecting the blue from above so they looked like pieces of fallen sky.

Charlie was humming again. Mr. Smith didn't seem to notice, and Reese had pretty well gotten used to it, too. After a while, the noise was like a radio playing in the other room: something that was there in the background, but you didn't really pay any attention to it. Mr. Smith cleared his throat as if he were going to say something. But then he fell silent again.

Reese thought they must almost be there. He looked at the clock on the car's dashboard: It was a little past 1:30 in the afternoon. He had his pocketknife out, and he was fiddling with it, opening and closing the blade. He thought of his dad, wondered how he was doing.

He realized then that he hadn't thought of his dad all day since leaving the Smiths' place, and he felt a little twinge of guilt about that.

He was thinking about this, opening and closing his knife, when suddenly something happened that made him jump. Charlie grabbed the dashboard and yelled, "*STOP! STOP!*"

Mr. Smith jumped, too, and the car lurched as his foot went from the gas to the brake and then back to gas again. "What's wrong?"

"Kitten!" Charlie said. He had turned around to look out the rear window, and then he spoke in such a rush Reese couldn't follow all of it. He heard "*Gonna get hit!*" and "*GO BACK!*"

Reese turned to Meg: "What's happening?"

"Charlie saw a kitten by the road, by itself," she said, "He's worried it's going to get hit by a car. He wants to go back to pick it up."

"Charlie . . ." said Mr. Smith.

"Go back, GO BACK!" Charlie said.

Mr. Smith sighed and, slowing, pulled the car over onto the shoulder. On Reese's side was a field of corn. The stalks were about waist high. On the other side were woods. "Where did you see the kitten?" Mr. Smith said. "Which side was it on?"

"That side." Charlie pointed toward the field. "It's gonna get run over. We have to save it!"

"Okay, okay, we'll go back and look," said Mr. Smith. "But wait until we stop and I get out. We can go look together." He checked behind him and then made a U-turn. "You tell me where to stop, Charlie."

They drove back slowly the way they had come, with Charlie leaning forward, his palms on the dashboard, scanning the road ahead. When they came to a curve in the road, he pointed into the cornfield. "There! It was there."

Reese wouldn't get this worked up about a cat, and he doubted his mom and dad would have gone to all the trouble Mr. Smith was going to if he did. But he tried to help by looking out the window, too, searching for the lost kitten. He didn't see anything but the field stretching away to a line of trees. If there were a kitten out there, it was a long way from any person who might take care of it. The closest house Reese had seen was a couple miles behind them probably. Maybe someone had dumped the kitten out on the road.

"I don't see anything now," Mr. Smith said.

"He's hiding," Charlie said. "We have to get out."

"Charlie, that's a huge field for one little cat to hide in," Mr. Smith said. "I bet its mama is out there and will find it." The car was creeping along, two tires on the road and two on the gravel shoulder. "Do you even have any idea what direction the kitten could have gone in?"

"No."

"Reese or Meg, did you see it?" Mr. Smith asked.

"No," Reese said.

"Me neither," said Meg.

"What color was it, Charlie?"

"Gray," Charlie said.

Mr. Smith sighed again and pulled over, just past the curve in the road. Charlie undid his seatbelt. "Easy, easy," said Mr. Smith. "Slow down. Wait until I get out."

But Charlie didn't wait. He opened his door and started to get out. "Charlie!" said Mr. Smith. "I said slow down!"

Mr. Smith began to open his door, and Reese heard something from behind them: an airy whistling. Then everything happened very fast.

Charlie came down onto the shoulder with both feet and dashed around the front of the car. Mr. Smith yelled, "*Oh my God!*" Reese heard a screech of tires, and a car, an old station wagon, was suddenly beside them, swerving, fishtailing, its tires smoking.

The car barely missed Charlie, who, instead of stopping, kept running, across the road and into the field. Mr. Smith was still half sitting behind the wheel, one hand on his door handle. "Oh Lord," he said. Then he was out of the car, running after Charlie.

The station wagon had pulled over a little way up the road,

and a man in a camo baseball cap and tan overalls got out, shouting at Charlie: "Are you stupid? What the hell are you doing? Why don't you look where you're going?"

Charlie had waded through the weeds along the edge of the field, and he plunged into the cornstalks, both hands on top of his head. He was making a strange sound, a wailing, that cut into Reese and made him scared that Charlie was hurt.

The driver yelled again: "What's wrong with you? You're going to get yourself killed!" His face had gone deep red.

Out in the field, Charlie kept up that terrible wailing.

Meg was out of the car by then, and she sprinted past Mr. Smith, going ahead of him into the field. When she got close, she reached for Charlie from behind. He was sobbing, and he turned and hit her with open hands, as if he were trying to push her away. But Meg wrapped her arms around him and pulled him to her.

Reese had also gotten out of the car. The man with the station wagon turned to look at him and Mr. Smith, as if they might be able to explain what had just happened. Mr. Smith walked over to talk with him.

Reese wanted to help, but he didn't know what he should do. Watching Meg and Charlie holding on to each other out in the field, he felt as if he were violating their privacy or something. He looked down at his feet, and he kept his eyes down until finally he heard the station wagon door slam and the angry man drive away.

CHAPTER 19

When Charlie had stopped crying and calmed down, they all walked the edge of the field, looking for the kitten. Reese saw no sign of it, and no one else did either. He heard only the whispering of the breeze in the cornstalks.

After a while, they drove home. Meg sat looking out her window. Charlie did the same. He didn't ask Meg to read.

When they pulled in at the house, Mrs. Smith was outside hanging laundry on the line, and Charlie got out of the car and ran to her. She hugged him and looked up, puzzled, at Mr. Smith. He just shook his head sadly. Meg and Reese got out, too. Charlie went into the house with Mrs. Smith, her arm around his shoulders.

"I'm very sorry," Mr. Smith said. "That was a bad end to a good day out. We appreciate you coming with us, though, Reese. And thanks for helping us look out there."

"I'm glad nobody got hurt," Reese said.

"The whole thing was my fault," Mr. Smith said. "I shouldn't have pulled over so close to the curve like that. It was dangerous, too hard for cars to see us. And I should have known Charlie might jump out ahead of me like that even though I warned him not to. He doesn't have a lot of self-control sometimes, and he won't let things go."

Reese felt uncomfortable listening to this: Mr. Smith, a grown-up, seemed to want his understanding. Or forgiveness. Or something. Reese wasn't sure what to say or do.

Meg, meanwhile, had turned and walked away, heading away from the house. Mr. Smith called to her: "Meg? Are you okay?"

"I'm just great," she said, sarcastically. She obviously wasn't okay.

"Can I do anything?" Reese asked Mr. Smith.

The old man shook his head. "Just give everyone some space, I guess. I'm sorry about all this."

Meg was walking down the slope to the river. Mr. Smith looked down at the bag from AutoZone in his hand. "I guess I'll get my tools and get going on this." He walked to the house, leaving Reese alone.

Reese went after Meg, because he was worried about her. She was almost to the dock when he caught up with her. "Can I do anything?" he asked.

She shook her head and then took off her shoes and sat on the edge of the dock, feet in the water. He hesitated a moment, not sure if she wanted him there. But then he took off his shoes, put his phone and his knife in one of them, and sat beside her at the end of the dock, with his bare feet in the cool water. He looked out over the sparkling river into the shadows of the flooded woods across from them and tried to think of something to do or say to make her feel better.

Meg had her chin raised, like she was listening for something, which Reese had figured out by then meant she was thinking hard. Suddenly she stood up. Reese squinted up at her, shielding his eyes from the afternoon sun. "What are you doing?" he asked.

"Nothing," she said.

Then she walked a few steps back on the dock, took a running start and jumped into the river.

She went under, in her T-shirt and shorts, with hardly a splash, her arms straight down against her sides. Reese, surprised, stood up. The ripples she had made spread out. The water sparkled. Reese felt a prickle of worry, like he didn't want her out of his sight. The ripples faded, and still no Meg.

He jumped in after her. When he opened his eyes underwater, he saw her floating upright, her eyes closed, her hair drifting around her face, her toes pointed at the bottom, wherever it was down there. He went to her, and when he touched her hand, she opened her eyes and looked at him.

Then she tilted her head up and pulled back to the sunny surface, and he followed. She lay out on the water, floating on her back, arms out, and looked at the sky. Reese floated next to her. After a minute she spoke: "How come you jumped in after me?"

"I don't know. I was scared, I guess."

"Scared of what?"

"I don't know. Forget it." He didn't want to say, because it sounded ridiculous: He had been worried for a second that she wouldn't come back up.

She let it drop. "Do you want to go back to the dock?"

"Whatever you want," he said.

"Let's go back."

They swam to the dock, pulled themselves out, and lay on their backs in the sun, side by side. Above them, two big black birds were circling each other as if they were tied together with an invisible string.

"Charlie has scared us like that before," Meg said. "Not exactly like that, but when he first came here, he hated every-thing so much that one day he just all of a sudden ran away from school. He went out a side door when no one was watch-ing and took off, like he was going to run all the way back to our old home. I was really, really frightened. We didn't know where he was for . . . I don't know how long."

"What happened?"

"The police finally found him when someone at a gas station saw him and got worried and called. Another time, he ran away from here when he got mad at our grandma about something, and my granddad had to chase him down the road."

She sat up and gathered her hair back, squeezed water from

it. Reese sat up beside her. She hugged her knees to her chest and then she looked at him, her eyes serious. "I love him so much, and I get so scared of losing him or him getting hurt or someone not understanding and being mean or rude, like that man in the car today. But sometimes I wish I didn't have to worry about him, and I get jealous of other kids with, you know, 'normal' families. I also used to get mad at him sometimes when our mom and dad would argue about him—or when I felt like he was taking all their attention. I used to blame him, even though I knew that was wrong. And when I think like that, I feel like a terrible person. Then when he got lost . . . or today when he almost got hit by that car . . . I just—" Her voice caught.

"You're not a terrible person," Reese said. "Sometimes you want hard stuff to just go away."

"I couldn't stand to lose him," Meg said. "He's all I've got, and I'm all he has."

"You have your grandparents," Reese said.

"It's not the same," she said.

She lay back on the dock again and closed her eyes. After a few moments, she said, "When our mom and dad died, he had trouble sleeping for a long time. He couldn't get to sleep without them there, and my grandparents couldn't really help. He would get out of bed, cry sometimes. Or he would half wake up in the middle of the night and call out for our mom. I'd hear him. It would wake me up, and it was awful. That's when I started reading to him. I'd read from our mom's books, and it would help him get to sleep. It made me feel better, too. It was like our mom and dad were in the room with us, sort of, only it was just us."

Reese looked up at the circling birds. Then he began to ask a question: "Can I ask . . ." He stopped, unsure if he should ask the thing he wanted to know. He was worried it would only make her sadder.

She turned her head to look at him. "What?"

"Never mind."

"No," she said. "Go ahead."

So he asked, "What happened to your parents exactly?"

She didn't answer for a few moments, which made Reese think that he had upset her or even offended her. "You don't have to talk about it if you don't want," he said.

She shook her head. "It's okay. They went out on a date and left Charlie and me home with a babysitter. They went to dinner, and they saw a movie. Then when they were coming home in the car, a truck coming the other way crossed over the center line and hit them. And that was it."

"I'm sorry," he said. His voice sounded flat, puny, swallowed up by the river and the sky.

"We went to bed not knowing," Meg said. "When I came downstairs the next morning, the babysitter's mother, who I didn't know very well, was sitting at the table in the kitchen. And when I asked for my mom and dad, she said they'd had an accident and were at the hospital. She said my grandparents were coming and they would explain everything." Meg shrugged. "Then my grandparents came. They told me and Charlie what had happened, that our mom and dad were dead."

This was the saddest, loneliest, most horrible thing Reese had ever heard from anyone.

"They stayed with us back home, until winter break," Meg said. "Then they moved us here."

They didn't talk at all for a while after that. Reese wanted to say something that would make everything better, but he couldn't think of anything at all. So he just lay back beside her in the sun until she stood up at last. They walked back to the house together.

They were sitting across from each other at the picnic table in the yard when Reese's mom came home from work. Their clothes and hair had dried by then. Meg was reading *Anne of Green Gables*, and Reese was reading the Spider-Man collection that Meg had picked out for him.

His mom pulled in by the light pole and got out holding a glass vase full of red and pink roses. "Where are those from?" Reese asked.

"Your father," she said. She smiled at Meg. "What are you two up to?"

Reese shrugged. "Nothing much." He wanted to know more about the flowers, but that was just between him and his mom.

"How was Goldsville?" she asked.

Reese looked at Meg. He didn't think Meg would want to talk about it anymore, at least right then. So he just said, "It was good. I liked the Indian food, and the comics store was fun. Meg and her granddad got me this." He held up his book.

"That's really nice," his mom said.

"I bet you'd like Indian food," Reese told her. "Dad might not, but I think you would. Butter chicken was my favorite, I think. That's Charlie's favorite, too."

"Mine, too," Meg said.

"And mango lassis," Reese said.

Meg smiled, and it made Reese feel good to see it. "Definitely mango lassis," she said.

"I'd like to try it all sometime," Reese's mom said. "Maybe next time y'all go, I can tag along. Would that be okay, Meg?"

"Sure." Meg stood up. "I guess I better go inside. I told my grandma I'd help her with the laundry today."

"Your grandma and grandpa are lucky to have you around," Reese's mom said.

Meg shrugged. "Bye," she said to Reese. Then she ran to the house and went inside.

"So today was really okay, with Meg and everyone?" his mom asked when she was gone.

"Yes," he said. "So how come Dad gave you flowers?"

"To try to say he's sorry, I guess. They're pretty, don't you think? They were waiting for me at the store when I got there. Hey, also: He called, and we talked about meeting him for supper at Hub's tomorrow. Is that okay?"

Reese looked at her closely. He wanted to ask her exactly

what she was thinking about his dad, but if things were going all right, he worried that speaking about it would just jinx it.

"Reese?" she said. "Is that okay?"

He nodded, and he followed her to the trailer. She put the vase of flowers on the kitchen table and took something else from her pocket: a little white envelope. She laid it on the table beside the vase. "Let me go to the bathroom, and then we can talk more," she said.

When she was gone, Reese heard the screen door at the house open and shut again. He looked out the trailer's kitchen window. Meg had come back out with her grandmother, carrying a laundry basket. They headed to the clothesline beside the house. Reese went back to the kitchen table and picked up the envelope. It was no bigger than the palm of his hand, and it had his mom's name written on it in his dad's handwriting. He looked at the bathroom door, which was still closed. Then he opened the envelope.

Inside was a note from his dad on a small white card: *Amanda, I love you and need you with me. Your Sam.*

He heard something clatter in the bathroom. His mom had dropped something. She turned on the faucet. He quickly put the card back in the envelope. He put it back beside the flowers and then moved away from the table to the kitchen sink, filling a glass to look busy.

Outside, Meg was taking clothes off the clothesline and putting them in the basket. Reese thought about what she had told him about losing both parents, finding a stranger sitting at her kitchen table when she woke, and then getting packed up and taken away from everything she and Charlie knew, all their friends, for good. He thought also about what she had said about Charlie, and how Meg, who was so smart and confident, also doubted herself, felt angry and helpless sometimes, just like he did.

Things were hard for him and his family, but the note with the flowers was a good sign: Maybe things were going to be okay. Maybe his dad was serious about doing what he had to do to get better and get the family back together. Reese might be able to go back home soon.

But for Meg and Charlie, there was no going back, ever.

CHAPTER 20

Reese's dad was waiting for them the next evening when they pulled into the parking lot at Hub's Home Style. He was leaning against the Barracuda, smoking a cigarette. The car looked freshly washed. He was dressed in sneakers and jeans and a black T-shirt. He waved when he saw them, dropped his cigarette and ground it out, and walked to them, coming up beside the Fiesta as they got out.

He looked better than he had the day he showed up at school; the bruise under his eye was fading. But he still seemed a little off, wound too tight. He didn't seem to know what to do with his hands; he put them in his pockets, took them out again, scratched his cheek. He looked at Reese's mom, who was standing with her arms crossed. "Hey, Amanda," he said.

"Hey," she said. It was not exactly an enthusiastic greeting.

"It's good to see you," he said.

She didn't respond at all to that. Reese, who was watching

her closely, trying to read her face and her tone, wondered if she was regretting meeting his dad for supper. His dad didn't look his best, but he looked good enough. Just nervous, Reese thought.

"Should we eat?" his dad said. "It's my treat tonight."

"You don't have to do that, Sam."

"Jimmy just paid me, and I want to treat. And I mean, c'mon: It's just Hub's."

Hub's Home Style was a diner at the edge of downtown Spendlowe, across from the Dollar General. It was a low building with plate-glass windows across the front and one of those rolling signs at the edge of the parking lot with the daily specials spelled out in movable plastic letters. Hub's was pretty shabby, actually: One of the windows was cracked, and inside, the red upholstery on the booths was worn and patched here and there with gray duct tape. They sure didn't serve fancy stuff like Indian butter chicken and palak whatever, and Reese thought Meg would probably think it was beyond boring. Lasagna was about as exotic as it got at Hub's. But for him, it was comfortable and familiar. He had been going to Hub's with his mom and dad his whole life.

The bell over the front door jangled, and he stepped inside ahead of his parents, into the familiar smells of French fries and coffee and the buzz of conversations. Someone had dropped a coin in the jukebox in back, and it was playing a country song with steel guitar and organ. It was an old song his mom liked, "Hello Darlin'."

The waitress, putting plates on a tray behind the counter, looked up as they came in. "Sit anywhere, y'all," she said.

They went for a booth in the rear left corner, which was one of their usual spots. Reese slid in first, on the side facing out into the room, and his mom sat beside him. His dad sat across from them and pulled three of the plastic menus from behind the ketchup and mustard bottles at the end of the table. He handed one to Reese and one to his mom. "You're in luck, Reese. Did you see tonight's special? It's your favorite, fried chicken. Think that's what you'll get?"

"Probably." The usual sounded good to him right then. No surprises: That was what he wanted tonight. He put his head down over the menu, but he looked out of the corner of his eye at his mom to check again how she was reacting. She was looking down at her menu, too, her hands clasped in her lap, with a look on her face that Reese thought was sad or worried. She hadn't smiled once.

"How about you, Amanda?" his dad asked her.

"How about me what?" she asked, not looking up, frowning a little.

"What are you going to have?"

"I don't know," she said.

"Look, the dessert special today is shoofly pie," Reese said, hoping to get her smiling. "You love shoofly pie."

She blinked and looked over at where Reese was pointing on his own menu. "That sounds good," she said.

"Is this okay?" he asked her. He didn't mean the pie or even Hub's. He meant being together, the three of them.

"Yes," she said. She sat up a little straighter, gave him a little smile. "Yes, it's fine."

Reese tried to think of something else to say to keep things moving. The waitress appeared and said, "Y'all know what you want?"

"I do," Reese's dad said. "But I think maybe we need a few more minutes. Amanda?"

"No, I'm ready," she said. She ordered a salad with grilled chicken. Reese ordered the fried chicken with mashed potatoes and coleslaw. His dad got a cheeseburger and fries.

"Anything to drink?" the waitress asked.

Reese's mom and dad just wanted water. Reese wanted a Mountain Dew. When she had written down their orders and left them, his dad said, "So I wanted to say something to you, Reese. I already said this to your mom, but I want to be sure I say it to you, too."

"We really don't need to go into this now, Sam," Reese's mom said.

"I think I need to," his dad said.

"It's okay," Reese said. Hub's was a safe place, he thought: The music from the jukebox and the buzz of conversation around them made it impossible for anyone in other booths to hear.

His mom lifted her hands, palms up, as if to say: *Fine, whatever.*

His dad put his hands on the table, palms down, as if he were bracing himself. "So, I want to say, Reese . . . I want you to know . . . that I'm serious about getting better. I know that I have a problem, and I'm going to fix it. Do you understand?"

"Why did you go so long without calling us?" Reese asked. "When you left, why didn't you call or answer my texts?"

"I was sick, Reese. I still wasn't thinking straight. And then I lost my phone. But listen, before I lost it, I got your texts, the stuff you sent about treatment centers and whatnot. I really appreciate you looking that up and sending it to me. I really do."

Reese's mom looked at him with raised eyebrows. "Reese, you didn't tell me you did that," she said.

Reese's face got warm. He worried she would be mad that he hadn't told her. He hoped his dad knew what he was doing by mentioning it in front of her.

"I was happy he did it, Amanda," his dad said. "I really was. Just like I appreciate you pushing me to get help. And Reese, what I want to say to you is that you don't have to worry about me anymore. Everything that's happened here recently, the trip to the hospital and then your mom walking out with you, it's been a wake-up call for me. And I don't blame your mom one bit for walking away. I let you both down, and your mom was right to draw a line. But look, this here, this kind of thing we're doing now, having supper together, being together . . . this means the world to me. You and your mom mean the world to me. I don't want to lose you two, and I need you with me to help me get better."

Reese looked hard at his dad's face, fair, blue-eyed—a face so much like his—and he wanted to believe. He searched for something that would tell him for sure.

His father shook his head. "What are you thinking?"

"I want us to be back together," Reese said. "When can we?"

His dad looked at his mom and then back to Reese. "We need to talk about that," he said. "Your mom and I."

His mom took a deep, deep breath. She was looking down at her hands in her lap, as if she was thinking this all over. Just then, their waitress came back, carrying their drinks. "Food will be up in a few minutes, y'all," she said.

"That's fine," his dad said.

"Do you need anything else?" the waitress asked.

"No," said Reese's mom, louder than she needed to. The waitress frowned a little, puzzled. "No, thank you," his mom said more quietly. "We're good."

When the waitress was gone, his dad said, "So, another thing I've been thinking about is your birthday, Reese. It's almost here, less than a week away! Do you know what you want to do to celebrate?"

Reese shrugged. "Not really."

"We need to celebrate," his dad said.

"He's right, Reese," his mom said, looking up, suddenly engaged. "You deserve it."

"Whatever," Reese said. "I don't care about my birthday."

"Well, I care," his mom said. "My boy's turning thirteen. A teenager!"

"*We* care," his dad said.

"Yes," his mom said.

We care. We. The words were there and gone, but they shone out to Reese as they passed, yet another hopeful sign: There was still a "we" for his mom and dad. His dad smiled and reached out and squeezed his hand. "Think about it, bud," he said. Then he looked at Reese's mom. "I want to ask something else in the meantime, Amanda," he said. "Kind of a favor."

"What?" His mom's eyes narrowed. She was wary again, suspicious, and Reese got worried that his dad was about to push too far and upset everything.

"It's not a big thing," his dad said.

"What, Sam?"

"Well, look," his dad said. "I'm working with Jimmy, and he says he's got lots of work for me. Money's coming in, so I'd like to contribute. I'd like to help even while we're working things out. Can I bring y'all groceries at least, for starters? I'd be very happy if I could go to the grocery store in the next couple days and get whatever you guys need and bring it out to you."

"Sam, I . . ." his mom began. She stopped. Reese held his breath.

"If it would make you uncomfortable, don't worry about it," his dad said. "Or if it would make these people, the Smiths . . . if it would make them uncomfortable, I won't do it. But it would mean a lot to me if you let me."

He had said "the Smiths," so Reese's mom had told him where they were staying.

His dad's question seemed to hang over their table. Reese's dad waited, and so did Reese. This was a chance for his dad to prove himself, Reese thought, and all his mom needed to do was say yes.

The waitress came with their food, and she set the plates in front of them. "Anything else?"

"No, thank you," Reese's dad said.

When the waitress was gone, his mom raised a hand and rubbed her eyes. Reese thought she was about to say no, and he would have to sit there and just take it. He couldn't start something in the restaurant, couldn't fight with her about it there, with all the people around them. His dad must have thought the same thing because he started to speak: "Amanda, forget it. It's okay to—"

But she held up a hand, stopping him. "It's fine, Sam," she said.

"What's fine?" Reese asked.

"I mean I appreciate your father wanting to do that, so it's fine. The answer is yes."

CHAPTER 21

The next day, his mom had to work an early-morning shift at the Kwik Stop, and Reese was still in bed when she came in about seven to say goodbye. "I'm going to have lunch or grab some coffee or something with your father while I'm in town," she said. "He and I will talk more about him coming out."

"Can I come to lunch with you?" Reese asked.

"I think he and I just need some time together alone to talk things over, okay?"

He sat up in bed. He was feeling a little better after the dinner at Hub's, like maybe things were moving in the right direction, and there was nothing much in town for him anyway. Tony had gone to church camp, and Ryan was still in South Carolina. So he said okay.

"What do you think you're going to do today?" she asked.

"I don't know," he said. "I'll think of something."

"Thank you, Reese," his mom said. "I really appreciate it.

Hey, and I've been thinking about something else, something your dad said last night about you texting him with treatment programs and that kind of thing. . . ."

"I'm sorry I didn't tell you," he said quickly.

"It's fine. I'm not mad or anything. But listen, we're on the same team here. You shouldn't be taking on things like that on your own. You shouldn't feel like you need to. Keep talking to me. I promise I'll keep talking to you, too. Okay? Is it a deal?"

He nodded. "Okay."

"Will you give me a hug, please?"

He stood up and gave her a hug. Honestly, it felt good to hug her. He made a promise to himself that he would try to help keep things on track by being very good: He would listen to his mom, keep talking to her, try to help, not stress her out by fighting or complaining.

When she had gone, he lay back down for a while and thought about drawing. But then he thought of something better: the basketball hoop outside. His own basketball was sitting back at the apartment in town, under his bed. But he remembered that Mr. Smith had said there was a basketball in the shed.

He went to the kitchen and ate a bowl of Cheerios. Then he got dressed, put on his sneakers, and went outside. The shed was red with spots of orange rust here and there, and when Reese pushed the door open, it squealed along rusty runners. He smelled motor oil and something else, like a damp basement—mold maybe. In the early-morning sunlight falling through the open door, he saw a bunch of junk in there: a lawnmower, a Weedwacker, a gasoline can, a big plastic bottle of weed killer, some cardboard boxes stacked on top of one another, and a dusty old bicycle set upright in a back corner. Down behind the boxes was the basketball. It was dusty and flat, but he took it out and felt it all over and it seemed fine, no holes. He looked around some more in the shed for a bicycle pump but couldn't see one.

He took the ball to the Smiths' back door and knocked. Mrs. Smith answered. She was still in her bathrobe. Behind her, Charlie was at the kitchen table in his pajamas, eating a plate of eggs. He said, "Hey, Reese!"

"Oh, you found our old basketball," said Mrs. Smith. "Are you going to play?"

"I was wondering if Charlie and Meg wanted to shoot baskets with me," he said. "I just need to pump up the ball. Do you have a bicycle pump?"

"In the basement, I think," said Mrs. Smith.

"I might just watch," Charlie said. "I don't really know how to play basketball."

"You don't have to play if you don't want to," Reese said. "But I could show you. You might like it. And anyway, it's kind of boring to shoot baskets by myself."

"I think that's a great idea," said Mrs. Smith. "Charlie, why don't you get dressed and get Meg up? Reese, I'll get the pump."

By the time Charlie and Meg were ready and came outside, Reese had pumped up the ball and was shooting baskets. He was wishing for an asphalt court like at school or the park in town, but the ground around the hoop was hard and level—good enough to take some shots. Just as Charlie and Meg came up to him, he made a perfect free throw.

"Hey, you're really good," Charlie said.

"Thanks," Reese said. "You've really never played?"

Meg shrugged and shook her head. "My granddad tried to get us to play a couple times."

"I can show you how to take a free throw like I just did, if you want."

"Sure, okay," Meg said. She smiled. "Don't laugh at me, though."

"Yeah, don't laugh," Charlie said.

Reese thought of roller-skating for the first time and how his dad had explained it all to him without making him feel stupid or too self-conscious. "I promise I won't laugh," he said. "Watch me shoot again, and I'll tell you what I'm doing step by step."

First he showed them how to stand, one foot just a little forward on the same side as your shooting hand, lined up with the center of the rim. "See how I'm at just a little bit of an angle to the basket? Not too much, but right foot forward, because I'm right-handed."

"It's like karate," Charlie said. "Like with your feet."

"What's that?" Reese asked.

"They work in karate on placing your feet in just the right way," Meg said. "What's it called, Charlie?"

"Your stance," Charlie said.

Reese remembered the karate trophies in Charlie's room. "That's a good point."

He talked through how to hold the ball and shoot: knees bent, ball low to start, down at his thigh, and then ball and body rising, shooting arm extending, all in one smooth motion, wrist snapping down at the end as the ball left his hand, like you're waving goodbye to it. "Don't look at the ball or at your hands," he said. "Keep your eyes on the rim."

He took his shot. It was perfect.

Reese handed Charlie the ball. "Try it," he said. "Are you right-handed or left-handed?"

Charlie raised a hand. "This one. Right."

"Okay, so right foot forward then just like I did." Charlie's first shot went wide, bounced away and hit the shed with a bang. The second one hit the top of the backboard and bounced off in the other direction. Reese ran down the ball each time and brought it back to him for another try.

"I don't think I can do it," Charlie said.

"You can do it," Reese said. "It just takes practice, like karate. You know what I'm thinking about right now, while I'm watching you? I'm thinking about all the times *I* missed when I was learning. Everybody does when they start."

The third shot hit the rim. "Missed again!" Charlie said.

"No, that was actually good," Reese said. "That was close. You're getting it."

Charlie's fourth and fifth shots were better, almost in. The sixth was closer still. Then, number seven: The ball hit the backboard, bobbled on the rim, and went in.

Meg cheered. "Yes!" Reese gave Charlie a high five.

Reese was surprised by how happy he was to see Charlie make that shot. He had been thinking he might show Charlie and Meg his backward free throw, but suddenly he didn't want to do it. It would have felt wrong somehow, like he was being a show-off and making the whole thing about him. He thought again of the night at the skating rink and the way his dad had hung back with him while he was learning, skating at Reese's pace even though he could have been hot-dogging.

Remembering this really made Reese miss his dad, and he wondered what his mom would say to him when they met in town. He felt a wave of worry that his dad would blow it some-how or his mom would get upset about something his dad did or didn't do. He wished he could be there to hear or to maybe kind of help steer things in the right direction.

Meg was looking at him with a funny expression, her head turned a little to one side like her grandma. It was like she could tell from his face what he was thinking. "You okay?" she asked.

"I'm fine," he said. "Here . . ." He threw the ball to her. "You want to try?"

It took her six shots, but then she made it, too.

They shot hoops until they were tired of it. Reese showed Charlie and Meg how to dribble and pass as well, and they picked it up fast. Reese told them about twenty-one, and they played that for a while. The sun was nearly overhead when they took a break for lunch. Mr. Smith made them turkey sandwiches and sliced apples. They ate in Meg's room, among her books and maps, and afterward, they went down to the river and paddled around in the canoe close to the dock. Reese sat in the middle while Meg and Charlie paddled, and then he switched places with Meg and took a paddle for a while.

They were up by the house shooting hoops again when Reese's mom came home from work a little after four. She looked tired when she pulled in, but she smiled when she saw them.

"Hey! That looks like fun!" she said.

"Do you want to play?" Reese asked.

He knew that his mom not only could play basketball, but she was good at it. She had been on her high school team back in Vera, and she had told Reese crazy stories about playing street ball as a girl with a big family of boys who lived just down from her house. She and Reese and his dad used to shoot baskets together at the park in town near one of their old apartments. In fact, it was his mom who had really showed him how to play, and his dad said Reese took after her in the way he moved on the court.

But they hadn't played like that for what felt like a long time. Since things had gotten bad with his dad, she had always been too tired or too busy. So Reese expected her to say no when he asked her then.

What she said instead was: "Give it here. Pass me the ball."

Meg had the ball, and she threw it to her. His mom dribbled once, twice, three times in place. Then she charged at the hoop, went around Reese and Meg, and went up for a layup, her blue Kwik Stop shirt untucked, billowing out. She made it.

"Woo-hoo!" Charlie said. "Go, Miss Amanda!"

Reese got the ball, and he went in for a layup, too, with his mom trying her best to block him. He was too quick for her, though, and he went around her and made the basket.

His mom laughed. "Good one, Reese!" she said. "You've really gotten fast!"

He got the ball and looked at Charlie. "You want to take a shot?" he asked.

"Pass it to me!" Charlie said.

"Mom, watch Charlie," Reese said.

Charlie dribbled once, twice. He set up the shot, just like Reese had showed him. Reese crossed the fingers of one hand, and he thought, *Come on, Charlie.*

Charlie took his shot. The ball left his hand, his wrist snapping down just right, and it arched over Meg, who stood watching with a smile on her face. And it went in: no rim, clean through.

CHAPTER 22

On Sunday, Reese went to church with his mom again without complaining too much. There were doughnuts after anyway. He and Charlie and Meg played basketball when they got back and swam in the river. He helped Charlie feed the cats and check on the kittens, which were sleeping in a pile beside their mother when they looked in.

Early that evening, before supper, Reese was drawing at the picnic table in the yard. He was working on some new ideas for monster trucks. Charlie was sitting across from him, watching while he brushed one of his cats. Meg was on the swing, turning slowly, her bare toes in the dirt.

The sun was going down, and the shadows were getting long. Mr. Smith was outside, too, working on his pickup again, which seemed to be a never-ending project. He had the hood up, a light hooked to it, shining down on the engine.

Suddenly, he looked up and then turned and called to them: "Someone's coming. Reese, I think it's probably your dad."

Reese heard it then, too: tires crunching on the dirt road. He had been looking forward to his dad visiting, but when he saw the Barracuda coming out of the trees, shining crazy green in the late-day light, he got worried. It felt as if all his family's troubles were rolling in with his dad in that rumbling car for the Smiths to see. He also realized suddenly that he had no idea how his dad would react to Mr. Smith and Charlie and Meg and all the rest of it—this place that Reese and his mom had gone when they left him. He stayed seated as the car came to a stop in the yard.

His dad got out. He looked okay, steady, which was a relief. He was dressed for work again: jeans and work boots, a white T-shirt.

Then Mr. Smith said exactly the right thing: "Now *that* is a nice car!"

Reese's dad smiled.

"A Barracuda!" said Mr. Smith, walking over, wiping his hands on a rag. "Don't tell me the year. Let me guess. Is it a 1970?"

"That's very close," said Reese's dad. "It's a '71."

"Who did the work on it?"

"I did everything but the paint job," his dad said. He took a step toward Mr. Smith and held his hand out. "I'm Sam."

"I'm Johnny," said Mr. Smith, taking his hand. "These are my grandkids, Charlie and Meg."

The trailer door opened, and Reese's mom stepped out, wiping her hands on a dish towel. His dad saw her, and he smiled and waved. Reese by then had gotten up from the table and walked to him. His dad put his arm around his shoulder. "Hey, bud," he said.

Mr. Smith was still admiring the Barracuda. "Can I look inside?" he said.

"Absolutely," his dad said.

Mr. Smith opened the Barracuda's door and whistled. "Beautiful inside and out. It's a V8?"

"It is. You're welcome to take it out for a drive if you want."

This was his dad at his best again: charming, generous, fun.

"I'd be afraid to mess with it," said Mr. Smith. "I'm happy just to look. My daughter and I worked on a '66 Chevelle back when she was in high school, and we got it running real nice. Then she went off to college and I wasn't really driving it much, so I sold it. I regret it every time I see an old beauty like yours."

"The Chevelle's a beautiful car," Reese's dad said.

Reese looked at Charlie and Meg to see how they were reacting. Charlie had gotten off the picnic table and was sitting cross-legged on the ground, brushing another of his cats. Meg was still sitting on the swing. She looked fine, just watching.

Reese's dad had turned his attention to the pickup truck. "So what's going on here?" he asked.

"I'm hoping nothing serious," said Mr. Smith said. "The

oil-pressure light came on yesterday, but the engine's running fine and the oil level is fine. I'm hoping it's just a bad sending unit. I'm fixing to pull it and check the pressure manually."

"No engine knock?" asked Reese's dad.

"Nope."

Meg had her head up, listening. "What's a sending unit?" she asked.

Reese knew the answer to that, because once he had helped his dad swap one out in the Barracuda. "It's the thing that tells you if have enough oil in your engine," he said.

"Right!" said his dad, and he smiled at him, which made Reese feel good, kind of proud of himself. His dad turned back to Mr. Smith. "Do you need help with it?"

"I wouldn't say no, but you should get on inside with your family."

"I think it's okay," Reese's dad said. "That's a fast job. Reese and I just need to get some groceries out of the car first." He turned to Reese's mom, who had walked up to them. "Amanda, do you mind if I help here right quick?"

"That's fine," she said.

She looked as if she were holding in a smile, and his dad said, "Are you laughing at me?"

"I am," she said. She spoke to Mr. Smith: "You have made Sam's evening. The only thing he likes more than talking about cars is messing around with them."

Reese's dad helped Mr. Smith after unloading the groceries, and the job only took about fifteen minutes. Then he came to the trailer with Reese and went to the bathroom to wash his hands. "Nice guy, Mr. Smith," he said when he came back out.

"They're both good people, him and Mattie," said Reese's mom, who was at the stove. "Did y'all figure out the problem?"

"He was right: The sending unit is bad. It's like forty bucks to fix." He sniffed the air. "Is that spaghetti and meatballs you're making? It smells great."

Supper did smell good, and it occurred to Reese then that the little table could seat three, so he took a chance and asked, "Can Dad stay for supper?"

"I don't want to intrude," his dad said. "Especially if you've only made enough for two. That's not why I came out."

"There's enough," Reese said, pushing his luck, before his mom could answer. "Mom always makes too much."

She didn't turn from the stove, but she said, "Set another plate, Reese."

"I don't want to cause any trouble," his dad said.

"We have enough," she said.

"I'll make a salad," his dad said without missing a beat. He really was doing all the right things that night. "You got a bowl I can put it in?"

"Cabinet on the right," his mom said, pointing at it with her spatula.

His dad took out some of the vegetables that he had brought, got the bowl, and set to washing the veggies and chopping. To Reese, standing there watching his dad and mom together in the kitchen, the crummy trailer suddenly seemed a little bit like home.

"Hey, Reese," his dad said. "I wanted to talk again with you about your birthday on Thursday. Have you decided what you want to do?"

Reese thought then of the moment during dinner at Hub's when his mom and dad both seemed to kind of light up as they talked about his birthday. And he had what seemed like a really good idea. "Can we have dinner at the apartment, just the three of us? Dad can make his steaks, with that rub of his. We could get a chocolate cake from Hub's. That's what I want."

His dad's steaks really were the best. He had a delicious dry rub he would put on them that he said was a big secret. It was spicy and sweet.

"You don't want to do something with your friends?" his mom said.

"Sure. But what I want on my actual birthday is Dad's steaks, with just us." Here was a perfect chance for his dad to show his mom that he was getting it together—and remind her that they belonged together, the three of them.

"I can't grill at the apartment," his dad said. "They don't allow grills outside there. So I don't know that I could really do the steaks the way you like."

"You can figure it out," Reese said. "Can't you make them in the oven? And if they're not totally perfect, who cares?"

His dad blinked, and for a second, Reese thought he was going to say no. But then he smiled, almost the old smile, and he said, "Okay! Let's do it. Thursday evening. Is that all right, Amanda?"

"I'm down to work a shift then, but I'm sure I can get an evening off for my boy's birthday. I'll talk with Larry. Are you sure you're okay with it, Sam?"

"Absolutely."

"Things are okay at work?" she said, which didn't seem connected to what they were talking about.

"Things are good," his dad said. "Things are great in fact. Jimmy has more houses for me to work on in the pipeline."

"That's good news, Sam," said Reese's mom.

His dad winked at him then, and Reese knew what that meant: *Everything's good, Reese. I got it under control.* To his mom, his dad said, "Do you have garlic powder? I could make garlic bread."

"In the drawer to your right," his mom said. She smiled then, which made Reese happy. Suddenly he was looking forward to his birthday.

CHAPTER 23

After supper, his parents took a walk down to the river so they could talk, just the two of them. They went across the yard, disappearing into the darkness away from the house. Reese sat on the picnic table to wait.

The frogs were singing around him, and he sat listening to them and watching for his mom and dad. After a while, the screen door at the house opened, and Meg came out. She stood on the top step in the light from inside the house. She looked behind her. Then she came down the steps, crossed the yard, and sat on the swing near Reese.

"What are you doing?" she asked.

"Nothing," he said.

"Are your mom and dad inside?"

"They took a walk, down to the river."

She lifted her feet and let herself slowly turn, so her back was to him. Then she turned back slowly, and when she was facing him, she put her feet on the ground to stop herself. "Charlie has to go to Goldsville tomorrow morning for a therapy appointment," she said. "You want to go canoeing with me? I was thinking about going all the way downriver to Whitchard's Landing. I can show you that spot my granddad says is the deepest on the river."

"Sure," Reese said. "I just have to ask my mom."

Meg lifted her feet and let herself slowly turn again, and this time, she went all the way around before stopping herself again. Two of Charlie's cats met inside the circle of light from the pole in the yard, and one began grooming the other, licking its face, which is something Reese had never seen cats do. It was funny how much the other cat liked this.

Meg was watching the cats in the light, too. "Those two are best friends," she said. "They're always together."

She went around on the swing again. Reese looked into the dark, wondering what his mom and dad were saying to each other. Meg must have guessed what he was thinking about, because she asked, "Do you think your mom and dad are going to get back together?"

"I hope so," he said.

The screen door opened, and Mrs. Smith appeared. "Meg?" she called. "Is that Reese out there with you?"

"Yes," Meg said.

"Please don't wander off, you two. It's getting late."

"We won't," Meg said.

When her grandmother had gone back inside, Meg said,

"He seemed like a nice guy. Your dad, I mean. He seems fun."

"He is," Reese said. Then he added: "He can be." *When he's healthy*, he thought.

He had an urge again to tell her everything. He figured she would understand and wouldn't think less of him and his family, because she had told him hard things, secret things, about herself and her own family. Maybe it also felt extra safe to talk about it now because things seemed to be looking better with his dad. He said, "Do you want to know why my parents were fighting?"

"If you want to tell me," she said.

He looked at the ground in the circle of light from the pole, thinking about how to begin. "A while back," he said finally, "my dad got hurt at work. He's an electrician, and he was working at a construction site when a board he was standing on broke. He fell two floors. He broke his hip and his arm, and he hurt his back really bad. He was in the hospital for a long time, and he couldn't work for months."

Meg lifted her chin and looked at him, listening.

"It hurt a lot, all the time," Reese said. "It hurt so much he couldn't sleep or lie still, so while he was in the hospital, the doctors gave him pills, some drugs, to make it not hurt. But then when he was supposed to stop taking them, he couldn't, not for very long. He'd stop for a while, but then he'd start again."

He looked at Meg. "Do you understand?" he asked.

"Maybe," she said. "I'm not sure."

"He got addicted to the pills."

And there it was: *addicted.* He had never said the word out loud, not even when talking to his mom.

"That's what my parents have been fighting about," he said. "He keeps taking the pills after he promises to stop and get help, and he keeps ending up in the hospital when he takes too much, when he overdoses. I found him the last time, right before we came here. He almost died."

"*You* found him?" Meg asked. "By yourself?"

"Yeah."

"Were you scared?"

"Yeah."

"What was it like? What did you do?"

"He was unconscious, on the floor, and I couldn't wake him up. I was worried about his breathing, and I—"

Reese felt his throat tighten, and he thought for a moment he was about to cry. Talking about that afternoon brought back a picture of his dad's face as it was then: pale, lips going blue.

"You don't have to talk about it," Meg said.

Reese shook his head. He swallowed hard. "It's okay," he said. "It's just that the pills can stop your breathing if you take too much, and that's why I was scared. So I called 911, told them what had happened, and an ambulance came and took him to the hospital. He really did almost die, but afterward he still wouldn't get help. That's when my mom said we can't be with him until he does. The pills can kill him, and she said we can't be around that anymore. So we left and came here."

"And now he wants you back," Meg said.

"Yes."

"Is he going to get help now?"

"He says he is," Reese said. "And he says he needs us with him to help him, too." He drew his legs up and hugged his knees. He thought of his mom crying, back at the apartment, on that horrible night when they had left to come to the Smiths'. He thought of his tug-of-war with her over the suitcase. He saw her falling.

"Sometimes," he said, "I get really angry at my dad for not stopping, because I feel like if he really cared about us, he'd do anything to get help and stop. And I get angry at my mom for leaving, because I feel like we need to be there for him. I get scared if he overdoses again and we're not there to help, he might die."

And there it was, all of it. Reese had laid it out for her, and he didn't feel embarrassed or ashamed like he had worried he would. He felt lighter somehow, relieved to have said it to someone.

"Wow," she said. "I'm really, really sorry." He could tell that she was—but not sorry *for* him, like she pitied him or something. Just sorry.

She didn't ask any more questions. Another of Charlie's cats, a striped tabby, crept into the light and out again. Something rustled in the grass at the other end of the trailer, another cat probably.

Then Meg turned in the swing and looked into the darkness.

"What's wrong?" Reese asked.

"I think your mom and dad are coming back," she said.

Reese saw a faint patch of white beyond the trees. The patch grew larger and came into focus: It was his dad's T-shirt. He and his mom came out of the darkness together, walking so close to each other that their hands brushed. His dad squinted into the light from the pole, and then he must have seen Reese because he smiled and waved.

"I should go," Meg said. "Remember to ask your mom if it's okay for you to come canoeing tomorrow."

"Okay," Reese said. "See you." He watched her go back to the house. His parents stood at the end of the yard, talking, and Reese stayed where he was, watching and waiting.

CHAPTER 24

Reese and Meg left for Whitchard's Landing before nine the next morning, right after Charlie and Mrs. Smith went to Goldsville. The day was already hot and humid, so they took it easy, paddling slowly down the river and staying in the shade of the trees as much as they could. Reese was up front, with Meg behind, steering.

"How far is it?" Reese asked.

"Not too far," Meg said. "We can be back by lunch. Maybe next time, if you want to come back, we can bring lunch and eat there. My mom used to take me and Charlie to the landing in the canoe, and we'd sit in this one old building without a roof and have a picnic. I'll show you the place when we get there."

"Why does it have no roof?"

"I think it burned, a long time ago," she said. "The whole place has been abandoned for a really long time, like a hundred years or something. More than that probably. There's an old house there, too, that I can show you. It's cool."

They paddled around a bend and caught a soft breeze, which brought just a little relief from the humidity. The leaves whispered around them, and then the breeze was gone, upriver. After a moment, Meg spoke again:

"Hey, can I ask you a question about something you were talking about last night?" she said. "It's about your dad."

"Okay."

"If you're addicted to drugs, how do you get un-addicted? You said your dad was getting help to stop, but how do people help you stop?"

"There are special treatment programs you go to," Reese said. "My mom says it's a sickness, and you have to get medical help to get well, just like with any other sickness. It's hard to just stop on your own. The pills are really, really addictive."

"Does it hurt to quit taking them, if you're addicted?"

"I think so," Reese said. His mom described addiction as a monster with claws that sink deep into you, and it must hurt to get the claws out. He had never spoken to his dad about it because he knew it was the last thing his dad wanted to talk about.

"Is that why he hasn't gotten help before?"

He stopped paddling and turned to look at her, in the back of the canoe. She had a baseball cap on, a Braves cap faded almost to pink that she said had belonged to her mom, and she had it pulled low, so her eyes were in shadow.

"My dad says he doesn't like doctors or anyone else who tells you what to do and kind of preaches at you," he said. "He says a man ought to think for himself and do for himself, take care of his own problems."

She lifted her cap and resettled it farther back on her head. "But he says he needs *your* help, you and your mom's," she said. "That's one of the reasons he wants you back, isn't it?"

"Yes," Reese said. He wasn't sure where she was headed with this one.

"So what can you do?" she asked.

He didn't understand. "We'll go back to him, I hope. I want my mom and dad to get back together."

"No, I mean if you and your mom move back with him— *when* you move back with him—what can *you* do to help him get better? What can you do that you haven't done already?"

He hadn't minded her questions up to then, but that one brought him up short. What was she getting at? Was she trying to say that they *couldn't* do anything for his dad, that they couldn't help him? "I don't know," he said. "How would I know that?"

Meg must have heard the edge in his voice because she said quickly, "I was only asking."

He felt bad then for snapping at her. "I just don't know," he said. And that was the truth.

"I didn't mean to make you feel bad or get you mad," she said.

"It's okay," he said. "Really. It actually feels good to talk about it with someone."

From back among the trees to his right came a faint splash, and he squinted into the shadows to try to make out what it was, but he couldn't see anything. He picked up one of the thermoses of water that Meg had brought. He uncapped it and tipped it, the ice sloshing, and he took a drink. The water fell cold into his stomach. He thought of his parents as they had been the night before, in the trailer: his mom smiling at the sink while his dad made a salad beside her. He tried to hold on to that picture, willed it to fill his mind so that it would crowd out other, not-so-good things that he didn't want to remember or think about.

"You want to keep going?" Meg asked.

"Yes, sure."

They kept on paddling, sliding along between the trees. On one stretch, they passed an open field like at the Smiths' place, this one filled with a half dozen cows. One of the cows was standing in the water just off the bank, and it watched them go by silently. Then the trees came in close again. Other than birds, those cows were the only other living things they saw.

At last Meg said, "We're here: Whitchard's Landing."

Reese could see wooden posts ahead, sticking out of the water in a line that led to a bank on their right. They paddled to them, and the canoe's bow bumped into one. The wood was black and rotting. "My grandpa says this was an old dock for steamboats," Meg said. "There was a store here and a warehouse, and the steamboats used to run back and forth to the Albemarle Sound, at the mouth of the river."

Looking at the bank, Reese could see only trees and bushes, a tangle of green, with brown vines hanging down. A jungle.

"Do you want to get out and look?" she asked.

He did, so she steered them in between the posts until the canoe nosed into the muddy bank. Reese got out first and then held the canoe for Meg. They pulled the canoe higher up the bank, out of the water. Then she led the way into the trees. Reese slipped once, the mud squishing beneath his sneakers, and he grabbed a branch of an overhanging tree to keep from sliding farther. He thought for a second that he was going to slip and fall into the water, which would have been embarrassing.

"You okay?" Meg asked.

"I'm fine." He straightened up and looked around. Now that they were on the bank, he could see what was left of an old building: no roof, just four crumbling brick walls and openings for windows and a door. A tree grew inside, out the top, where the roof had been.

"That's the building I told you about," Meg said. "That's where my mom and Charlie and I used to have picnics."

The air was perfectly still among the trees. Even the birds had gone silent. He went to the doorway of the ruined building. The floor was hard-packed dirt. The bricks in the walls looked very old. The mortar between was crumbling, leaving some gaps that you could see through. If he ignored a little modern trash that was in one corner—a few empty soda and beer cans, a Styrofoam cup—he could have believed that he and Meg were the first people to come there in a hundred years or more. He stepped inside and looked up. It was a strange feeling to be inside but with only blue sky over him.

He turned to Meg, who had come in behind him. "What was this building?"

"My granddad says this was the warehouse, where they would keep stuff that was coming in or going out by boat. Farther back were a store and a few other buildings and the house I told you about, which I think is where the family who ran the store and the warehouse lived."

"What happened to this place?" he asked. "Why did everybody leave?"

"They just weren't needed anymore, I guess," Meg said. "The boats stopped coming at some point, when the roads got better and people weren't traveling on the rivers as much, so they didn't need places like this. Come on, and I'll show you the house."

He followed her out of the building and around to a dirt path that led into the trees behind. She pointed to a vine growing up a tree. "Do you know what poison ivy looks like? That's it right there. It's all over back in here, so watch out. One time, before I knew what it looked like, I touched some and rubbed my face, and I got so bad my eyes swelled shut."

"Oh, man," Reese said. "I've never had it." And he didn't want it. He edged sideways around the tree, keeping his eyes on the vines, like they might reach out and grab him.

The woods were so thick and he was so focused on watching for poison ivy that he didn't see the house until they were right upon it. They stepped out of the deep shadows of the woods, into the clearing, and there it was: just a skeleton of a building, gray boards with gaps between, windows like empty eyes, a rusty gray metal roof. It was two stories, or more like a story and a half: the top windows were half the size of the ones below. It was raised a few feet off the ground on supports made of brick. Below was just empty space, no basement. The house had a small front porch, but the steps were gone. Someone had placed some cement blocks where the stairs used to be so you could get up.

"Can we go in?" he asked.

"We can go on the first floor, but watch where you step," she said. "My granddad says the floors are rotted in places, so it's way too dangerous to go upstairs. You might fall through and break a leg or something."

They went up the cement blocks and through the open doorway. It was trashed inside: Big chunks of the plaster had fallen off the walls, revealing the wooden boards beneath. Pieces of the plaster ceiling had fallen, too. The floors were covered with the chunks of plaster and leaves and cans and crumpled-up cigarette packs. At one end of the room was a brick fireplace.

Looking up, Reese could see why Mr. Smith didn't want them going upstairs: There was a big gaping hole in the ceiling, and through it, right at the edge of the hole, Reese could see the end of an old iron bed, covered with dust. Hanging on a wall near the bed was what looked like an old calendar, yellowed and faded. He couldn't read the year from where he was standing, but it gave him a feeling like time had stopped inside the house, like he was somehow standing in the past surrounded by the ghosts of the people who had lived here, who had slept in that bed up there and marked off the days on that calendar one by one as they passed.

It was spooky, but in a fun way, not actually scary. It was like they were explorers, discovering some long-dead town back in a jungle somewhere.

He looked at Meg, who had her head in the fireplace, looking up the chimney. "Hey," he said.

She straightened up and looked at him. "What?"

"This is really cool."

He had meant to say more than that, but he didn't know how to say what was on his mind without sounding mushy or weird. He was thinking that he was glad he had met Meg and Charlie, even though he wished it hadn't been because of his parents splitting up.

Meg smiled. "Do you want to keep looking around? There are four more rooms here, and back the other way through the trees is the store. It burned down at some point, so it's just a bunch of burned wood and bricks, but Charlie once found a really old quarter there, from 1840 or something, when he was digging around. And I've found some cool old bottles, like medicine bottles."

"Sure," Reese said.

They didn't find any old coins or anything else valuable, but it was fun to poke around and imagine what it all used to look like when Whitchard's Landing was a real place, alive. And when they had seen enough, they circled back to where they had left the canoe, got back in, and pushed off again into the river to head back home.

They passed the stumps of the old dock, and then Meg steered them into the river's middle, under the open sky and the sun. Reese told her to paddle hard with him then to see how fast they could go, and the faster they went, the lighter and freer he felt. When they were tired, Meg splashed him with her paddle, and he splashed her back, both of them laughing.

They were getting close to the Smiths' place when something caught his eye: It was the white bleach jugs they had looked at earlier, strung in a line between the trees, the trotline baited for catfish. One of the jugs was bobbing in the water, jerking, as if it were alive.

"What is that?" he asked Meg.

"I guess they caught something," she said.

They eased in, and as they came close, the jug dipped hard, almost beneath the surface, and then popped up again, sending ripples across the water to touch their canoe. "They caught something *big*," Meg said.

It was a turtle.

From the river's black water, it looked at them sideways, with one dark eye. Sticking out from one cheek, behind its beaked mouth, was the wicked-looking barbed end of a fishhook. The turtle had swallowed it. From the hook's shank, heavy fishing line ran to the bleach jug.

Meg leaned over to examine the turtle and whistled. "That's a big old snapping turtle. We had one come up in the yard a while back. Charlie found it. It might have been this one."

Without thinking, Reese reached out to touch it, to try to help, but Meg leaned forward to put her hand on his arm. "Stop!" she said. "Keep your hand away from him. He'll bite through your finger."

"I want to help," Reese said.

"I know that, but he doesn't, especially when he's scared. He'll try to bite you. Charlie got too close to the one in our yard and tried to touch it, and it snapped at him. It just missed his hand. My grandma screamed."

Reese looked around, as if there might be someone else who could help even though obviously they were alone. He asked, "What'll happen to him?"

"I don't know. Even if we could get a hold of him to get the hook out, we'd probably get bit. We could maybe cut the fishing line, but with that hook in his mouth, I don't know that he could eat. He'd probably starve to death."

"We can't just leave him here," Reese said.

"I'm sorry," Meg said. "Sometimes I guess there's nothing you can do to help."

Staring down at the hooked turtle, Reese wished they had gone past without looking so he wouldn't have had to see this. He felt as if he were about to cry, which was ridiculous.

The turtle sank into the still, black water, until only its eyes and the end of its snout broke the surface. "He looks worn out," Reese said.

He turned to Meg, and she blinked and looked away. She looked like she was about to cry, too. Then he made up his mind: He reached into his pocket for his Buck knife, the one his dad had given him, and he pulled out the blade. Rising a little from his seat, he reached quickly into the water, took hold of the fishing line, as close as he dared to the turtle's head, and put his blade to it. The canoe tipped.

"What are you doing?" Meg asked. Alarmed, she started to rise, too, and the canoe rocked more.

"Whoa!" Reese said. "Hold still. Sit down. I'm going to cut him loose."

He had to saw and pull to break the line. The turtle thrashed, churning the water around it, snapping blindly as Reese worked. Then, with a pop, the line broke, and the turtle dove immediately. It disappeared into the blacker depths of the river.

Reese and Meg watched the water until the last ripples had faded away. Reese asked, "Do you really think he's going to starve?"

"I don't know. He looked tough, though, and we gave him a chance, right?"

"I wish he would've let us help him," Reese said. "I wish he would've let us take the hook out."

"Me too," Meg said.

The water was still again. It was a smooth, dark mirror

reflecting the trees and the sky and clouds above them, in inky tones. Reese thought of the turtle's eye, staring. In that eye was no sign at all that the turtle understood what was happening to it. There was nothing but glassy green and yellow, and in the center, the black pupil, like a bottomless hole.

Reese leaned over the edge of the canoe and looked into the water, trying to make out the turtle. But he saw only his own face reflected back at him.

CHAPTER 25

Reese's mom was on the phone the next morning when Reese woke up. He saw her outside the trailer, sitting at the picnic table, the phone pressed to her ear. She looked fine, calm, so it wasn't bad news, anyway. She was even smiling a little.

It was Tuesday, two days until his birthday.

Across the yard, Mrs. Smith was hanging laundry on the line, and she was looking over at his mom from time to time. His mom laughed into the phone.

Reese got up and went to the kitchen. He was pouring himself a bowl of Cheerios when she came back into the trailer. "Who was that?" he asked.

"It was your dad," she said. "He says he's got a day off today, and he was wondering if you wanted to hang out with him, run some errands, take a drive. He has to run to the junkyard to look for a part for Trey's truck first thing, so he's heading this way, and he thought you might want to go along."

"Sure," Reese said. "Is Trey coming?"

"I don't know. I don't think so, though."

Reese could take or leave Trey, who was an old friend of his dad's, but he loved the junkyard, which was called Petty & Sons Salvage. It was the place where his dad had scrounged many of the parts for his Barracuda, including the transmission. You never knew what you might find there. Once, the Pettys had hauled in an airplane—an old crop-duster—and Reese had spent an hour climbing through it and all over it. Another time, they had an Army jeep.

Reese also saw this day with his dad as another good sign: His mom was trusting his dad, opening up to him even more.

"When will he be here?"

"About an hour, maybe less. I have to go to the store for a while later, so I told him he can drop you off there after."

Reese finished eating breakfast. Meg and Charlie had left a little earlier with their grandfather. They were going to visit some old relative and were supposed to be gone all day. When Reese had gotten dressed, he went out to the swing, and he was sitting on it when the Barracuda pulled in, its engine rumbling.

Mrs. Smith came out of the house then, with some more laundry to hang on the line. His dad got out, and he raised a hand to her. "Hey, I'm Sam," he said. "Are you Mattie?"

"Yes," she said. "Nice to meet you."

"I'm just picking up Reese for the day," he said. "You ready to go, bud?"

Reese's mom came out of the trailer then, and his dad gave

her a quick little kiss on the lips. Mrs. Smith saw it, too, and Reese could have sworn that she frowned before turning away, back to her laundry. Reese looked at his mom to see if she had noticed anything funny. He wondered suddenly if Mrs. Smith was unhappy about his dad coming around, didn't approve of it.

But his mom was focused on his dad. "I'm off at four-thirty, Sam," she said. "So no later than that, okay?"

"Absolutely," he said.

"Trey's not coming?" Reese asked.

"Nah. He's working today. I told him I'd help out and look for the part he needs at Petty's. So it's just you and me today."

"How come you're off today?" Reese asked.

"Jimmy doesn't have much for me this week," his dad said. "And I thought, 'Why not spend today with my boy?'"

"Didn't you tell Mom the other day that Jimmy had lots of work?" Reese asked.

"He does, he does. When exactly he needs me just kind of ebbs and flows, depending on where he's at with framing and whatnot. But hey, listen here: How about if we do maybe a quick run out to Petty's first, and then we can go somewhere and throw the ball around a little. Is that okay? I got our baseball gloves in the car, and it's a nice day."

That was okay by Reese. The day was sunny and not too hot. He tried to remember when he and his dad had last played catch. It had been a while. Their last apartment before their most recent one had a small open field behind it where they could throw the ball around, so they used to walk over there pretty often to play. Their current apartment had no grassy spots. Playing on a parking lot wasn't much fun, and the ball got all scuffed up.

Reese climbed into the front seat of the Barracuda and touched the warm grip of the shifter between the seats. Before getting in, his dad leaned over to rub a little something off the gleaming front fender, and then he said goodbye to Reese's mom. When he turned the key in the ignition, the big engine roared to life. Reese loved the sound of that V8, and he liked to see people's heads turn on the street at the deep rumble of it.

"You strapped in?" his dad asked.

Reese nodded. His dad put the car in gear, and they pulled away, through the trees to the front road.

"Are you still okay with my birthday dinner on Thursday?" Reese asked.

"Sure," his dad said. "I'll get the steaks tomorrow. T-bones okay?"

"Okay," Reese said. He couldn't resist adding, "Maybe Thursday night we can talk to Mom about moving back to the apartment for good."

His dad looked at him quickly and then turned his eyes back to the road. "Let's not push your mom so hard, bud," he said. "And let's not turn this into a big make-or-break thing, okay? I mean it's your birthday and all, but I . . ."

He stopped. Reese turned a little to look at him. "But what?"

He dad shook his head. "Nothing. Let's just enjoy your birthday. That's all I'm saying. I don't know if those steaks are going to be perfect, because I'm going to broil them, rather than cook them over charcoal. But my rub is killer, right?"

"Right," Reese said.

His dad reached out and patted his leg. The bruise under his eyes was just about gone. His eyes were clear, sky blue. He gave him a smile. "It's all good," he said. "Today, let's hang loose and have fun."

"Okay," Reese said. He tried to shake off his worries, push the frowning Mrs. Smith and whatever it was she was thinking out of his mind, too. His dad had this, he told himself. Thursday *was* going to be good. And today was going to be good, too.

They drove out to the junkyard, and his dad found the part he was looking for right away: a fuel pump for Trey's Ford pickup. They wandered around the junkyard for a while after that, looking at the cars, talking about ones they'd buy and fix up if they had the money and the time. His dad picked a Cadillac Coupe de Ville, long and red with a white top, that they found on blocks in the back. Reese picked an AMC Matador Coupe from the 1970s because he liked the lines of it. "You've got a good eye," his dad told him, which made him feel good. Reese wanted to be as good with cars as his dad someday.

From Petty's, they went back to town, had lunch at the Hardee's out at the bypass, and then went to play ball at Walker

Park, which was near Reese's school. His dad got their gloves and a ball from the trunk. The park was quiet. They started walking to an open area, and partway there, his dad tapped him on the back and said, "Race you."

He took off surprisingly fast. Reese put his head down and ran hard to keep up with his dad's long, loping strides. When they reached the open field, they squared off, and his dad wound up and let the ball fly. The throw went into the dirt. "Crap," his dad said. "Wow, I'm rusty."

Reese tossed the ball back underhand. His dad's second throw went wide, and Reese had to chase it down. "Sorry, Reese," his dad said. "Bear with me here. I got to get warmed up." He shook his arms, punched the air. He wobbled his head, jumped up and down, getting loose. He was smiling, though, playing it for laughs.

"Okay, all right, all right," his dad said. "Ready?" His next throw was better. Reese stepped, reaching, and got it with the tip of his glove.

The next one was perfect, right into Reese's glove with a satisfying smack. He didn't even have to move. It came in hard, and it stung a little.

"All right, all right, that's the way, that's it," his dad said. "I'm back."

Reese smiled, and he threw the ball back into his dad's glove: *Smack!* "Good one," his dad said. "Let's count. That's two. What's our record? How many throws in a row without a miss? Forty in a row? Do you remember?"

"Something like that," Reese said. He loved this, just tossing the ball around with his dad, not thinking about anything at all but throwing and catching, back and forth. They had done this off and on, not as much as he would have liked, but pretty often, for as long as he could remember. He didn't think he'd ever get too old for it.

"Can we break the record?" His dad threw: *Smack!* "Three!" he said.

They went on like that. They reached thirty-two before one of Reese's throws went a little wide, and his dad missed it. They started over and reached twenty-four before Reese missed a catch. They began again. "No stopping until we beat the record," his dad said.

When at last the forty-first throw landed safely in his dad's glove, Reese yelled, "New record!" They kept going, and they got to forty-six before his dad reached and missed. He called for a water break then, and they walked together to a fountain by the playground, not far from the parking lot. His dad looked at his watch. "Your mom said to be back by four-thirty, so we still got some time. Want to go for a ride?"

"Where?"

"Just around."

After getting a drink, they put the ball and their gloves in the Barracuda's trunk, and Reese climbed up front again beside his dad. They took off, heading south down Main Street and then out into the country. The sun gleamed off the Barracuda's hood scoops. As they passed the town limits, a big man in overalls on a riding mower in front of a house looked up and waved. Reese's dad honked his horn.

"Do you know him?" Reese asked.

His dad looked in the rearview mirror. "Nope," he said. "I don't think so. He's probably just into cars and waving at the Barracuda."

They rolled the windows all the way down, and his dad turned the stereo up: It was rock radio out of Goldsville, playing a classic rock song that Reese knew.

"'Rock of Ages'!" said his dad, his voice raised above the rumble of the engine and the whistling of the wind.

"Turn it up!" Reese said.

His dad turned it way up. The wind whipped around them, a slip of paper rising and floating between them. Reese put his arm out the window, surfing the air with his open hand, feeling nothing but free and happy. Their shadow stretched way out on his side, across the open fields. He waved to it out the open window, saw the long shadow of his arm, above the car, waving back at him.

"Hey, do you want to shift?" his dad said, nearly shouting to be heard over the wind and the radio. He tapped the gear shift between them. "You shift. Into fourth. I'll say when, and you pull it toward you and then down. Ready?"

When they hit a straightaway, his dad floored it, and the Barracuda leaped forward, like it was alive. The acceleration pushed Reese back into his seat. "Now!" his dad said. Down went his foot on the clutch and up came his foot from the gas.

The engine spun free. Reese pulled the gearshift toward him and then down, smoothly. Up went the clutch, and down went the gas, all the way to the floor.

They were flying then, between the shoulder and the double yellow lines. Reese looked at his dad, and his dad smiled that smile of his. Reese thought of him and his mom walking so close in the night, their hands almost touching. He thought of the flowers and the note that his dad had sent his mom. He thought of watching his mom and dad skating together so gracefully at the roller rink.

And then there was today: a perfect day.

They sang along with the radio at the top of their voices as they flew down the road with no destination, just enjoying the ride.

CHAPTER 26

Charlie came looking for Reese after supper. He knocked on the trailer door, and Reese's mom answered. "Hi, Charlie. What's going on?"

Reese came up from behind. "Hey, Charlie."

"I have something to show you," Charlie said to Reese.

"I'm supposed to do the laundry," Reese said. His mom had asked him to bring the dirty clothes over to the Smiths' house to put in their washing machine, and he had agreed without complaining. Since his dad seemed to be doing so well, he was thinking he and his mom would only be there a little while longer, so he didn't even mind facing Mrs. Smith and her frowns.

But his mom said, "I'll take the laundry over. You go on with Charlie. Don't stay out too long, though. It's fixing to rain."

Reese went out into the early evening. "What's happening?" he asked Charlie.

"Their eyes are open," Charlie said.

"Whose?"

"The kittens," Charlie said.

Reese followed him to the woodshed. The sun was sitting, fat and red, in the top of the trees. Dark clouds were piling up, too, above the sun. At the woodshed, Reese and Charlie squatted together at its open side. Just inside were two bowls, one with water, the other with a little kibble. And behind the bowls were Mama Cat and her kittens. When Reese inched closer, he saw their tiny eyes.

Charlie reached out and picked up the gray one. "Is that okay to do?" Reese asked.

"It's okay," Charlie said. "You have to pick them up like this every day if you don't want them to be wild." Mama Cat stood up and stretched, seemingly unconcerned. Charlie said, "Do you want to hold it? Hold out your hands, like a cup."

"Okay," Reese said. Charlie placed the kitten in his hands. It mewed. Reese touched it, and it wriggled. Its eyes were like little blue gems. Its ears were tiny and flat against its head, barely visible in the fur. Mama Cat was looking at them with half-closed eyes. Her other kittens were nosing her belly, mewing.

"Which one is your favorite?" Charlie asked.

"My favorite kitten? I don't know. Which one is your favorite?"

"I like that one," Charlie said, pointing to the one Reese was holding. "I like gray cats."

"How come?"

Charlie shrugged. He reached out and picked up the black

one, which mewed. He petted it and set it down and then picked up the other gray one. "You have to pick them up every day, so they don't go wild," he said again. "That's what I'm going to do." He looked at Reese. "Have you tried to draw my cats yet?"

"No," Reese said.

"You should do that," he said.

They sat in silence for a little while. Reese stroked the tiny gray cat in his hand with one finger. The fur was softer than anything he had ever touched. He looked back at the house and the trailer. When his dad had dropped Reese off at the store after their good day together, after the drive in the Barracuda, his mom had let his dad kiss her again, a peck on the lips. "I love you," he had told her.

"I love you, too, Sam," she had said.

Reese thought of this, and then he said to Charlie, "I'm going home soon."

"Okay," Charlie said. "We can walk back."

"No, not to the trailer. I mean I'm going back to live with my dad. We're going back home, my mom and me. We're going to celebrate my birthday on Thursday, and I think we'll decide after that when we'll move."

He didn't know this was true at all, but he had this urge to say it anyway. Saying it out loud felt good and made it seem real. Maybe his mom *would* agree to return after his birthday supper. He thought again about how she had looked when she said goodbye to his dad. Reese knew she didn't want to see him alone. She was as worried about him as Reese was.

"You're leaving?" Charlie said.

He sounded upset, which took Reese by surprise. "Not exactly right away," he said, trying to soften it a little.

"When?"

"I said I don't know exactly. But I'll visit. It's not like I'll be going far."

Charlie put the kitten he was holding down beside its mother. "I don't want you to go."

"I have to leave, Charlie," Reese said. "This isn't my home. The trailer's not my home. My mom and I have to be with my dad."

Charlie didn't say anything for a moment. Then, his eyes still fixed down, he abruptly took the kitten from Reese's hands. The kitten cried, high-pitched, and for just a moment, Reese had the crazy thought that Charlie was going to throw the kitten at him or at the side of the woodshed. But Charlie set it carefully next to its mother. Then he stood and, turning away, said, "You're scaring the cats. You need to get away from them."

The cats hadn't moved. Mama Cat's eyes had opened wide, though: She was looking at Reese, as if she were waiting for him to answer Charlie. From above, he heard a rustling and creaking: The trees were moving in the wind. Charlie began walking away. His hands were balled up in fists at his side. Reese followed him.

"Hey, Charlie!" he called. "Stop, Charlie. Let me talk to you."

But Charlie kept walking to the house. Reese was faster, and when he got close, he reached out and touched his arm. Charlie shook him off. Reese suddenly feared what Charlie would tell Mr. and Mrs. Smith. His mom liked them, and she wouldn't be the least bit happy if they got mad at him for upsetting Charlie. Then he thought of Meg, and he worried about what Charlie might tell her. He didn't want her thinking he was a jerk, mean or ungrateful. He needed to calm Charlie down. He reached out and touched his arm again. "Please," he said. "Stop. I want to talk to you."

Charlie stopped. "What?"

"I'm sorry I upset you," Reese said. "You and Meg and your grandma and granddad, you've all been really good to me and my mom. But I have to be back with my family, where I belong. This isn't my home. Wouldn't you want to be back—" He stopped. He had almost asked Charlie if he wouldn't want to be back with *his* mom and dad.

"What?" Charlie said again.

"Wouldn't you want to be back with Meg and your grandparents, if you got lost or stuck somewhere else, away from them? Wouldn't you?"

Charlie didn't answer. He kept his eyes down.

"Wouldn't you?" Reese said again. Charlie still didn't answer, so he kept talking: "I'll come back and visit you, I swear. Of course I will. And I'll help you feed the cats. Okay? Is that okay? Can I come and help you feed the cats?"

Charlie looked up at the sky behind them. Reese turned his

head to see what Charlie was looking at. He saw only the sky and the rainclouds. A gust of wind moved through the big tree near the house, shaking its crown.

"You won't remember," Charlie said.

Reese shook his head. "What won't I remember? To visit? I'll remember. My mom and dad can drive me, and my mom will see your grandma at—"

But Charlie didn't let him finish. He took off running to the house.

Reese ran after him for a few steps, but then, feeling foolish, he stopped. He stood alone while Charlie went up the steps and through the back door, which fell shut with a bang.

CHAPTER 27

There was something strange about the light: The dark clouds had continued to pile up above the trees beyond the barn, and the fat sun was caught in a thin, bright band of clear sky between the belly of the clouds and the treetops. The light was orange and hard. The greens of the pines seemed to vibrate in it.

After Charlie went inside, Reese walked restlessly to the bank of the river, worrying about what he was going to say to Meg, and not sure what to do. Lightning arced across the clear strip of sky above the trees, and a gust of wind blew across the field and the river. A few moments later came a rumble of thunder. His mom had been right: The rain was almost there.

He walked back to the trailer and up the steps. Inside was dark. He called out: "Mom?" He turned on the lights and went to the back bedroom. It was empty. She must still be at the Smiths' doing the laundry.

He decided he would go to the house, too, and talk to Charlie and Meg, try to clear the air before Meg got the idea he was a jerk for getting Charlie upset. When he went outside, the wind had picked up. It danced in his direction, whirling dead leaves and a scrap of newspaper. He crossed the yard and went to the Smiths' back door.

The kitchen window was open, and through it he could see his mom and Mr. and Mrs. Smith. They were at the kitchen table, and Mrs. Smith was talking, one hand tapping the table-top to the rhythm of her words: "What I'm saying is it's too soon."

Reese froze. He held his breath and strained to hear.

His mom said, "I hear you, Mattie. I get it. But even after everything, I love him, and I believe he loves me. I know he loves Reese. You should hear him talking about planning for Reese's birthday on Thursday. He wants to do the right thing."

"How many times has he made these exact same promises to you?" said Mrs. Smith. "I'm sure he means it when he says it, but you've told me yourself that he has broken these prom-ises every time."

Reese's stomach had gone cold, and the chill spread up and outward, through his chest and down his arms to his fingers. Charlie had blabbed, he thought. He had come inside, and he had told his grandparents what Reese had said about going back to his dad, and now here was Mrs. Smith tearing his dad down. Part of him wanted to shout, to tell her she was dead wrong, but his tongue was frozen.

Reese's mom began to speak again, "I think what we're—"

But Mrs. Smith didn't give her a chance to finish. "What I'm saying," she said, "is that you've made the right decision in leaving, and now you need to be strong and stay the course. I mean, how long has it been? A week? Ten days?"

"Eleven days since we came out here," Reese's mom said.

"So less than two weeks," said Mrs. Smith. "You're welcome to stay here as long as you need to, and we also would be very happy to help you find another place in town for longer term. I truly think that's what's best for you and for Reese. And I think that's what is best for Sam, too. You're not doing him any favors by propping him up and covering for him. I'm sure he's scared of being on his own and having to get a grip on this by himself. But I don't think he'll ever really face this until he *has* to face it on his own. Has he followed through on all this talk about going into treatment? Do you know if he's actually been going?"

"I know he's found an outpatient program."

"Has he been going regularly?"

"I think so," his mom said.

"You need to verify that he's going," Mrs. Smith said, "and you need to see long-term commitment from him to staying clean, at a minimum, before you think about going back. I can see how much you love him, Amanda, and I know how badly you want this just to be over, with Sam better and you and Reese back with him. With my dad and his drinking, I wanted so badly to fix everything, and there were so many times I thought he had turned a corner at last. He did eventually, but it took a long, long time. He didn't get there in a straight line, and it only happened once he *really* admitted that he needed help."

Mr. Smith pushed back from the table then and got up. "I think I just heard the washer click off downstairs, Amanda. I'll go check on your laundry."

"I'll get it, Johnny," Reese's mom said.

"No, you two talk," he said. "I got it."

When he left, Reese's mom said, "I hear what you're saying about your dad, Mattie. I'm not saying I expect miracles."

Mrs. Smith said, "My point is you can't let your hopes run ahead of reality or you will just step right back on the same old roller-coaster ride with Sam. You said it yourself, Amanda: You can't cure him, and you and Reese can't keep living with it the way you have. You can't let Sam's problems keep dragging the two of you down. You should be putting energy into getting yourself on your feet. Fight for that raise at work. Go for manager. I'm sorry to have to be so blunt, but I'm scared for you and Reese. You say you love Sam, but love isn't enough sometimes."

Here was where his mom would stand up and tell Mrs. Smith she was dead wrong, Reese thought. She would tell the old lady that his dad at last was committed to getting better, and that she and Reese needed to be with him to help him. Reese stood at the window waiting for her to do it, to say the right thing. But she didn't say anything at all. Mrs. Smith just sat there looking hard at her, and after a moment, his mom got up, the feet of her chair scraping across the linoleum. She came to the window at the sink, and Reese ducked, like she might see him. But with the light on inside, she couldn't have seen him standing out there in the dark of the coming storm even if she had been looking right at him.

As angry as he was, she looked so sad that it made his heart hurt. He heard the clink of dishes, the sound of the kitchen tap running.

From across the field, the thunder rumbled.

Then the skies opened up and the rain came crashing down. Reese ran to the trailer, because he had no other place to go. He went to the bedroom and lay on his mattress, listening to the rain drum on the roof. He didn't know who to be angriest at: Charlie for telling? Mrs. Smith for talking down his dad, trying to keep his family apart? Or his mom for not sticking up for his dad? She had said absolutely nothing back to Mrs. Smith, which he thought was as good as agreeing with her.

Everyone seemed to be lined up against his family getting back together. He couldn't trust anyone.

Even Meg, now that he thought of it, had seemed to be taking sides against his dad, when she asked on the river what Reese and his mom could do to help him if they got back together. He had shaken it off, but now he wasn't so sure. Maybe she'd been listening to her grandparents talking about how Reese and his mom were better off without his dad.

He was angry at his dad, too. Reese himself had looked up information about programs and groups, so he knew for a fact that help was out there. He had shared it all with his dad: names, addresses, phone numbers. Had his dad started treatment like he had promised, or hadn't he? If he had, shouldn't he have said something about it earlier?

When his mom returned to the trailer from the Smiths' house, he wouldn't talk to her. He couldn't. He was too angry and disgusted. He couldn't even look at her when she tried to get him to tell her what was wrong.

"I don't understand," she said. "You were in such a good mood."

He just lay there until she left him alone, and then he started thinking about what he could do to fix this. His dad had seemed fine recently, but Reese knew how everything with him could blow into a million pieces at any moment. He needed to warn his dad before they went to the apartment for his birthday on Thursday, let him know how much depended on him keeping it together and pulling off a good evening. A supper, a cake, no letdowns, no ugly surprises.

His dad needed to know everything: what Mrs. Smith was saying and how his mom was listening to her.

He looked at his phone, and he thought about calling him right then. But there was no privacy in the trailer, and he couldn't go out into the rain to call. He didn't mind getting wet, but his mom would get suspicious if she saw him standing out there in the downpour talking on his phone. He couldn't text either, because it was too complicated. He needed to say it.

He was still thinking about all of this when his mom came back to check on him one last time before going to bed. The window next to him was open, and gusts threw cold spray through the screen. He felt the wetness on his cheeks.

"Reese," she said, "I'll ask you one more time before I go to bed. Do you want to talk about it?"

He turned his head to look at her. She was standing in the doorway, a silhouette against the light from the tiny trailer bathroom behind her. "No," he said. He turned away.

"Well, look," she said, annoyed with him, "I'm not a mind reader, so if there is something on your mind, you need to speak to me, with actual words, and not just make ugly faces."

He shrugged.

"It's up to you," she said. "You know where to find me. And please, close that window. The rain is blowing in all over the place. It's going to make the carpet in here disgusting."

He couldn't imagine how anything about that trailer could be more disgusting than it already was. "There's no air in here," he said.

"We can't just— Oh, for God's sake." She disappeared for a moment, and when she returned, she threw a towel at him. It landed on his face, and he snatched it off angrily and sat up. "At least put that under the window to catch the water," she said.

She stood there until he did as he was told. Then she clicked off the bathroom light. When she was gone, he lay back down and rolled over on his side. A little light filtered in from the back bedroom, but after a while, it went off. In the darkness, he felt more alone than ever.

══ ══

First thing the next morning, with one day to go until his birthday, he went outside and around to the back of the trailer, so no one could see him, and called his dad. He touched the number in his contacts, and it rang once, but then he got a message, a woman's voice saying, "The number you are trying to reach has been disconnected or is no longer in service. Please check the number and dial again."

He thought at first something had gone wrong with the call, like it had been sent to the wrong number or something, so he hung up and tried again, dialing the numbers directly this time. He got the same message: "The number you are trying to reach . . ."

Then he remembered that his dad had lost his regular phone and had been using a prepaid phone. Reese got that number from his texts and called it. But he got the same message.

He had to ask his mom for help. He went inside and found her in the back bedroom, changing the sheets on the bed. He told her what had happened. "Maybe you misdialed," she said.

She picked up her phone and tried dialing. "You're right: It's not working. I guess maybe he got another new phone. If he doesn't call, we'll see him tomorrow and we can ask him then."

He didn't know what his next move was. He was about an inch from telling her what he had overheard.

"What?" she asked. And she sounded so annoyed at him that any urge he might have had to talk to her instantly vanished.

"Nothing," he said.

The only other thing he could think to do was try to reach his dad at his apartment, so when it was time for his mom to go in to work, he hitched a ride with her to town, telling her he wanted to meet Tony and Ryan at the park. They were both still out of town, but his mom didn't know that. When they got to the store, he walked alone to the apartment. But the Barracuda wasn't there, and of course it shouldn't be, because it was a workday. He went into the apartment and left a note for his dad on the counter, telling him to call. He couldn't explain everything in a note, and he didn't want it laying around for his mom maybe to find the next day. He needed to *talk* with his dad, and hear his voice, to know that everything was going to be okay.

He didn't know what to do next. He wandered away from the apartment complex. If Tony and Ryan had been in town, he could have texted them to see if they wanted to meet at one of their houses or go to the park or something. But even if they had been around, he didn't really want to see anybody then or talk with anyone other than his dad.

He wound up back at the Kwik Stop. Maybe his dad would stop by to talk with his mom, and Reese could catch him there.

He was sitting by the side of the store, messing around with his knife, when Larry came out with a bag of trash to put in the bin. "Hey, Reese," he said. "I didn't know you were here. What are you doing?"

He shrugged. "Nothing."

Larry frowned. "You okay, buddy?"

"Sure, fine," Reese said. He dropped his knife point down into the dirt, picked it up, and dropped it again.

"Hey, Reese, seriously," Larry said. "You okay?"

Reese looked down, then back at Larry's face, then over at the trash bin. "Yes," he lied. "I'm totally fine."

Larry didn't look like he believed it, but he said, "If you say so. I'll leave you be." He tossed the trash into the bin.

Reese looked down again and, flicking his wrist, drove the blade of the knife hard into the ground, the deepest cut yet.

CHAPTER 28

Reese called to his mom from the door of the trailer: "Come on, let's go!"

It was almost half past five on Thursday, his birthday. They were supposed to be at the apartment to meet his dad at six, but his mom was still in the back bedroom with the door closed. He sat on the trailer's steps and brushed a speck of lint from the knee of his pants. He was wearing khaki pants and a good shirt with a collar because his mom had said it would be nice to dress up a little for supper, make it more special.

He had never managed to reach his dad to tell him what he had overheard at the Smiths' window, but he had talked himself around, convinced himself that it was going to be okay. His dad was going to be fine. Still, he was anxious to get there, wanted to get this over with, *see* that it was fine.

Charlie came out of the house with bowls to feed his cats. Reese got up quickly and went inside the trailer. He didn't want to talk with Charlie: The more Reese had thought about it, the more obvious it seemed to him that it was Charlie who had triggered Mrs. Smith's big lecture to his mom by blabbing about what Reese had said about him and his mom going back to his dad.

His mom was out of the bedroom finally. She was wearing one of her best dresses, black, down to the knees, with thin shoulder straps. Her hair was up in a bun, with not a hair out of place, and she had on the sparkly earrings, her favorites. Reese knew they were his dad's favorites, too. She was also carrying a big present, in blue paper, with a white bow. "What did you get me?" Reese asked.

"You can open it with Dad."

When they went out to the car, Charlie came over to them, smiling. "Hi, Charlie," Reese's mom said.

"You want to help feed the cats?" Charlie asked Reese.

Reese couldn't really look him in the eyes. "I can't," he said. "We have to go meet my dad." He got into the car.

"That's okay," Charlie said.

"I'm sorry," Reese's mom said, which annoyed Reese. They needed to get moving, and Charlie was holding them up. She came around to get into the driver's seat, and when they were headed up the drive, she asked, "Are you okay? You were a little short with Charlie."

"We're just late."

When they were out on the front road, he got to thinking that he didn't want his mom in a bad mood when they got to the apartment, so he said, "I'm sorry. You were right: I was kind of rude to Charlie. I just want to get to dinner."

She reached out and squeezed his leg. "You can say sorry and explain everything when we get back. But look, forget it for now. Let's have fun. It's your birthday."

As they drove along, back to town, Reese's mood lifted again. Hadn't his last day out with his dad been just about perfect? His dad was okay. He would have T-bone steaks, and they would have corn on the cob and potatoes and the chocolate cake from Hub's.

But the important thing was they would be together, celebrating as a family, and his mom would see what a terrible mistake it was for them to be apart.

When they pulled in at the apartment, the Barracuda was in its usual spot in front of their building. The complex was quiet. "Why don't you take the present and carry it in," Reese's mom said. "Just don't shake it or you'll spoil the surprise."

He stepped out of the car and got the present from the backseat. It was pretty heavy and hard. His mom walked ahead to the door of the building, and Reese couldn't resist giving the present a little shake. He heard something rattle. Pieces of wood maybe? He couldn't tell what it was.

He followed his mom into their building, but she stopped just inside. "What's that smell?" she said.

Reese smelled it, too. "Something's burning," he said.

His mom began climbing faster, and the smell got stronger as they rose. By the time they got to the next landing, it was clear that it was coming from their apartment. The smoke alarm wasn't going off, but maybe the batteries were dead, because Reese could definitely smell smoke. His mom knocked, pounded. No answer. She pounded harder. She cursed. She dug into her bag for the keys.

Reese's heart was in his throat. "It's going to be okay," he said, like saying so would make it okay. "Everything's fine."

She fumbled the keys. Her hands were shaking. Then she unlocked the door, and they stepped into a kitchen filled with smoke. It was coming from the oven.

His mom turned off the oven. "Reese, open the window." He held his breath and opened the window while his mom went into the next room.

Then, from the other room, he heard his dad's voice, slurred, muffled: "Wha's happening?"

"Reese's birthday supper is burning, that's what's happening," his mom said. "Get the hell up."

"Wha' time's it?"

"How dare you," his mom said. "How dare you, Sam."

Reese went to the dining room. He felt stunned, like he had fallen and hit the ground hard and all the wind had been knocked out of him. Everything had come undone in an instant. His dad was standing beside the sofa in the living room, swaying, his hair a mess. His eyes were red. His mom's eyes were on fire. "How dare you!" his mom said again. "Today, Sam? *Today?*"

"It's okay," Reese said, and his voice cracked. "He's fine. It's okay. We can order out." Like supper even mattered anymore. Like calling for a pizza or something could fix this.

His dad turned to him and gave him a look like he thought Reese could save this. "Reese . . ." he said.

"OUTSIDE, Sam," his mom barked. "Get outside now. Reese, you stay here."

She stood there, her arms crossed, until his dad went through the smoky kitchen and into the stairwell. He stumbled once, grabbed the doorframe to steady himself.

Reese was still standing there holding the present like a fool. He put it down on the dining table. Then he went out to the stairwell, too. He stopped at the little window on the landing one flight down and looked out. His parents were standing in front of his mom's car. He couldn't hear through the glass, but he could see that his mom was chewing his dad out, poking her finger into his chest, way beyond caring if anyone around saw or heard.

His dad stumbled again, caught himself, put one hand in the pocket of his jeans. He turned away from her—to the Barracuda.

His mom lunged at him, grabbing at something. She looked scared suddenly, and Reese knew what was happening because he had seen it before. His dad was about to drive away, and his mom was trying to get the keys from him because he was in no condition to drive.

Reese cursed at his dad's stupidity, and he came unstuck. He was scared and angry now. He went clattering down the stairs, and he heard the Barracuda's engine roar to life just as he got to the bottom. He burst out of the door, yelling, "DAD! Stop!"

But it was too late. His dad was backing out. The car headed for the apartment complex exit, and then, tires squealing, it hit the street, turning wide, too wide, across the double yellow line. It was going the wrong way, into the path of a pickup. The pickup honked and swerved. Reese closed his eyes, and then . . . nothing.

When he opened his eyes, the street was empty. His dad was gone.

"Reese, I'm very, very sorry," his mom said. She wiped her hair away from her eyes. Her hand was shaking. Her face was pale. "I wish I knew something to say to make this better."

"I want to go," he said. He couldn't stand to be there one more minute.

"Get in the car," she said. "I'll get the food out of the oven and lock up. I won't be long."

He went without another word. When she came back to the car, she put his present in the backseat. She tried to speak: "Your father—"

But Reese didn't want to talk about it. "I just want to go."

They drove back to the Smiths' place in silence, and when they got to the trailer, he left his present in the car and went straight to his bed and lay on his back, staring up at the stained ceiling. His mom went back to her bedroom and changed out of her dress and the fancy earrings and put on shorts and a T-shirt. Then she went to the kitchen, and after a moment, he heard pots clanking. She was making supper for them, although Reese wasn't hungry. When she called to say she had grilled cheese if he wanted it, Reese said he didn't want anything.

He thought that he should be crying or yelling or trying to think of some way to fix this, but he just felt empty.

The sun went down behind the trees. He had been lying there for what felt like a very long while, listening to the frogs singing, when he heard a car coming down the drive. He sat up and looked out the window. He saw a yellow light through the trees at the end of the drive by the house. Then the car appeared, engine rumbling.

It was the Barracuda.

His mother spoke from the kitchen: "Oh my God."

Reese sat there looking out, feeling sick to his stomach. He couldn't stand to see his dad like this again, like he had been at the apartment, and he didn't want Meg and Charlie and the Smiths to see him like this either. He should have guessed who it was the moment he heard the car coming, and he should have run out and up the drive to try to head his dad off. Now it was too late. He wanted to hide.

The Barracuda stopped under the light pole in the yard, so close to it that the bumper nearly touched it. The engine gunned, the gears clunked, and the car backed up a few feet. Then the engine died. His dad got out, swaying. He put a hand on the car's top to steady himself. His shirt was untucked and twisted, like he had the buttons in the wrong holes. He yelled, "Amanda!"

"Stay inside," his mom called to Reese from the kitchen. She went out, the door falling shut behind her. Reese heard her say, "What the hell are you doing here, Sam? You're lucky you didn't kill someone on the way over. You shouldn't be driving."

"I'm here because I need my family," he said. "And I need to be with my son on his birthday. I have a right to be with my son on his birthday."

"Sam, don't you bring this here," his mom said. "This is someone's home. These people don't deserve this."

"These people." His dad spat the words. He took a step forward, stumbled left. "They put this idea into your head in the first place . . . you leaving."

The light on the back door at the house came on, the screen door opened, and there was Mr. Smith. Behind him were Meg and Charlie. Now they were seeing it, the whole horror show: just how completely screwed up Reese's family was.

"Stop this, Sam," Reese's mom said. "This is disgraceful. You are embarrassing yourself and us. Give me the keys and get inside. Get in the trailer. Now. Let's take this inside."

"Amanda?" Mr. Smith said. "Do you need help?"

Reese's mom shook her head, and then she spoke to his dad again: "Do you see this, Sam? You are disturbing them, and you are shaming us in front of them. Haven't you done enough already? You've already ruined your son's birthday, and he gets just one thirteenth birthday. Don't you think that's enough damage for one day?"

Inside the trailer, Reese had stood and gone to the door. He put his hand on the handle of the screen door, feeling like he should try to talk with his dad, but wondering if he could bear to go out with Meg and Charlie watching.

"Fine," his dad said. "I'm an embarrassment. Excuse me. I'll take my embarrassing self somewhere else."

"Don't you get back in that car," his mom said. "You are absolutely in no state to be driving."

It was happening again, just like at the apartment. His dad was moving to the Barracuda. "I thought you wanted me gone," he said.

"Get inside the trailer," his mom said. "For God's sake."

His dad stood there, swaying. He was looking up into the darkness past the circle of light from the pole. For a moment, Reese thought he was going to listen to his mom this time and come in, give her the car keys.

Then he said, "Nope. I'm out of here."

"Don't you get into that car!" his mom said.

"You all have a great evening," his dad said, and he was getting into the car. "Happy birthday, Reese!"

His mom lunged, going for his hand to take the keys. But his dad slammed the door. Reese yelled, "DAD!" He pushed the screen door open and jumped over the steps, landing on the dirt. At that moment, he didn't care about Meg or Charlie watching. He needed to stop his dad from doing something so stupid.

The Barracuda's engine roared, and his dad threw the car into gear and floored the gas, spitting gravel, spinning around in reverse. His mom turned and stepped toward the car, but slipped, one foot going out from under her. His dad threw the shifter into first and floored it again, the Barracuda's rear end fishtailing. Then it was headed up the drive, headlights off. It disappeared among the trees.

Reese's mom turned to him, her eyes wide.

There was no warning for what came next. No squeal of tires, no horn.

There was just the sound of the crash: metal crunching, glass shattering.

Reese's mom yelled, "Oh my God!"

And then the lights went out.

Every single light around them went dark: the light on the pole in the yard, the lights in the house and trailer. The darkness dropped around them as if someone had thrown a master switch.

Mr. Smith, still standing on the back steps of the house, yelled, "Mattie, call 911!"

Reese's mom had taken off running up the drive, and Reese went after her, his heart pounding. He ran fastest, overtaking her and then pulling ahead, not caring where his footsteps fell in the dark, just wanting to get to his dad. His mom called after him, "Reese! Stop!"

He broke out of the trees into the light of a half-moon. The Barracuda was across the road, and at first Reese couldn't get his head around what he was seeing. It was the car, the front end horribly crushed, and what he thought was a tree leaning over the road with a tangle of ropes or wires hanging over it all. Then he realized the tree was a utility pole. The car had run into it, splintering it, pitching it forward.

"Reese! Oh my God! Stop! Don't you move! Those are power lines!" His mom had come to the top of the drive, breathing hard. "Those lines on the ground could kill you. Don't step into the road." She put both hands on top of her head. "Oh my God, oh my God. Sam!"

The car door opened with a crunch and a groan of bent metal, and Reese's dad was there, in the driver's seat. He was holding his head, and all down his face and his shirt was what Reese thought at first was oil. It looked black in the moonlight. Then he realized it was blood.

"I feel sick," his dad said.

He slumped sideways and down, out of the car, and he threw up.

CHAPTER 29

Reese recognized the lady at the ER admissions desk from the last time they were there, and he thought she recognized him, too. When their eyes met, she smiled at him. He looked away. He felt on display there, the poor kid with the addict dad. He'd turned off his phone. Tony and Ryan had been texting, wishing him a happy birthday. They had no clue what was going on, living their normal, happy lives, and he couldn't stand right then to read their normal, happy messages.

The TV in the ER waiting area was tuned to some Disney Channel show, and Reese couldn't stand that either: all the happy talk and people laughing their heads off. He got up and spoke to the only other person in there, a man with a big black mustache who was looking at his phone.

"You care if I turn that off?" he asked him.

The man just raised his hands, palms up, and shook his

head. He either didn't understand or didn't care. The ER nurse spoke then: "Do you want to change the channel?"

"I want it off," Reese said.

She looked at the man in the corner, and when he didn't object, she said, "Sure." She raised a remote and, *click*, the screen went black.

He sat back down and stared at his hands until the nurse returned to her work. Then he checked a clock hanging in the hallway. His mom had been gone for about a half hour, talking to his dad and the doctor.

He watched the clock face, the second hand sweeping around. It went around once, twice, three times. Then his mom reappeared. She sat next to him and put a hand on his arm. "Reese . . ." Her eyes were red, her face was puffy.

"What did the doctor say?" he asked.

"They just did some x-rays and other tests. He has a broken leg, and a concussion, and that gash in his head needed stitches. He's also bruised up bad, and he hurts all over. But it could have been so much worse. We can both go back to see him now."

She patted his arm and stood.

He didn't move. He had been terrified that his dad was going to die in that wreck. Now his fear had been replaced by anger. His dad had blown everything. *Everything*. Again.

His mom was looking closely at his face. "He's asking for you, but you don't have to go back now if you don't want to," she said.

Reese got up, avoiding the gaze of the nurse at the desk.

They went down a hall, turned right, and went through double doors into a large room with a nurse's station in the middle and small open rooms along the walls, with only curtains for privacy. "I'm back with my son to see Sam Buck," his mom said to a nurse at a computer.

"You can go on in," the nurse said.

Reese's dad was in the far corner. The curtain was half open. He lay in a bed with his broken leg in a cast. The head of the bed was raised, so he was half sitting up. He had a white bandage on his head, and the right side of his face was swollen and purple. He seemed to be sleeping.

"Sam?" his mom said. "Reese is here."

He opened one eye, the left one, and it was like a dark hole. His other eye was swollen shut.

He said, "Can I talk with Reese alone, please? Just for a few minutes. There are some things I need to say to him."

His mom's mouth drew tight, and Reese thought she was about to say no. But then she said, "I guess that's up to Reese."

A big part of Reese had wanted her to say no for him, wanted her to take his arm and lead him away. But his mom had left him hanging, with nothing to do but nod okay.

"I'll be close by," his mom said. She went out, pulling the curtain shut behind her.

Reese stood at the foot of his dad's bed as if he were nailed to the spot. The electric clock on the wall buzzed and clicked as another minute dropped away. It was after eleven p.m., although inside that windowless room, it would have been impossible to tell whether it was night or day.

His dad looked at him with that one dark eye. He said, "Will you come closer?"

Reese took a couple of steps forward, to his dad's side. His dad reached for him, took hold of his wrist. "I'm so sorry, Reese," he said. "I'm sorry for everything . . . for ruining your birthday, for letting you down again . . ."

Reese's anger boiled over then, and he pulled his arm away. "Why can't you just *stop*? Why do you keep doing this? What do we have to do *to get you to just stop*?"

His dad tried to answer: "I—"

But Reese cut him off: "I texted you all the information about treatment. I gave you phone numbers. You *told us you were getting help*. You told me you had this. But this just keeps happening, over and over and over. It doesn't get better. It just keeps getting worse."

His dad took hold of his wrist again. "Reese! Reese! Listen to me! You're right. You are absolutely right to be angry with me. That's what I need to talk to you about."

Reese wanted to pull his arm away again, but he didn't move. His dad closed his one good eye again and said nothing for a few moments. The clock on the wall buzzed and clicked.

Then his dad said, "I want so bad to kick this once and for all. I really do. I want to be clean, and for a while I'll feel like I got it. But time after time it just slips through my fingers. One of the things I need to tell you . . . admit to you . . . is that this week, on Monday, I took something before work, and I"—he swallowed and shook his head—"I just have to say it: I showed up high at a job. I was messed up, and Jimmy could see it, and he said he can't hire me anymore to work on his houses. He fired me."

Reese pulled his arm away. "*You what?* Why would you do that?"

"I don't know why I did it, Reese. It's always 'just this once,' just one more time to kind of get me through or whatever. It doesn't make any kind of sense. But it happened. That's why I was free the next day when you and I went over to Petty's and all that. And I don't blame Jimmy. He has given me a second chance and a third chance, and I've blown it every time. Just like I keep blowing my chances with you and your mom. That's what I was thinking about this afternoon, before you came over for your dinner. I was thinking about how bad I want you and your mom back, how scared I am of losing you two, and how disappointed and angry you both would be when you found out what happened with Jimmy. And I thought: 'I'm losing everything.' It's like everything is falling into this black hole. My work. My family. Me. I'm falling into the hole."

"Stop talking like that," Reese snapped. "Just stop it."

"It's what it feels like, Reese. I was sitting there in the apartment today, thinking about how bad I keep screwing up and about how all this week, since Jimmy cut me loose, I've been lying to you and your mom, pretending that it's all good. Now it's your birthday, and I thought how much you deserve a good birthday and how much I want to make you and your mom believe that I'm okay and everything's going to be fine. And I just freaked out. That's what happened: I freaked out, and I took something, thinking maybe it would calm my nerves, help me through. And one thing led to another."

He shifted positions, sucked in his breath. "Lord, it hurts. It hurts like hell right now. I wouldn't let them give me anything but Tylenol for the pain. I didn't want any more of the—I don't want it. I want my head to be clear. And it is clear. What I understand now and what I need to say to you is that your mom is right: I can't be the dad you need until I get clean and get a handle on this. And until I do, you two are better off living your life apart from me."

This Reese hadn't expected. At all. *"What?"*

"I am dragging you both down. I'm doing nothing but hurting you. So what your mom has done is what's best."

Reese felt as if the lights had suddenly dimmed. His dad's bruised, swollen face looked as if it were underwater. "Best for who?" he said.

"Best for you and your mom. You don't need me around like this. You don't need—" He shook his head. "Reese, I want so bad to get better. I want so bad to be the dad you deserve. I want to be the man your mom deserves. But I'm so scared. I'm scared that I never will be."

He put his hand to his mouth, and then tears were rolling down his cheeks. He was crying, his shoulders shaking.

Reese thought he should hug him, put his arms around him,

tell him that it would be okay, that he loved him no matter what. But he couldn't bring himself to touch him. He felt disgusted with his dad for crying, for being weak, for failing him and his mom and himself, and he was ashamed of himself for being disgusted by the weakness of someone he loved.

What had he expected his dad to say when he yelled at him for letting everyone down? He had wanted his dad to say that at last he saw everything clearly and was going to make this right. He had wanted him to say that he had let Reese down horribly, terribly, the worst yet—but at last this was the wake-up call he needed to quit the drugs forever.

Instead, he was lying there crying and saying he might never get better.

Reese had been looking forward to a rescue from the trailer, from his family's separation, from their problems. But the rescue he was looking for wasn't coming, not for any of them, he thought. They were stuck, forever and ever.

He turned and walked out.

His dad called after him: "Reese? Reese! Come back!"

His mom was hunched over in a chair at the entrance to the ER, with her elbows on her knees, her face in her hands. She looked up when she heard the curtain rattle. She had red rings under her eyes. Her hair was down and tangled. "Reese, what happened?" she said.

"He's giving up," Reese said. "Just like you're giving up."

"What are you talking about?" his mom said. "What did he say?"

"He says he might never get better. He says he's hurting us, so we're better off without him. Everything is just going down a big black hole. That's what he said. Him, us. Oh, and he lost his work with Jimmy. Did he tell you that? He came to a job messed up, and Jimmy says he won't hire him anymore."

"Oh, Lord." She stood. "Yes, he told me about Jimmy. But, Reese, no one is giving up."

Did she really think he was that stupid? Did she think he didn't understand what was happening? "I *heard you*," he said. "I heard you and Mrs. Smith: I heard her tell you that we're better off without him dragging us down, and you didn't say anything back. You didn't argue."

His mom shook her head. "What are you talking about? The other night in her kitchen?"

"I was coming to the house, and I heard you through their window. I heard her tell you that he needed to deal with this on his own, and you needed to get on with your life. That it's what's best for everybody. And that's what Dad just said: It's what's best. Everyone is saying that. But don't I get a say in what's best?"

"Reese, please, you don't understand. You misunderstood what Mrs. Smith was saying. It's complicated. What she—"

He wasn't going to let her finish. He pushed open the double doors and went through, into the hallway beyond, and let the doors shut on his mom. But he heard the doors swing open a moment later as she came after him. She reached for him and took his arm, pulling him up short. She grabbed his arm so tight it hurt, and she turned him around. Her face was red.

"Don't you walk away from me, Reese Buck."

She was losing it, and through the windows of the double doors, he saw the nurse at the ER station look up, frowning, probably wondering if she should call security. "Keep your voice down!" Reese hissed. "Be quiet!"

"I will *not* be quiet," she said. "And you need to stand there and listen. No one is giving up on anyone. And I do not believe your father is giving up, as upset and scared as he is right now. But he has a big, scary problem that he can't handle on his own, and he's got to admit to himself that he can't handle it and then get help. He's the *only* one who can do that. I can't do it for him. Neither can you. And we can't cure him. Neither of us has any control at all over this. Zero. We have to accept that we can't control this, and we have to take care of ourselves and try to live our lives. *That's* what Mrs. Smith was saying. We can't let this take over everything and just stop us in our tracks until your father gets better. Do you understand me?"

But he had turned his face away. He wouldn't look at her. She put a hand, a gentler hand, on his arm. But he shook it off. That feeling like a fist in his chest was back, hard as stone.

CHAPTER 30

Reese was lying on the bed in the trailer. It was nearly nine in the morning, the day after his birthday, and he hadn't gotten out of bed. Now his mom was at the door. She said, "You can't lie there all day. You have to eat something at least."

"No."

"I'm staying home from work," she said. "I should have called in sooner. This is no day for me to be gone. If they can't find someone else, they can close the store."

"No," he said. "You need to go." He wanted to be alone.

"I'm staying home."

"Go," he said, his tone like a hammer pounding a nail.

She came in and sat on the edge of the mattress, and she put a hand on his leg. "I keep telling you: You have a right to be angry. You have a right to be sad, scared, let down, all of it. But you have to get up and keep moving. I need your help, for one thing."

Reese kept his eyes fixed on the ceiling, just wanting her to leave him alone. His mom shook her head and stood. "So, you're just not going to talk to me or move?"

"Right," he said.

"I guess there really is nothing for me to do but go to work."

She left him then. She got dressed, said goodbye, and then got in the car and drove away. He lay there, too depressed to get up, as the sun rose overhead and the shadows shortened. Someone came out of the house, and Reese rose a little on his elbows to peek out. It was Mrs. Smith, hanging laundry on the line. He was sure she was thinking how she had been right all along about his dad. The trees behind the trailer whispered and creaked in the breeze. He heard a bird call from somewhere close, a *brrrp!* sound, and he thought that Meg probably could tell him what bird it was, from her books.

Thinking about Meg made him feel even sadder and more alone. She had not come over to check on him, and he wondered what she thought of him now. He had seen her and her grandfather go out earlier that morning and walk up the road, probably to look in the daylight at the mess his dad had made. Then they had come back and gone inside the house.

The power had come back on a short while after that, so the power company must have fixed the wires and put up a new pole to replace the one his dad had smashed.

His dad's car, the beautiful and powerful Barracuda, was gone forever. By the time Reese and his mom had returned to the Smiths' place from the hospital, someone had hauled it away. The one question Reese had asked his mom on the drive back was about the car: "Can they fix it?"

"No," she had said. "It's totaled."

Reese stayed on the mattress until finally he couldn't stand it anymore. He had gone to sleep in his clothes the night before, and he didn't change now or brush his hair. He just got up and went into the kitchen.

On the table was his present from the day before, still wrapped. He didn't want to open it.

He put on his shoes and went outside and stood at the bottom of the trailer steps, blinking in the bright sun. Mrs. Smith had gone back inside. He tried to think what to do or which direction to go, and he was at a loss. He was stuck. He thought of his dad, with his swollen face, lying in that hospital bed, looking at him with that one open eye. He had stayed in the hospital overnight. Reese wasn't sure whether he'd be released that day or not, and he hadn't asked. Reese didn't want to see him.

He looked back at the trailer, this place where he had been dumped. Every flaw, every crack and spot of rust, stood out to him. He looked around at the patchy grass, the hard-packed dirt. He was so far from what he wanted, from any place he wanted to be. Even the air was disgusting: It was heavy that morning, hot and wet.

Then the back door of the house opened, and out came Charlie.

Reese turned away and started walking to the end of the trailer, hoping to slip around the back of it before Charlie spotted him. But it was too late: Charlie called to him, "Reese, wait up."

Reese stopped. "What?"

"You can come with me to see the kittens if you want." Charlie said this as if nothing had happened, like it was a normal day. "I'm going to bring Mama Cat her food."

"No," Reese said. He turned to walk away, up the dirt road.

Charlie followed. "You don't want to see the kittens? You can help me pick them up. Remember, you have to pick them up every day."

"You've told me that a hundred times," Reese said. "I don't care."

"I don't understand." Charlie had come close. "You like the kittens, and they're our secret."

All the anger and hurt that had built up inside Reese welled up then. He wanted to punch something, and the world seemed to narrow to Charlie, pushing in, crowding him.

"I don't care about your kittens," Reese said. "Do you hear me? I don't care about your cats." It felt good to say it, a release. "I want you to get away from me," he said. "Just leave me alone. Do you hear me? Leave me alone!"

The last thing he saw before he turned away was Charlie's open mouth, his eyes wide. He looked as if Reese really had punched him in the gut and knocked the air out of him.

Reese ran as hard as he could, so angry at everything and at the same time so ashamed of himself that he felt like he might throw up. He went up the dirt road, through the fields to the front road, and then turned left. He kept running along the road's shoulder until his sides ached. He slowed to a walk.

He didn't know where he was headed except away.

He kept going until the road ended in a T intersection with another road that looked just the same. He turned left, the direction picked at random. He walked as the sun rose higher in the sky. He walked until he reached a fork in the road with a gas station in the middle. It was a blue cube of a building that looked as if it had sat there for about a thousand years. It had a faded metal sign on the side that read, **GAS CIGARETTES SNACKS COLD DRINKS RESTROOMS**.

He stopped. His mouth felt as if it were full of cotton, and his head ached. He needed water, so he went into the store. An old woman with short gray hair was sitting on a high stool behind the front counter, looking at her phone. She looked up. "Yes, son?"

"Can I have a drink of water?" he asked.

"Bottles of water are in back, in the cooler," she said.

"I don't have any money."

She squinted hard at Reese, as if she were just really seeing him. She rose a little from her seat and looked over his shoulder, outside. He turned to see what she was looking at, but it was just the empty parking lot. "Where's your ma and pa at?" the old lady asked him.

She sounded suspicious, as if she thought Reese was up to no good. "They're at home," he said. "I'm just taking a walk."

"To where?"

"Nowhere," he said, truthfully. "Just walking."

"Well, there's a spigot in the bathroom," she said. "Around back."

"Can I have the key?" he asked.

"You don't need no key," she said. She went back to her phone, as if he were already gone.

He went around to the back of the building and found the restroom, which smelled of pee and Pine-Sol. The sink was streaked with something black, as if someone had washed grease off their hands. He turned on the water and used his cupped hands to get water. He drank until he felt a little better. Then he went out. The bathroom and the lady in the store had knocked out of him any desire to run away—if that's even what he was thinking about doing in the first place.

He had just wanted to run.

But suddenly, what he wanted most was to see his mom. He went back to the road, walking wide around the gas station to avoid the eyes of the old lady inside, and he started back the way he had come, along the road's shoulder. A tractor-trailer was approaching with a load of cages piled high on it, and when it drew even with Reese, he saw each of the cages had a white chicken crammed inside. The truck blew by, trailing a cloud of feathers.

The sun had slipped past its high point, and the day was hotter than when he had started. He thought about Charlie, the look on his face, and he felt ashamed again, deep down, at the way he had treated him.

It was cruel: He saw that clearly. Charlie wasn't to blame for his problems with his dad. Neither was Mrs. Smith. He didn't know how he would face them now. He hoped he could slip into the trailer without anyone seeing him.

He was thinking about this when someone blew a horn behind him. It was Mr. Smith in his pickup truck.

Reese had a crazy thought that he should run, but he was tired of running. He just stood on the side of the road as Mr. Smith pulled up. The windows of the pickup were down, and inside Mr. Smith looked sad or angry or both. He said, "Have you seen Charlie? He's run off again."

When he heard that, Reese felt again like he would throw up. "I don't know where he is," he said.

"Get in, help me look," said Mr. Smith.

"What happened?" Reese asked after he had climbed in beside Mr. Smith.

"Charlie got upset about something, and when his grandma went out and tried to calm him down, he knocked her down and ran."

Reese swallowed hard. This was getting worse and worse. "He knocked her down?"

"When she tried to take his arm, he shoved her away. She lost her balance and fell."

"Was she hurt?"

"No, no, she just sat down hard is all. But now we can't find Charlie anywhere. He took off running to the front road and Mattie came up behind as fast as she could, but he was gone by the time she got up there. Last time he did this, he didn't get far, but now he's just gone. Did he say anything to you? Do you know why he might be upset?"

"No, I don't," he lied. He couldn't bring himself to admit the truth to Mr. Smith.

"Was he outside when you left the trailer?"

"No, sir," he said. Another lie.

Mr. Smith cocked his head back to look at him more closely. "Where were you going?" he asked.

"I don't know," Reese said. "I was just walking."

Mr. Smith kept looking at him until Reese was sure that the old man had seen right through his lies. But then Mr. Smith nodded and said, "I'm going to drive a little more and if we still can't find him, we'll have to call the sheriff."

This was the worst yet. Everything was spinning out of control. "Why do you have to call the sheriff?" Reese asked.

"To help us look," Mr. Smith said. "Now keep an eye out on your side, will you? If you see anything at all, tell me."

Reese nodded. "Yes, sir." He turned to his side of the pickup, but he saw nothing but the field and the trees and the dome of the sky, a landscape big enough to swallow someone whole.

CHAPTER 31

They didn't find Charlie, and when they got back to the house, Mr. Smith called 911. Two deputies came quickly in a patrol car and spoke with the Smiths. Reese, afraid and ashamed, watched from inside the trailer.

Meg came outside, and when she looked over toward the trailer, Reese ducked out of sight. She came his way, but when she knocked on the trailer door, Reese hid in the bathroom until she went away.

Silence fell over the trailer, and sitting on the toilet seat, he felt like a coward. He also had never felt more alone in his life. He stood up and looked at himself in the mirror. He made a face, eyes screwed up, tongue out. He looked like a devil. He thought again of his dad's face, bruised and swollen, with just one good eye.

He thought about calling his mom, but he already knew what he had to do: He had to tell. He couldn't hide behind her, and he couldn't sit in that little bathroom, all alone and afraid, until she came home. It wasn't right. The Smiths needed to know exactly what had happened with Charlie. Reese wasn't sure if it would help them find him, but maybe it would.

What made him really sick was thinking about how disappointed and angry Meg was going to be. He knew what she would think of him: He was a massive jerk. He was cruel. He couldn't be trusted. She would never speak to him again.

He took a deep breath and let it out to steady himself. Then he went out—out of the bathroom and out the trailer door. He walked across the yard, past the picnic table and the swing, and he knocked on the Smiths' back door.

Mrs. Smith answered. "Oh, Reese. We were worried about you. Meg just came over to the trailer to see how you were."

"I have something to tell you," he said.

Mrs. Smith's eyebrows came together. She looked puzzled. "Come in, please," she said.

Meg was at the kitchen table with a map spread out in front of her, helping to plan the search for Charlie probably. She looked up at Reese when he came in and frowned a little.

Reese looked down at his shoes and then up at Mrs. Smith. He couldn't look at Meg. His head felt as if it was going to float off his body. "I yelled at Charlie," he said. "That's why he was upset. That's why he ran away. It was my fault. I did it."

Mrs. Smith looked really puzzled then. "What on earth are you talking about?"

Reese wanted to get this over with fast, now that he had

started. "I yelled at Charlie," he said again. "And he got really upset. I was upset about my dad, and when Charlie came to ask me if I wanted to look at his kittens, I took it out on him. I told him to leave me alone. I told him I didn't care about his cats. And then I ran away. I left him."

Mrs. Smith's hand went to her throat. "What kittens?"

This was not what Reese had expected, and he opened his mouth to answer. But just then, Meg's chair fell over with such a loud clatter that he and Mrs. Smith both jumped, as if a gun had gone off. Meg had stood up so fast she had knocked it over. Her eyes narrowed. Then she swept the map to the floor and ran out, though the back door. "Meg!" called Mrs. Smith.

Reese ran after her. He had thought he was strong enough to live with her hating him, but it turned out that he wasn't. He had to catch her and try to make it right. Mrs. Smith called out to him, but he kept running, out the back door and down the steps. Meg was heading for the river. "Meg! Please!" he called. "Please, wait up. I want to explain."

She stopped, halfway to the river, but she didn't turn around. She stood with her back to him, breathing hard, her hands clenched at her sides. He stopped a few feet from her. "Meg . . ." he began, uncertain now what exactly to say.

"What?" she said. Her tone was sharp, angry.

"I'm sorry," he said. "I was upset about my dad, and your . . ." He almost told her about overhearing her grandmother talking to his mom about his dad. But he didn't want to turn things back onto her family; it wouldn't be fair. He said, "You saw what happened to my dad. You saw it. You saw everything."

"Yes," she said, still facing away. "And my grandma told me what happened with your birthday."

He thought maybe her tone had softened a little, and he pressed ahead, words tumbling from him: "I'd thought . . . I'd hoped . . . that my dad was finally getting better. But he isn't. He lost his job, too. And now the car. He says he wants to get better, but he's scared he never will. And he says we're better off without him dragging us down. Then he cried. When he was talking to me at the hospital, he started crying. And I walked away. I couldn't stand it."

He thought of his dad in the hospital bed, trying to explain himself to Reese just like Reese was trying to explain himself now to Meg. She probably wanted him to stop talking, just like he had wanted his dad to shut up. Meg was worried about Charlie, and here he was feeling sorry for himself. He felt light-headed again, and he squatted in the grass. "I couldn't touch him or tell him it would be okay, because it made me so mad and scared," he said. "This isn't how things are supposed to be. Everything's gone wrong, and I can't fix it. I can't fix anything. I'm just stuck with it. And when Charlie came, talking to me about the cats, I just . . . I don't know . . . I just wanted to push everything away. This isn't how things are supposed to be with my dad or my family. I shouldn't be here like this, and I took it out on Charlie. Do you understand?"

For a moment, the only sound was the breeze whispering in

the trees. Then Meg turned. Her face was flushed, and her hair had fallen over her eyes. "Do you think you're the only one?" she said.

He didn't understand. "Do I think I'm the only what?"

"I am sorry about your father," she said. "I know you're scared. It's horrible. But do you think you're the only one stuck with a life that doesn't look like it's supposed to? Do you think you're the only one who's stuck with problems they can't fix? Do you think my life or Charlie's life looks anything like we want?"

He felt ashamed of himself again. "No," he said.

"You said you can't fix the things that are wrong in your life. Well, my parents are dead. Can I fix that? Can I fix that for me and Charlie? And now he's run off, and if something happens to him . . . if we can't find him or he gets hurt . . ."

"I'm so sorry," Reese said. The words sounded weak. The breeze just carried them away like dust.

"Do you know what else we're stuck with?" Meg said. "Do you know that Charlie and I haven't made a single real friend here? Not one. I don't fit in at my school. I'm like an alien, the weird orphan smart kid from up North. Charlie gets stuck in this tiny special-education classroom every day at his dump of a school, with no one for company but a boy who can't speak, and no one will sit with him in his other classes or at lunch. And I can't fix that. Don't you think I'd like to push all that away? But I can't. He's stuck with it, and I'm stuck with it."

Reese opened his mouth to . . . what? To apologize again?

"And I thought you were different," Meg said. "I thought you understood. I thought I could trust you, that you were a friend. And Charlie believed you were his friend. Did you know that? He talked about you all the time, how much he liked you and how happy he was to have you here, helping him with his cats, showing him how to play basketball. That's why he got so upset when you were mean to him."

"I *am* your friend," Reese said. "And I'm Charlie's friend. I want to be."

Meg looked at him for a moment more, and then she sat down in the grass. She put her face in her hands. He stood and went to her. He sat beside her.

"I really am so sorry," he said, and with her so close to him, the words seemed to carry weight this time. He wished he had something else to say to make it better.

She wiped her nose with the back of her hand and shook her head. He thought that she didn't believe him, was shaking his apology away. Then she said, "I know it. I know you are. And I really am sorry about your dad. I wish he would get better, and your family could be back together again. And I wish you'd had the birthday you wanted."

After a moment, he put an arm around her shoulders. He was worried maybe she would shrug him off, but she didn't. In the middle of the field, between the house and the river, the two of them sat for a long while.

CHAPTER 32

Reese was sitting with Meg by the swing outside the house when Charlie came home that evening. They had just fed his cats. The sun had gone down, and they saw the headlights of Mr. Smith's pickup truck through the trees as it drove down the dirt road to the house.

The sheriff's department had found Charlie walking behind the county landfill, about four miles from home. He was lost and thirsty and hungry and upset, but not hurt. He wouldn't get into the squad car with the deputies, so they had called the house and Mr. Smith had gone in the pickup to get him.

"He's going to hate me," Reese said. "And I don't blame him."

"It'll probably take time, but you'll figure out how to fix it," Meg said. "I know you will."

The pickup pulled in, and Charlie stepped out. His skin looked greenish under the security light. He had a smudge of dirt on his cheek and mud on his knees. When he saw Reese walking to him, he spoke first: "No," he said.

"Charlie," Reese said. "I'm sorry."

Charlie turned away. "No," he said again. "I don't want to talk to you."

Reese took another step forward. He began: "I wanted—"

But Mr. Smith cut him off: "Reese, let's give Charlie a little space right now."

Reese's mom had come out of the trailer. He had told her everything when she got back from work, and she put her hands on his shoulders now and said to Mr. Smith, "We understand. Please, let us know if there's anything we can do."

Meg stood, looking sad. "I'll see you later," she said. She went to Charlie and put her arm around him, and together with their granddad, they went inside the house, leaving Reese and his mom alone in the yard.

Reese turned away, out of the circle of light, into the shadows. His mom took him by the arm. "Hey," she said. "Hey, look at me. Are you crying?"

He was, and it was embarrassing. He'd been holding it in for what felt like forever. He hadn't even cried after his dad's wreck or at the hospital, but now it just came pouring out.

"You did the right thing by telling everyone," his mom said. "I'm proud of you for doing that."

"I'm sorry for everything," he said.

"You don't have to keep saying that," she said. "You just need to remember you're not alone here. *We're* not alone. And you have to keep talking to people. If you can't talk to me, talk to Meg or whoever. Okay? If you hold this stuff inside, you end up blowing up, and then all you do is spread the hurt around."

She put her arms around him, and he let himself be held. He pressed his wet cheek into the warm fabric of her shirt. "I love you," she said.

"I love you, too," he said.

"And look, I meant what I said at the ER: No one is giving up on your dad. I just talked with him on the phone again. He's scared and in pain, but I think he's maybe in a little better place. After we left, he talked with a counselor at the hospital about drug treatment. They released him this evening. Trey took him home, and we'll go visit him tomorrow at the apartment, probably in the afternoon. Okay? If you're feeling up to it."

He wiped his eyes and nodded. "Okay," he said.

"He's got to do this for himself, but we're not turning our backs on him. Hey, and you know what? I just thought of something else: You never opened your birthday present. It's sitting on the table inside."

"I don't want it," Reese said. He had forgotten about it.

"I think you'll want it when you see it. Let's go in and open it. Do it for me, even if you don't feel like it. It would cheer me up."

She had him sit on the sofa inside, and she got the present and handed it to him. He ran his hand across the paper. It was a flat box, a little wider than his lap. He put his fingers under the fold in one end and tore, pulling away the paper.

It was a wooden box, light brown, with black metal hinges on one side and a black clasp and two little wooden knobs on the other. "Open it," she said.

He undid the clasp and lifted the lid. When he saw what was inside, he smiled. "It's an art case," he said.

"Do you like it?"

He nodded. It was a gift he hadn't thought to ask for, but he couldn't think of a better one. He opened it all the way up, and the lid pulled up two shelves on folding arms, which was cool. In each shelf and in the bottom were compartments with pencils and paints and brushes nestled inside. There were so many colors—deep reds running through yellows and greens to blues and blacks and grays. "The man at the art store in Goldsville told me this should have everything you need right now," his mom said. "It's got acrylic paints and watercolors. It's got pastels and colored pencils. And here, look at the bottom: little tubes of oil paints."

"I don't know how to use oil paints," Reese said.

"You can learn, if you want," she said. "Oh, and hold on . . ." She went to the back bedroom and returned with a plastic bag. "I forgot to wrap this. I thought it would be better than scrap paper from the Kwik Stop or whatever."

It was a drawing pad, with big sheets of heavy paper.

"What do you think?" she asked.

"It's great," he said. "It's awesome."

And when he smiled, she smiled back, a real smile that went all the way to her eyes. "Happy birthday," she said.

CHAPTER 33

The next day was Saturday, and Reese's mom talked with his dad again on the phone in the morning. She and Reese would go visit him in town that afternoon. Until then, from inside the trailer, Reese kept an eye out for Charlie.

When Charlie finally came outside, Reese went out to try to speak with him. Charlie was taking dry clothes off the clothesline, putting them in a basket, and when he saw Reese, he ducked his head and turned away.

Reese asked, "Can I help feed the cats when you do that?"

"No," Charlie said.

"I really am sorry for what I said," Reese said. "What I said wasn't true. I do care about your cats and about the kittens."

Charlie ignored him. He snatched the last few pieces of clothing off the line, threw them into the laundry basket, and went back inside.

Reese stood alone in the yard for a few moments, looking

at the back of the house. It was a beautiful day, not too hot or humid. The sky was high and blue. But Reese just felt sad. When he went back to the trailer, his mom was at the kitchen sink. She was peeling carrots. "He still didn't want to talk?" she asked.

"No. I wish there was something more I could do."

"Give him time."

The same thing happened later in the morning when Charlie came out to go to the woodshed and check on the kittens. Reese tried to talk to him; Charlie wouldn't talk. Reese was running out of ways to say he was sorry.

Back inside the trailer, he sat on the sofa, depressed. Through the window, he could see two of Charlie's cats, sunning themselves on the picnic table. One of them, a tiger-striped tabby, rose and stretched, tail straight up. Reese noticed the high curve of its back, the tilt of its head. He shifted in his seat and then stood and went to the window. The cat gathered itself and sat, its head slightly lifted, sniffing something on the breeze. Reese looked closely and he noticed that the cat made a rough triangle, ears at the tip, haunches at the base.

Then he had an idea.

He picked up his new drawing pad and opened it to the first, clean, perfect page. He opened his art box beside him, the two shelves rising smoothly on their brackets. He took a charcoal pencil from the second shelf.

"What are you going to draw?" his mom asked.

"A cat," he said.

"That's a new subject for you. I thought you were all about cars and trucks."

He got a chair from the kitchen and brought it close to the window, where he could see the cats outside. He looked carefully again at the tabby and put pencil to paper. He drew the line of the back first, a curve to the top of the head. Then he began to draw the head and . . . "Crap," he said. It wasn't right. He went back to the art box and got an eraser and tried again. And again, it wasn't right. He erased it.

He kept at it, drawing and erasing, drawing and erasing, until he wore a hole in the paper. The cat jumped down off the picnic table and walked away, across the grass, tail up. Reese threw his pencil down, frustrated. "I can't do it," he said.

"Take a break," his mom said. "What's so important about it anyway?"

"Nothing," he said. He didn't want to talk about it with her, partly because he was shy about it and worried it wouldn't work out. But mostly he didn't want to talk about it because it was between him and Charlie.

They went to the apartment in town later that day to visit his dad. His friend Trey was staying there to help take care of him, although it turned out it wouldn't be for long: Reese's dad was going to a drug treatment program in Goldsville first thing on Monday. The counselor he had talked with at the hospital had made some phone calls and found an unexpected opening for him. He would be in for at least thirty days, maybe longer.

"We'll drive you over, Sam," Reese's mom said.

"Trey can do it."

"We'll take you. I told you we would, and we will."

"Can we visit you?" Reese asked.

"Not at the start, anyway," his dad said. "I guess they want everybody to just focus on getting better. They won't even let me have my phone."

He was lying stretched out on the sofa in the living room in a T-shirt and shorts, with his broken leg propped up on a pillow. His bruised face and swollen eye still looked terrible, and somehow he looked smaller to Reese, kind of deflated. His skin was pale, his good eye was rimmed with red, and his hair was a mess. It looked like he hadn't slept well at all.

His dad hadn't apologized any more for the mess he had made, for ruining Reese's birthday, and Reese didn't want him to. What he wanted was what his dad was doing: getting help.

"How are you going to do the program with your leg broken?" Reese asked.

"We'll make it work," his dad said. "I got crutches. Maybe they'll push me around in a wheelchair if I get tired." He shifted his weight and winced. "Amanda, this counselor I met at the hospital, I talked with him a lot about what I've been going through . . . about what *we've* been going through. He's a good guy, and he says when I get out, I can call him if I need help, like connecting with a support group or something."

"That's good, Sam," Reese's mom said. "I'm glad you're

talking to him. And are you sure we can't get you anything while we're in town? Something for tonight, or anything you'll need while you're in the program?"

"I'm good," his dad said. "Although actually, Reese, later on there is one thing you can maybe do for me: Your mom says she gave you that art set. What do you think?"

"I like it a lot," Reese said. "Thank you."

"At some point, would you draw me something? I don't know if I can get mail at this place I'm going, but maybe. Or you can give it to me when I'm out."

"Sure," Reese said. "What do you want me to draw?"

"You pick," his dad said. "Surprise me."

And Reese would, although he'd have to think hard about what to draw for him. He wasn't sure whether his dad would want a picture of a car, and Reese wasn't sure if he wanted to draw one right then anyway. He didn't want to be reminded of the Barracuda and how it used to be. It was too sad.

He also had to finish Charlie's picture first. He got back to work on it when he and his mom returned to the Smiths' place, and then kept at it the next morning, Sunday, trying to get it right. After everything that had happened, his mom and the Smiths slept in rather than going to church, but Reese got up early to draw. Sitting at the window, looking out into a new day, he could see six cats in various poses. But he wanted to be closer, so after a few minutes, he picked up his pad and pencil and went to sit at the picnic table. He kept working.

After a while, Meg came out of the house. When she saw

what Reese was working on, she knew right away what he was up to. "Oh, he'll like that a lot," she said.

"I can't get it to look right," Reese said. "I'm terrible at drawing animals."

"However it looks, it'll be right," she said.

She sat on the swing and watched him draw for a while before going in to help her granddad with lunch. Reese stayed and kept working.

It took another hour and four more sheets of paper before Reese had a drawing that he thought was good enough for Charlie: It was of a cat sitting upright, with its paws in close and its tail wrapped around its haunches, which Reese thought was the handsomest pose. The cat's head was tilted slightly up, ears forward.

He took the final drawing inside the trailer to show his mom. "I like it," she said. "You really worked hard on it."

"I'm going to give it to Charlie."

"Oh," she said. She got a funny look on her face.

"What?" he asked. "Is that a bad idea?"

"Nope." She shook her head. "I think it's exactly the right idea."

When Charlie came outside to feed the cats, Reese went out with the drawing. Charlie again put his head down and turned away. Reese said, "I have something to give you."

Charlie stopped, not looking at him. "What?"

"This." Reese held up the drawing, and when Charlie looked at it, he offered it to him. "I made it for you, like you asked."

Charlie put the bin of cat food on the ground and took the picture. He looked at it without saying anything for what felt like forever. Then he said, "I like it."

"I'm glad," Reese said.

"It's for me?"

"Yes," Reese said. "I'm sorry it's not better. I did my best, but I've never drawn a cat before."

"I like it," Charlie said again.

"I got a new art box for my birthday," Reese said. "It has paints in it, which I don't really know how to use yet. But I can learn, and then I can add color to the drawing, if you want. I can paint the cat any color you want."

"Okay," Charlie said. He just stood for a few moments looking at the drawing, as if he was thinking about how it would look in color.

Reese asked, "How are the kittens?"

"You don't care," Charlie said, not looking up from the drawing.

"I really do care," Reese said.

The screen door at the house opened then, and Mr. Smith stepped out. He stopped when he saw Reese and Charlie together in the yard. Then he raised a hand to them and went back inside the house, and Reese was grateful to be alone again with Charlie.

"I really didn't mean what I said to you," he said. "It wasn't true at all. It wasn't true that I don't care about your cats. I was upset about something else."

"Meg told me about your dad and your birthday and everything," Charlie said. "It's really sad."

"I'm glad she told you," Reese said. "I was upset about that, about him. I was scared, too . . . I *am* scared . . . and I took it out on you, which was wrong."

"Is your dad going to be okay?" Charlie asked.

"I don't know," Reese said. "I hope so. He's going to a place to get help, but it's up to him to get better."

Charlie didn't say anything right away to that, and Reese just waited. Then Charlie said, "I have to feed the cats."

"Can I help?" Reese asked.

Charlie nodded. He took Reese's picture into the house to keep it safe, and then he and Reese together put out the bowls of food. Then they walked to the woodshed to check on the kittens. Mama Cat was lying just inside, and her kittens were up and moving. One of the gray ones was just outside the woodshed, walking in the grass. Charlie scooped it up and put it back next to its mother. "I've been picking them up every day so they don't go wild," he said.

"I remember," Reese said. "Can I hold one?"

"Which one? Which one is your favorite?"

"I like the one you just picked up," Reese said. "The one who was wandering."

Charlie picked up the kitten, which mewed loudly, and he placed it in Reese's outstretched hands. Its blue eyes were bright and wide open. Reese rubbed behind its ears, along the top of its head, which felt so small and fragile. Charlie was watching him, his face serious.

"How am I doing?" Reese asked.

"You're doing good," Charlie said. "Can you make it that color?"

"Make what?"

"Your drawing, the cat you drew for me: When you learn how to use your paints, can you make it gray like that kitten?"

Reese smiled. "I can."

CHAPTER 34

Reese was in the Smiths' kitchen making mango lassis with Meg. A month had passed, and finally he was ready to celebrate his birthday. He had asked to have Indian food for his party, and Mr. Smith had gone to the place in Goldsville to get it. The food was in aluminum foil trays on the kitchen table, everything on the list that Reese and Meg and Charlie had written out together: murgh makhani, palak paneer, pakoras, and a cauliflower and potato dish that Charlie had suggested called aloo gobi.

Meg had the idea of making fresh lassis for everyone, and Reese's mom had googled a recipe and gotten what they needed at the grocery store in town: yogurt, milk, bags of frozen mango chunks, and a little jar of a spice that Reese had never heard of, cardamom.

Now they had the blender on the counter, measuring everything out. "Is everyone going to want one?" Meg asked.

"Probably," Reese said. "I think we should make enough for everybody. It's Tony and Ryan and maybe Tony's dad, plus us, so nine. Maybe we should make enough for ten, just in case?"

"Better too much than not enough," Meg said. "I'm sorry again your dad can't be here."

Reese shrugged. "It's okay," he said. His dad thought treatment was helping and had decided to stay another thirty days. He was allowed visitors now, though, and Reese and his mom were going to drive over to Goldsville to see him in the coming week. Reese was planning to bring the picture his dad had asked for: an AMC Matador Coupe like the one he had spotted at the junkyard on their last good day together, but fixed up, as they had talked about. He drew it with racing stripes and fat tires, following a country road on a sunny day, with his dad driving and Reese waving from the open window.

Reese got the frozen mango out of the freezer. Making lassis, it turned out, was super easy: just dump everything in the blender and hit the smoothie button.

When they were finished and put the lassis in the fridge, they went outside with Charlie and played basketball for a while. The old hoop in the yard was looking awesome: Reese had helped Mr. Smith paint the backboard and hang a new net.

His mom came out of the trailer. She looked a little tired, but happy. She had been up late the night before moving boxes to their new apartment, not far from his school. They were going to leave the trailer and move in officially the next day.

She had also been working a lot. She had finally demanded that the owner of the Kwik Stop give her more money and more of a say in how the place was run. He had not only given her the raise but made her the manager of a new location, Kwik Stop II, that was opening out on the bypass. She had been setting up the new store and hiring staff and stocking the place. It meant more hours, but she seemed much happier.

She shot a few baskets with Reese and Meg and Charlie before setting the picnic table for the party. Earlier she had put out folding chairs so everyone would have a place to sit and eat. Tied to one end of the table and bobbing a little in the breeze was one of those goofy, giant Happy Birthday helium balloons. His mom had gotten it for him at Food Lion, which was silly, but Reese didn't mind. It made him smile.

Under the table were Mama Cat and her kittens. She had brought them out from the woodshed, and they were spending most of their days near the house, playing and exploring, joining the other cats around the bowls at suppertime.

At the basketball hoop, Reese was going in for a layup when Tony and Ryan arrived. Mr. Alvarez had driven them over, and he waved as he pulled in beside Mr. Smith's pickup truck. He and Mrs. Alvarez both knew everything about what was going on with Reese's dad and his family. Tony and Ryan also knew. Reese had told them. He told them about Meg and Charlie, too, and now they were all there together for his belated birthday party.

When Tony and Ryan got out of Mr. Alvarez's SUV, Reese

introduced everybody. "Tony and Ryan, this is Meg and Charlie."

He was a little nervous about trying to mix his friends, old and new. He wasn't sure what Tony and Ryan and Meg and Charlie would all think of one another. But Tony just said, "Nice to meet you. Cool farm."

"Hello," Charlie said. "Thank you."

"Where's the river at?" Ryan said.

They had come wearing their swimsuits, because Reese had told them about the river and the dock and the canoe. Reese and Meg and Charlie were in their swimsuits, too. His mom said, "Why don't y'all go right down to swim for a while before you eat?"

That was good for everyone, so Charlie and Meg led the way, down the grass. The river was shining in the morning sun.

"Awesome," Ryan said.

"It is awesome," Reese said.

Charlie broke into a run across the grass, stripping off his T-shirt as he went, and he was first to the dock. He kicked off his shoes, and then with a whoop, he did a cannonball that sent a spout of water so high it splashed everyone. Ryan laughed, and he jumped in after him. Tony followed.

Reese smiled. Maybe mixing his friends wasn't going to be such a big deal after all.

"You going in?" Meg asked him.

Of course he was going in. He took off his shoes and T-shirt, and he walked to the back of the dock. Then he took a running jump and leaped. He went in feet first. He heard Charlie whoop again, and then the silence of the river closed over him.

As he hung between the sunlit surface and the bottom, he thought of his dad, who he was sure did want to be there today. Reese pictured him as he had last seen him, walking into the treatment center on his crutches. Before the swinging doors closed, he had given Reese that smile of his.

Reese wanted so badly for his dad to get well. Maybe someday they could work together on an old car to replace the Barracuda, bring another classic, like the Matador, back from the dead.

But Reese didn't look for any promises this time. He had said goodbye to his dad and then walked out of the treatment center with his mom for the drive home to his friends. He had a whole summer to look forward to with them, swimming, canoeing, playing basketball. Then came eighth grade.

From above on the river's surface came the muffled sounds of laughter and yelling. Then Reese heard a splash and felt the water move around him. A hand touched his shoulder. It was Meg, her hair floating around her face. She smiled, and then together they pulled to the sunlit surface.

"Race you to the other side," Meg said. "I'm going to beat you this time."

Reese laughed. "In your dreams," he said.

And they were off, reaching and kicking, and Charlie and Tony and Ryan followed after.

AUTHOR'S NOTE

The story of Reese and his family was inspired in part by my own family experiences. I have watched people I love struggling with addiction, and I wanted so badly to make them better, but did not know how.

Many, many other people have been there, facing a loved one's addiction, or they are there right now, at this very moment, feeling powerless and scared. That includes millions of kids. The most recent national report on substance use and addiction in families estimated that 8.7 million young people under eighteen—one in eight—lived with at least one parent who had a drug or alcohol problem. That means that in any given classroom in a school, chances are good that not just one, but two or even three kids are dealing with this issue.

So if you are one of these kids, remember that you are not alone. Far from it. And know that you don't have to hide your worry and pain or feel ashamed. People around you—your friends, other family, your teachers, counselors, or other trusted grown-ups—can listen, help you sort through what you're dealing with, and find a positive way forward. This problem is so widespread that when you begin to talk about it, you might very well find that the person you are confiding in has been there, too.

People who help kids cope with drug use and addiction in

their families often talk about something called the Seven Cs, developed by counselor and author Jerry Moe. It's a brief credo that has helped me, and I kept it in mind as I was writing this story. Here it is:

> **I didn't cause it.**
> **I can't control it.**
> **I can't cure it.**
> **But**
> **I can take care of myself**
> **By communicating my feelings,**
> **Making healthy choices,**
> **And celebrating myself.**

The first half of this credo is about accepting the hard things you are facing and recognizing what is beyond your control. The second half is about focusing on what you *can* do: You can connect with other people, opening your heart to friends and trusted grown-ups about your feelings and needs, and accepting their help and support. You can make positive, healthy choices for yourself. And you can celebrate the good in life, your blessings and milestones, big and small, and do things that make you happy and lift your spirits. The Seven Cs can also extend beyond addiction to help people touched by grief, mental health issues, and other difficult things in life.

If you'd like to connect with other people who have gone through this experience, or find resources and guidance, there are groups out there that can help. Among them:

- Eluna has resources and information for kids, parents, teachers and others on their website: **https://elunanetwork.org/resources/**. Eluna also runs a year-round program called Camp Mariposa for kids ages nine to twelve who have been affected by a family member's substance use: **https://elunanetwork.org/camps-programs/camp-mariposa/**.

- The National Association for Children of Addiction has resources and information for teens, younger kids, and families, as well as ways to get involved in helping improve the lives of others facing this problem: **https://nacoa.org/families/**.

- Boys Town has a crisis hotline to connect you to counselors who can help: **https://www.boystown.org/hotline/**. You can text VOICE to 20121 to connect to someone who speaks English or Spanish. Translation services are available for more than one hundred other languages. Those with speech or hearing impairments can email: **hotline@boystown.org.**

- Childhelp has a 24/7 national hotline to contact if you or a young person you know is being harmed or neglected, physically or emotionally: **https://childhelphotline.org**. You can live chat through the website, or you can call or text 800-422-4453.

- Crisis Text Line can connect you with trained volunteer crisis counselors when you're feeling scared, depressed or anxious and need to talk with someone: **https://www.crisistextline.org**. Text HOME to 741741. You also can text or chat through the website or connect via WhatsApp.

If you have a friend who is affected by drug use or addiction in their family, you can be there for them by listening and letting them know you care and that you understand how traumatic and painful this is for them. Show them that they are not alone. Help them believe it.

ACKNOWLEDGMENTS

Working on this book reminded me how blessed I am to have many smart, creative, and supportive people in my life. I could never have written *Breaking into Sunlight* and seen it through to publication without their help.

First and foremost is my family: my wife, Kelly, and our kids, Maren and Liam. Maren was an important early reader of the manuscript. Her criticism was dead-on and unsparing, which helped me get the story on track. As I drafted and redrafted, Kelly read each version, improving the manuscript with her questions, thoughts, and ideas. She never wavered in her support and her faith in me and the story, and she was always available to talk when I needed to work through a problem with the story. My sister, Ann, and mom, Peg, also were always ready to listen and offer suggestions and encouragement. Thank you to Ginny and Rose Kelly for reading an early draft and giving me valuable feedback.

I want to thank my wonderful agent, Isabelle Bleecker of Nordlyset Literary Agency, and editor, Cheryl Klein of Algonquin Young Readers. I am forever indebted to them for fishing my manuscript out of their piles of submissions, helping me refine it, and then taking it out into the world.

Friends and fellow writers also were incredibly generous with their help along the way, carefully and thoughtfully reading the manuscript, correcting errors, offering ideas and criticism, and sharing essential guidance and contacts as I worked toward publication. They are Judy Christie, Suzanne Garofalo, Jake Halpern, Jennifer Howard, John Lawson, Elissa Leif, Katherine Marsh, Beth McMurtrie, Donna Lawless Newell, Valerie Nieman, John Robinson, Benjamin Soskis, Debra Spearman, and Ed Williams.

Finally, thank you to Ashley Stainback Kress of the Rise School in Houston, Texas (https://www.riseschool.org/), for reading my story and giving me her thoughts and insights on my portrayal of Charlie and Down syndrome.